"Grappling with the word wi[...]
troversy. But Dr Woodard e[...]
us, the fortunate reader, the [...]
catalyst for social change, hea[...]
navigating the crossroads of gender, sexuality and power, this book invites readers to reconsider long-held narratives and confront the enduring legacies of misogyny, oppression and fear. Thoughtfully written and deeply impactful, this book is an essential and enjoyable read!"

Sarah Robinson, author of *Kitchen Witch: Food, Folklore & Fairy Tale*, *The Witch and the Wildwood* and *Witch Country: Seeking the Witch in the British Landscape*

Witchcraft

From fairy tales and fiction to TikTok, the specter of the witch has cast a long shadow over women and popular culture. *Witchcraft: Gendered Perspectives* traces the history and evolution of the term "witch" across six centuries.

Tracing the history of witchcraft from the publication of the *Malleus Maleficarum* to its contemporary representation and reclamation, this volume takes a gendered and intersectional approach to the cultural and historical shifts which have both demonized and democratized the witch online and in public discourse. Amongst these are:

- The witch trials in Scotland, England and America
- Literary and screen reimaginings of the witch
- The rise of Wicca as an alternative religion.

Witchcraft: Gendered Perspectives is an invaluable resource for graduate and undergraduate students across gender studies, queer history, religious studies, media studies and European and North American history.

Jennie Woodard is Assistant Professor of History and Women, Gender and Sexuality Studies at the University of Maine, Augusta, USA.

Gendered Perspectives

Gender pervades every aspect of everyday life, from political decision making to the clothes that we wear. Taking an explicit interdisciplinary and intersectional gender studies approach to everything from the environment to social media, the *Gendered Perspectives* series provides an accessible and comprehensive insight into contemporary concerns, their historical and social context, and possible future directions. Often challenging gendered presumptions about a subject, the series shows us the nuances of gender and sexuality in the world around us.

Recent titles in series:

Witchcraft
Gendered Perspectives
Jennie Woodard

For more information about this series, please visit: www.routledge.com/GenderedPerspectives/book-series/GenPers

Witchcraft
Gendered Perspectives

Jennie Woodard

Routledge
Taylor & Francis Group

LONDON AND NEW YORK

Designed cover image: Shaiith, Getty Images

First published 2026
by Routledge
4 Park Square, Milton Park, Abingdon, Oxon OX14 4RN

and by Routledge
605 Third Avenue, New York, NY 10158

Routledge is an imprint of the Taylor & Francis Group, an informa business

© 2026 Jennie Woodard

The right of Jennie Woodard to be identified as author of this work has been asserted in accordance with sections 77 and 78 of the Copyright, Designs and Patents Act 1988.

All rights reserved. No part of this book may be reprinted or reproduced or utilised in any form or by any electronic, mechanical, or other means, now known or hereafter invented, including photocopying and recording, or in any information storage or retrieval system, without permission in writing from the publishers.

Trademark notice: Product or corporate names may be trademarks or registered trademarks, and are used only for identification and explanation without intent to infringe.

British Library Cataloguing-in-Publication Data
A catalogue record for this book is available from the British Library

ISBN: 978-1-032-71724-1 (hbk)
ISBN: 978-1-032-71205-5 (pbk)
ISBN: 978-1-032-71722-7 (ebk)

DOI: 10.4324/9781032717227

Typeset in Sabon
by Apex CoVantage, LLC

To John and Phoebe, who bring magic and whimsy to my world

Contents

Acknowledgments   *x*

Introduction   1

1 "The Wickedness of Woman": The *Malleus Maleficarum*, or "The Hammer of Witches"   11

2 "Something Wicked This Way Comes": The Witchhunts of Scotland, England and Salem   30

3 "Garmented in Light": Reimaginings of the Witch Through Nineteenth-Century Poetry   48

4 "An Ye Harm None": The Rise of Wicca in the Twentieth Century   63

5 "Normal is Not Necessarily a Virtue": TV and Movie Witches of the Twentieth and Twenty-First Centuries   82

6 "The Power to Write Your Own Story": The Witch as Reclamation in the Twenty-First Century   99

Conclusion   115

Bibliography   *123*
Index   *133*

Acknowledgments

I am deeply grateful to all the people and organizations, both known and unknown, that helped bring this book to fruition. I could not have done any extensive research without the meticulous organization of online archival primary sources through Cornell University, the National Archives of Scotland and the Essex Institute. The Nottage Library at the Bangor campus of the University of Maine at Augusta, Fogler Library at the University of Maine in Orono and the Bangor Public Library each held valuable tomes necessary to my research. Both Nathan Godfried and Olivia Johnson were essential to the initial stages of writing and editing this book's proposal. The enthusiastic cheerleading of Jason, Sam, Mimi, Melissa and Jody gave me the confidence and support I needed to get the ball rolling in the earliest stages of writing and research. One of my dearest friends and longtime colleagues, Rebecca, not only provided enthusiasm and support, but became a sounding board when I needed to get ideas off the ground, gave excellent suggestions for history and gender studies resources, edited chapters when I most needed help and joined with me for many hikes, cups of coffee and crafting sessions when what was most called for was a break. Finally, an extra special thanks to my partner, John, and daughter, Phoebe, who supported me unequivocally through the process. John provided insight into the history of yuta within his Okinawan heritage and Phoebe helped me to navigate trends on TikTok, neither of which I would have been able to do without their knowledge and experience. More importantly, however, they brought encouragement, made me laugh, sang loudly in the car with me and continued to bring the joy and magic they always infuse into everyday life.

Introduction

Elizabeth Johnson Jr was a witch. At least, that's what she said in her confession on August 11, 1692. The 22 year old had admitted that "Goody Carrier baptized her when she Baptized her Daughter Sarah and that Goody Carr'r told her she Should be Saved if she would be a witch."[1] Born in North Andover, Massachusetts in 1670, Johnson, described as "simplish at best" by her grandfather, possibly did not know what she was agreeing to when Goody Carrier presented her with the option of baptism. She was then sentenced to death, only to be "saved by then-Gov. William Phips, who threw her punishment as the insanity of the accusations started to become clear."[2] Despite being saved from execution, her name was not formally cleared before her death in 1747. Reading this history, two things are highly likely: one, Johnson was targeted due to her perceived difference and two, she was not a witch yet became entangled in the hysteria, almost losing her life as a result.

In 2023, *Ms. Magazine* featured filmmakers Annika Hylmö and Dawn Green, whose in-progress documentary *The Last Witch* follows the journey of a group of eighth graders from Andover, Massachusetts as they try to clear the name of Elizabeth Johnson Jr. Both teacher and students recognized that Johnson, one of over 200 people accused of witchcraft during the infamous trials in Salem, was neither wed nor a mother and suspected to be mentally ill, making her easy prey for those on the hunt for supposed witches and evil doers of the time.[3] Exonerations for the accused and executed began in 1697, shortly after the mania in Salem had died down, when Judge Samuel Sewall expressed remorse for his part in the proceedings, and, by 1702, the trials had been declared unlawful. In 1697, Thomas Fiske, who had been the foreman of the jury in Rebecca Nurse's trial, declared, with other jurors, that they had played a role in the "miscarriage of justice" and expressed sorrow at enacting such cruelty when they had been supplied with little evidence.[4]

Despite the earnestness of these sentiments, it would be another 9 years before the final confession would be heard and nearly 330 years before Johnson would be the last witch exonerated for her "crime." Carrie LaPierre, a teacher at North Andover Middle School, first heard of Johnson in 2019 and decided to introduce the case to her class. What began as a lesson on

DOI: 10.4324/9781032717227-1

the Salem trials became a year-long project toward a bill that would lead to Johnson's exoneration. LaPierre said that the students

> spent most of the year working on getting this set for the legislature – actually writing a bill, writing letters to legislators, creating presentations, doing all the research, looking at the actual testimony of Elizabeth Johnson, learning more about the Salem witch trials, [and] it became quite extensive for these kids.[5]

For LaPierre, it became "a matter of justice," as she saw the injustice against Johnson and the other accused as similar to injustices against the LGBTQ+ community, racial injustice and more.[6]

Today, the influence of witches and witch culture can be seen in all corners of Western society. Where once books on crystals, spell work and the Goddess would be relegated to the alternative religion section of major bookstores, information on these practices and more is displayed prominently on shelves in Target and reviewed by TikTok influencers with thousands of followers. Romantasy (a genre that combines romance and fantasy) regularly features novels with witchy protagonists, such as *The Crimson Moth*, that are prominently featured on BookTok and BookTube. Witches are on television, are the cute protagonists in video games and college courses teach the history of witchcraft. Beyond representation in media and consumer culture, the witch has become an increasingly significant part of identity and belonging. In 2020, an estimated 1.5 million people identified their spiritual practice as Pagan or Wiccan, a radical increase from the approximation of 8,000 practitioners in 1990.[7] As will be discussed in the last chapter, many practitioners have claimed the identity of witch as part of their own resistance against institutions, such as Christianity, that have oppressed or rejected other aspects of their being, such as their race, sexuality or gender identity.

Popular conceptions of a witch often revolve around specific symbols and iconography: the pointed black hat, a broomstick, a cauldron, perhaps a black cat or a toad. She – and the witch is almost exclusively portrayed as a woman – is often depicted as old, haggard and stooped, with a crooked nose and a wart or two spread across her face. We can see this depiction with the Evil Queen's transformation into a witch in Disney's 1937 classic *Snow White and the Seven Dwarves* and later in 2001 with Yubaba in Ghibli Studio's *Spirited Away*. At times, the witch is depicted with green or purple skin, such as *The Wizard of Oz*'s Wicked Witch of the West (as well as the 2023 film adaptation of the musical *Wicked*) and Madam Mim in *The Sword in the Stone*, respectively. The primary objectives of these witches include the desire to steal beauty and youth, enact revenge on those who have wronged them and obtain some form of magical or societal power otherwise denied to them. They are seen as a threat to the moral integrity and gendered order of the society around them. The girl-next-door beauty and goodness of Dorothy Gale, who describes herself as "small and meek," must stand up to the Wicked Witch of the West. *The Sword in the Stone* depicts Madam Mim as the antithesis to those with power and potential (the male characters), particularly up against Merlin's bumbling bookish wizardry.

Today's witches seek to rewrite the narrative of what it means to be a witch, clapping back against the gendered stereotypes of beauty and historical beliefs in the practice as evil and diabolic. Instead, witches today focus their identities and practices around ideas such as healing, community, connecting to the earth, standing up to oppression and reclaiming spiritual and cultural heritages. Yet how does one define a witch? Prominent scholars of witch and witchcraft history, including Richard Kieckhefer, P.G. Maxwell-Stuart, Ronald Hutton and Lyndal Roper, have grappled with the language and discourse around the word "witch." After all, it was the inquisitors as well as religious and political leaders that constructed the definition of what it meant to be a "witch." Those who might have practiced holistic healing or sought alternative practices to Christianity were not given the opportunity to display any agency over their own identities. Thus, the lore surrounding the witch matched the descriptions and definitions of those in power.

Despite these depictions, the witch narrative remained anything but stagnant. In *The Witch in the Western Imagination*, Roper wrote that the witch was "never one thing . . . [but] was several different beings at once, and she invaded many areas of thinking and writing accruing new association and new layers of meaning as she did so."[8] Not only did those with religious and political power shape the definition of what it meant to be a witch, but artists, writers and others who created cultural mediums helped to deepen and redefine the idea of "witch." Though the narrative of the witch as ugly, haggard, evil and in league with the devil remained, more narratives emerged: she was an ethereal Goddess, a seductress, a healer and much more. By the Victorian era, "the word 'pagan' had become equipped with connotations of freedom, self-indulgence, and ancient knowledge," connotations that persist in varying degrees to this day.[9] Though, as seen by the proliferation of movie and cartoon witches in the twentieth century, these newer narratives and interpretations failed to supplant the old ones.

This book is a broad journey through these narratives, emerging partially out of my own personal interest in earth-based spirituality and feminist histories. My first foray into earth-based spirituality came during my college years around the turn of the millennium, when I began to explore connections between Goddesses and nature. I taped printed black-and-white images of Goddesses such as Isis, Brigid and Amaterasu on a mirror in my studio apartment and engaged in meditation, burned sage and read about the associations of each Goddess. Over twenty years later, a desire to return to this type of spirituality beckoned, but, with two decades of feminist ideology and pedagogy under my belt, I found myself with newer insights and observations, primarily that such practices were less of a secret than they had been even during my college years. More people were out of the broom closet and engaging in practices openly on social media. Books on spellcasting, tarot and oracle cards, and other tools one might use in their practice, appeared to be far more readily available. Following the 2016 election, more groups calling themselves witches declared their intentions to hex the patriarchy and fight for social justice. I decided to explore this most recent transformation of witch culture in one of the ways I knew best: through teaching. I designed a course on a broad history of witchcraft, examining the evolutionary trajectory of the witch from the fifteenth century to the present day. Throughout the course, I found my curiosity brewing and curated more questions for myself, chief among them, "How did we get here? How did the mere whiff of witchcraft lead to someone's execution 400 years ago, yet now witchcraft can function as a business, a social movement, a spiritual practice and a reclamation of identity?" History has taught us that progress, whatever the meaning of the word might be, is not linear, so to chalk it up to "we know better now" wasn't enough of an answer.

The first chapter, "'The Wickedness of Woman': The *Malleus Maleficarum*, or 'The Hammer of Witches'," examines one of the most famous documents that associates the witch with evil and dealings with the devil. Published by Catholic Inquisition authorities in Germany in 1486, the *Malleus Maleficarum* (translated into "The Hammer of Witches") posits that "all wickedness is but little to the wickedness of woman . . . what else is woman but a foe to friendship, an unescapable punishment, a necessary evil."[10] This chapter will illustrate that the *Malleus Maleficarum* played a central role in the positioning of "witch," almost always female, as sinful, lustful, evil and diabolic. Prior to the publication of the *Malleus Maleficarum*, the word "witch" was not generally a part of popular imagination. Women had been accused of heresy, seduction and temptation, of cavorting and working with evil spirits, but not until the *Malleus Maleficarum* had those actions and accusations fallen under one singular category of witch. This chapter will provide the history and background of the *Malleus Maleficarum*'s publication and illustrate that the attempt to define the evil woman now referred to as a witch through a diabolic lens proved successful, setting the stage for the pervasive stereotypes and assumptions that would lead to countless accusations and thousands of executions, as well as literary and artistic representations that persist to this day.

Chapter 2, "'Something Wicked This Way Comes': The Witchhunts of Scotland, England and Salem," explores three cases in each of the regions as examples of the broader implications of the hysteria and mania surrounding witchcraft. The first case, from 1590 to 1592 involving Agnes Sampson of North Berwick, Scotland, illustrates the threats many believed witches imposed, including the ability to strip a monarch of his power. Having heard rumors that witches were plotting his murder, either through enchanting and then destroying a wax figure made in his likeness or obtaining poison from various "magical" sources, King James VI "took a personal interest, and indeed part, in the subsequent interrogations of those arrested."[11] The second case, the Pendle witches of Lancashire, illustrates the way hysteria overtook the judicial order, including the role misgivings, rumors and insubstantial evidence, as well as the evidence of a 9-year-old girl, that played into the deaths of ten accused witches. The third case examines the testimony of Tituba, one of the first accused in Salem. Though she confessed to having practiced witchcraft, only later to recant her testimony, Tituba's story illustrates the intersectional nature of the witch trials, where her position as a slave left her with no power or agency in which she could make any other choice but to confess.

Chapter 3, "'Garmented in Light': Reimaginings of the Witch Through Nineteenth-Century Poetry," examines the Romantic era of poetry, where the witch began to take on more beautiful, mystical and ethereal connotations, such as in Percy Bysshe Shelley's "The Witch of Atlas." Other poets, such as Mary Coleridge and Emily Dickinson, used the witch as a symbol of both injustice against women and their own resistance, even defiance, against the institutions of marriage and other constructs of traditional femininity. Here we see the idea of Roper's "layers" develop. Several female writers of the era

> evoke the female monster in their novels and poems [and] alter her meaning by virtue of their own identification with her. For it is usually because she is in some sense imbued with interiority that the witch-monster-madwoman becomes so crucial an avatar of the writer's own self.[12]

As the chapter will illustrate, Coleridge and Dickinson took the established histories of women accused of witchcraft and applied them not only to their own experiences but to the misogynistic and patriarchal systems in which they lived.

Chapter 4, "'An Ye Harm None': The Rise of Wicca in the Twentieth Century," explores the mythologies and popular books that construct the Wiccan religion. Gerald Gardner, often considered the "father" of modern Wicca, makes for a complicated and puzzling subject. As the chapter will demonstrate, Gardner's influence on modern practices of paganism and witchcraft is undeniable, including celebrations and rituals such as the Wheel of the Year. Yet Gardner proved to be a problematic figure, considered a manipulator and media-hungry by some, and was purported to hold both sexist and homophobic views. Others, such as Doreen Valiente, a High Priestess in Gardner's coven, recognized these issues and spoke out against Gardner. The chapter ends with an exploration of the intersection between Pagan spirituality and the American feminist movement of the 1970s, demonstrating that ideas associated with Wicca were adapted and utilized to empower and enhance the political, spiritual and cultural agency of those in the movement.

Chapter 5, "'Normal is Not Necessarily a Virtue': TV and Movie Witches of the Twentieth and Twenty-First Centuries," continues the book's trajectory of Roper's "layered" narrative. Many of the witches in the movies and films examined in the chapter, including the Owens sisters in *Practical Magic* and the assembled coven in *Agatha All Along*, have complicated associations and generational trauma because of the witch trials, particularly in Salem, yet clearly borrow from aspects of medicinal and herbal healing and include Wiccan and Pagan influences. The chapter argues that many of these witchy characters must conform to a feminine standard of "normal," hiding who they really are, to find acceptance within their community. Those who don't, or can't, suffer rejection, are targets of persecution or commit wicked deeds due to repeated ostracization in society. Though more recent iterations of the witch tend to blur these lines and represent a more diverse array of identities, there is still a repeated emphasis on marriage, beauty and motherhood as part of the normalizing process.

Chapter 6, "'The Power to Write Your Own Story': The Witch as Reclamation in the Twenty-First Century," examines common themes that account for the rise in witchy and Pagan practices in the twenty-first century, particularly online and through social media. These themes include: witchcraft as resistance against a capitalist-driven society of productivity; a space for social justice and social justice movements; a place of belonging and inclusivity; and a connection to ancestry, culture and heritage. This chapter demonstrates that, in addition to the spiritual practice of the craft, those who engage with Wicca, paganism and/or witchcraft are drawn to their practice because of cultural connections, political alignments, resistance to dominant systems and/or experiences with prejudice and oppression.

The book begins in 1486 with the publication of the *Malleus Maleficarum* and ends in the first quarter of the twenty-first century. Covering nearly 600 years of history is no small task and I had to make significant choices as to what to include, leaving out much more history than can be covered in one text. These choices were based on my areas of expertise and access to various materials and resources. Specific narratives should be read as general examples of broader concepts and not as a monolithic representation of experience. I have made conscious efforts to be inclusive regarding representation and diversity. Though arranged chronologically, this book should not be read as though the ideas of the past no longer exist once a new chapter is begun. Roper's idea of the increased layers of meaning and symbolism is significant to the layout of this book. Each historical point written is intended to provide context for how the word "witch," so often associated with fear and power, has morphed, changed and been reclaimed at several points throughout the last several centuries.

This book also has Western Europe and the United States as its central focus. This is largely due to my fields of expertise as well as having to make significant decisions to include nearly 600 years of history in one volume. However, the claims made within these pages pertain to those geographical regions and should not be broadly applied to other areas of the globe. As stated at the beginning of this Introduction, the witch trials in Salem were considered unlawful by 1702, yet there is evidence of people in areas of the world being tried and convicted of witchcraft today. For example, in the East African nation of Tanzania, women have been targeted as witches, accused of murdering albinos and attempting to use their body parts for magic and power. Vigilantes have come after women they believe have committed such crimes, including 58-year-old Jane Faidha Bakari who was burned alive in front of her husband, Moses, under the belief that she had used witchcraft to kill.[13] As with so many injustices and oppressions, studying witchcraft persecution through the lens of history does not mean that it is a thing of the past.

There is data and scholarship that links connections between exoneration of accused witches in the past to the possibility of ending the practice of persecution in the present. Brendan Walsh of the University of Queensland has demonstrated that "the witchcraft exoneration movement isn't simply about addressing past injustices. Violence directed at suspected witches persists across the world today and, alarmingly, seems to be intensifying."[14] In a March 2020 report, the United Nations noted at least 20,000 alleged witches were killed globally between 2006 and 2010.[15] With more attention and emphasis on the injustices of the past as well as the oppressive systems that not only allowed but participated in such persecutions, more emphasis might be placed on the persistence of such practices. In 2021, the Human Rights Council of the United Nations passed a resolution condemning acts of violence and harmful acts in the name of supposed witchcraft, addressing the vulnerability of certain populations and acknowledging the rights of individuals to practice witchcraft and paganism.[16]

It's also important to note that this book relies on court records and other primary documents that almost exclusively refer to white cisgender heterosexual women. Cases of women of color, such as Tituba, are few and far between, while primary sources regarding queer practicing and/or persecuted witches prior to the twentieth century are nearly nonexistent. Yet scholarship is moving rapidly in the direction of uncovering more of these histories. Anya Topolski, a professor of philosophy, has written about the intersection of race, religion and witchhunts in the recent book *Purple Brains: Feminisms at the Limits of Philosophy*. Other scholars, such as Peter Geschiere and Amber Murrey, have examined the colonization of witchcraft, including the centralization of Europe in its histories. Several historians have examined the intersections of immigrant, slave and Native American populations during the Salem witch trials. One example, Elaine Breslaw's 1996 work *Tituba, Reluctant Witch of Salem: Devilish Indians and Puritan Fantasies*, uncovers more of Tituba's identity as Arawak, illustrating more of her intersecting identities and allowing her a complexity not included in the court records and trial notes of the Salem era. In her 2000 work "Purloined Identity: The Racial Metamorphosis of Tituba of Salem Village," Veta Smith Tucker argued that Tituba's intersectional identities have been erased at various points of scholarship with an emphasis on her African origins in nineteenth-century scholarship, where scholarship of the 1990s focused more on her Indian culture, yet "in the absence of incontestable evidence indicating a precise racial identity for Tituba, contemporary readers rely on today's racial categories and import 20th-century notions of racial exclusivity into their racial reconstructions of Tituba."[17]

There is a significant connection between beliefs about witchcraft and the devil and prejudices against Native Americans in areas of Massachusetts, as far north as what is now Maine. Countless volumes have been written on King Philip's War 15 years prior to the Salem witch trials. Many scholars of the subject argue that accusations of witchcraft against Native American tribes go beyond innate prejudice but have colonial claims to Native lands at their core. In "American Indians, Witchcraft, and Witchhunting," Matthew Dennis demonstrates that the language used to accuse witches, such as being in league with the devil, is the same language colonists used to describe Native American tribes, including their homes as the "devil's den."[18] Scholars Emerson W. Baker and James Kences noted that the witchcraft judges owned land in what is now Maine, and further colonial speculation for Native lands in areas of Massachusetts and Maine fueled hysteria and fear about the Godless "heathen" Native Americans.[19]

Though there is less scholarship in the realm of queer identities in relation to witch trials and history prior to the twentieth century, various artists, scholars and writers have examined the parallels between the witch and queerness, particularly how these identities appeared as threats against the norms of sex, sexuality, gender and Christianity, yet homophobia existed within the craft as well. In the early days of Gardnerian Wicca, homosexuality was viewed as unnatural and anyone within the LGBTQIA community would automatically be denied initiation into the coven. Scott Cunningham, author of *Wicca: A Guide for the Solitary Practitioner*, emphasized inclusivity due to his own experiences with rejection as a result of his identity as a gay man. Furthermore, Wicca's emphasis on the male/female and masculine/feminine binaries of the God and Goddess has led to the exclusion of trans and nonbinary people from the practice. Michelle Mueller has examined this tension in her work "The Chalice and the Rainbow: Conflicts Between Women's Spirituality and Transgender Rights in US Wicca in the 2010s," noting instances where changing language within Wiccan practices has resulted in more inclusive spaces for those who reject or identify outside of the gender binary.[20]

Across geographies and historical time periods, including the present day, women beyond childbearing years, roughly 50 and older, had been common targets of witchcraft accusation. Historian Brian Levack argues that, with the data and records available, the most common victims of the witch trials were women over 50, as this was "considered to be a much more advanced age than it is today."[21] Deborah Willis argues that elderly widows, no longer able to reproduce, and largely unable to work or provide themselves with basic securities, became economic burdens on society. She notes that as such a woman was "increasingly resented as an economic burden, she was also perceived by her neighbors to be the locus of a dangerous envy and verbal violence."[22] As evidenced in areas such as Tanzania and Ghana in the twenty-first century, the persecution of older and elderly women continues to persist.

As illustrated above, this book is in no way meant to be read as a complete and comprehensive history of witchcraft. Instead, this work intends to be a starting point to draw connecting threads between a time when notions of the witch had the real possibility of leading to death and existing today in public spaces and institutions, including the digital world. Each chapter provides an overview of various historical points of access regarding the history of witch trials, representations of witches in poetry and media entertainment, various religious and spiritual traditions connected to witchcraft, and the connection between witchcraft, community and social justice.

Notes

1 Dudley Broads, "Examination of Elizabeth Johnson Jr" (Peabody Essex Museum: Essex Institute Collection, August 11, 1692), https://salem.lib.virginia.edu/n83.html.
2 Lauren Tousignant, "Woman Cleared of Witchcraft 300 Years Later, Thanks to Eighth-Grade Class," *Jezebel* May 26, 2022, www.jezebel.com/woman-cleared-of-witchcraft-300-years-later-thanks-to-1848983594.
3 Emmaline Kenny, "The Last Salem Witch Has Been Exonerated," *Ms. Magazine*, October 30, 2023, https://msmagazine.com/2023/10/30/salem-witch-trial-exonerated-movie-documentary/, accessed January 21, 2024.
4 Richard Francis, *Judge Sewall's Apology: The Salem Witch Trials and the Forming of an American Conscience* (New York: Harper Perennial, 2006), 184.
5 Brigit Katz, "Last Convicted Salem 'Witch' is Finally Cleared," *Smithsonian Magazine*, August 3, 2022, https://www.smithsonianmag.com/smart-news/last-convicted-salem-witch-is-finally-cleared-180980516/, accessed January 13, 2024.
6 Anonymous, "The Last Witch: A Documentary 330 Years in the Making," https://www.thelastwitchfilm.com/.
7 Benjamin Fearnow, "Number of Witches Rises Dramatically across U.S. as Millennials Reject Christianity," *Newsweek*, March 25, 2020, https://www.newsweek.com/witchcraft-wiccans-mysticism-astrology-witches-millennials-pagans-religion-1221019.
8 Lyndal Roper, *The Witch in the Western Imagination* (Charlottesville: University of Virginia Press, 2012), 6.
9 Ronald Hutton, *The Triumph of the Moon: A History of Modern Pagan Witchcraft* (Oxford: Oxford University Press, 1999), 27.
10 Christopher S. Mackay, *The Hammer of Witches: A Complete Translation of the Malleus Maleficarum* (Cambridge: Cambridge University Press, 2009), 162.
11 P.G. Maxwell-Stuart, "A Royal Witch Theorist: James VI's *Daemonologie*," in *The Science of Demons: Early Modern Authors Facing Witchcraft and the Devil*, ed. Jan Machielse (London: Routledge, 2020), 167.
12 Sandra Gilbert and Susan Gubar, *The Madwoman in the Attic: The Woman Writer and the Nineteenth-Century Literary Imagination* (London: Yale University Press, 1979), 53.
13 Tonny Onyulo, "Witch Hunts Increase in Tanzania as Albino Deaths Jump," *USA Today*, February 26, 2015, https://www.usatoday.com/story/news/world/2015/02/26/tanzania-witchcraft/23929143/.
14 Brendan Walsh, "'Witches' Are Still Killed All Over the World. Pardoning Past Victims Could End the Practice," May 10, 2024, https://www.uq.edu.au/research/

article/2024/05/%E2%80%98witches%E2%80%99-are-still-killed-all-over-world-pardoning-past-victims-could-end-practice.
15 United Nations, "Concept Note on the Elimination of Harmful Practices Related to Witchcraft Accusations and Ritual Killings," March 19, 2020, https://www.ohchr.org/en/documents/tools-and-resources/concept-note-elimination-harmful-practices-related-witchcraft.
16 Manny Moreno, "UN Council Adopts Historic Resolution Condemning Harmful Practices Related to Accusations of Witchcraft and Ritual Attacks," July 28, 2021, https://wildhunt.org/2021/07/un-council-adopts-historic-resolution-condemning-harmful-practices-related-to-accusations-of-witchcraft-and-ritual-attacks.html.
17 Veta Smith Tucker, "Purloined Identity: The Racial Metamorphosis of Tituba of Salem Village," *Journal of Black Studies* 30, no. 4 (March 2000), 631.
18 Matthew Dennis, "American Indians, Witchcraft, and Witchhunting," *OAH Magazine of History* 17, no. 4 (July 2003), 23.
19 Emerson W. Baker and James Kences, "Maine, Indian Land Speculation, and the Essex County Witchcraft Outbreak of 1692," *Maine History* 40, no. 3 (2001), 158–189.
20 Michelle Mueller, "The Chalice and the Rainbow: Conflicts between Women's Spirituality and Transgender Rights in US Wicca in the 2010s," in *Female Leaders in New Religious Movements*, ed. Christian Giudice (Gothenburg, Sweden: Palgrave Macmillan Cham, 2017), 260.
21 Brian P. Levack, *The Witch-Hunt in Early Modern Europe* (London: Routledge, 2006), 129.
22 Deborah Willis, *Malevolent Nurture: Witch-Hunting and Maternal Power in Early Modern England* (Ithaca: Cornell University Press, 1995), 65.

1 "The Wickedness of Woman"
The *Malleus Maleficarum*, or "The Hammer of Witches"

Introduction

In the fifteenth century, the devil was afoot. Binary in nature to God himself, the devil used a wellspring of manipulation and trickery in order to see his evil bidding done on earth. Yet, there were many who didn't believe that the devil himself roamed the Earth but instead had representatives to do his bidding for him. Just as the church and its leaders were God's representatives in the name of righteousness, theologians of the time saw witches (most often women) as the dealers of Satan's evil on Earth. Often referred to as "heretics," "diabolics" or "sorceresses" rather than witches, these women were viewed as sexual temptations and seductresses, vengeful and vindictive, often raining plagues, devastation and starvation onto those in her path, particularly those who dared say no or challenge her in the name of God.[1]

As dramatic as this sounds, one document demonstrates that the belief in such a perilous evil at the hands of women was not only sound, but reasonable. Two inquisitors given special authority via papal bull written in 1484 to find such heretics, Jakob Sprenger and Heinrich Kramer (known by his Latinized name Institoris[2]), wrote the *Malleus Maleficarum*, translated to "The Hammer of Witches." This work detailed their argument in three parts: Part One, scholastic reasoning; Part Two, their experiences; and Part Three, the step-by-step process for accusing, trying and punishing the heretic. This book would become the cornerstone of future witchhunts, trials and executions, a manual that the witchhunters, judges and executioners relied upon for instruction and, most importantly, justification for their actions.

Heinrich Institoris and Trouble in Germany

A Dominican friar, Institoris was well into his fifties by the time he began work on the *Malleus Maleficarum*. Born in Schlettstadt, Germany, Institoris entered a Dominican monastery as a young man and continued his education in advanced theological studies, eventually earning his doctorate in 1479. Institoris became well known for his "aggressive zeal" against any heresy or stances against the Christian faith and, as early as 1467, had been awarded a special place in the papal commission to "preach against heresy and collect money," later given the authority to absolve sins and collect indulgences. By 1474, Institoris had been named an inquisitor and had been given the authority to act as such in provinces where there was no such position. In 1479, Institoris began work with fellow inquisitor Jakob Sprenger, and the two actively engaged in witchhunts in "Upper Germany."[3]

The following year, Institoris had become obsessed by the idea of witchcraft and traveled to Ravensburg in the northern part of Germany to preach against the diabolic infiltration. In various reports, including the *Malleus Maleficarum*, Institoris claimed to have been responsible for the execution of more than 200 witches, though historians such as Joseph Bergin, Tamar Herzig and others have demonstrated that the inquisitor likely took great liberty in his account and that he had only been involved with the witch trials in Ravensburg in 1484 and Innsbruck in 1485.[4] Whatever the claim, Institoris led a headstrong campaign against suspected witchcraft and by 1484, a total of eight women had been burned for the crime of heresy.[5]

Despite the apparent support Institoris received from town authorities in Ravensburg, he had amassed a great deal of opposition when he attempted to stretch his power to other regions. Having already gained a reputation for overstepping his bounds and slanderous speech, even being threatened with prison by the emperor in 1474, as well as scandals that involved embezzling funds, Institoris had become widely disliked for his arrogance, belligerence and unwavering zeal.[6] In order to gain further authority, particularly in areas where he met opposition, Institoris went to Rome with a letter signed by himself and his colleague, Sprenger, claiming that the devil and witchcraft were running rampant and undermining the sacred and righteous place of Christianity. In response to this plea, Pope Innocent VIII issued the famous papal bull entitled "Summis desiderantes," an official letter that addressed the disastrous weather and ill fortune affecting areas of Germany. The "Summis desiderantes" laid blame for the calamities at the feet of magic, heresy and witchcraft and granted both Institoris and Sprenger the authority to persecute those suspected of witchcraft in what was called "Germania superior," which historian Johannes Dillinger describes as "an ill-defined term that is probably best understood as today's South Germany and the Eastern Alpine region."[7]

Though there is ample evidence that Institoris believed that heresy had gained traction throughout Germany, by 1480 he had come to specifically believe that witches and witchcraft had become a widespread threat due to climate conditions across Germany. As a result of the Little Ice Age, climate change had affected weather patterns and crop yields in areas all over Europe. Intense rainfall and unseasonably cold weather in Germany left farmers without a productive harvest and what plants did grow succumbed to disease, resulting in starvation and illness in animals and humans alike. Witches, in league with the devil himself, and their sorcery became the scapegoats for this great misfortune.[8] Though there had been suggestions since the 1430s that unusual weather patterns could be a result of witchcraft, the papal bull of 1484 solidified the Catholic Church's official position on the matter.[9]

Buoyed by the papal bull and his strengthened authoritative power to persecute witches by any means, Institoris turned to the media to widely distribute information about how to identify and try suspected witches. By 1486, the first printing of the *Malleus Maleficarum* emerged, serving as both a "how to" manual and as the leading authority on witches, witchcraft, trial and execution. Largely due to the growing popularity of the printing press, the *Malleus Maleficarum* gained rapid traction, and went through 20 editions between 1486 and 1520 with another 16 editions between 1574 and 1669.[10] Through the *Malleus Maleficarum*, Institoris painted an image of a witch as performing feats of mal-intentioned sorcery, who has the ability to fly and, of course, manipulate the weather. The *Malleus Maleficarum* also makes it abundantly clear that the witch is almost always a woman, and the emphasis on gender cannot be overstated. Within the first part of Christopher Mackay's translation of the *Malleus Maleficarum*, the word "woman" appears 79 times, with the plural "women" and other words such as "sorceress" appearing just as often.

Due to their fragility and gullibility, Institoris argued that women were easily manipulated by the devil and would be unable to discern the seriousness of doing his bidding. In addition, the sin of Eve led to women having a natural impurity, and, as a result, they could possess a lust so great that they could make good Christian men give in to their carnal desires. As stated within the *Malleus Maleficarum*, even a woman's appearance could be an indication of her wickedness. Quoting Aristotle, Institoris wrote,

> For the eyes infect the adjoining air for a predetermined distance, in the same way that when mirrors are new and pure, they attract some impurity from the sight of a menstruating woman, as Aristotle says in the book *Sleep and Wakefulness* [...] In this way, then, when a soul is strongly impelled in the direction of evil, as happens to old women in particular, the sight of her is rendered poisonous and harmful in this manner, especially for children, who have tender bodies that are easily receptive of an impression.[11]

The implication of the old woman as being "strongly impelled in the direction of evil" would automatically render her a terrifying sight, "poisonous" especially to young children. It is no coincidence that, in the centuries to come, fairy tales and literature would have elderly female witches not only serve as the antagonists, but be haggard in appearance, in possession of poisonous objects and both threaten and frighten young children.

A Note on Translations

Between the initial publication in 1486 and 1669, the *Malleus Maleficarum* went through 36 editions, and by the twentieth century had undergone a number of translations in a variety of languages. As countless scholars have demonstrated, these translations were often sensationalistic and lacked focus on the complex academic, judiciary or theological implications of the text. This is especially true of the 1928 translation by Rev. Montague Summers, who held a deep fascination with the subject of demonology, witchcraft and the supernatural, writing dozens of books and articles on the occult, vampires and more. His translation of the *Malleus Maleficarum* dominated the twentieth century due to its availability and completeness, though his use of later editions of the work caused him to use "witch" and "witchcraft" when the 1486 edition relied more heavily on the language of *maleficarum*. As Joseph Bergin et al. have pointed out,

> Prior to the fifteenth century, people spoke in terms of heretics, of *maleficium*, of monstrous female spirits – the *lamiae* and *strigae*, but not of a single composite category, "witch." By the mid-sixteenth century, however, educated men generally agreed upon the definitions of "witch" and "witchcraft," definitions which drew upon, but were clearly distinguished from, older categories.[12]

In addition to altering the original language of the text in his translation, Summers also used language that tended to add more than was necessary (particularly obvious when compared to more recent translations). This included taking quotes, such as from literary scholars or the Bible, that appeared in the *Malleus Maleficarum* and occasionally translating them into his own words.

The translation used in this chapter comes from the 2009 publication of Mackay's *The Hammer of Witches: A Complete Translation of the Malleus Maleficarum*. Though there are many translations worth noting, including a 2000 German translation by Wolfgang Behringer, this chapter will primarily rely on Mackay's, as it is a complete translation and provides detailed notes on the various works cited within the *Malleus Maleficarum*. Though the Maxwell-Stuart translation is abridged and uses a 1588 edition of the *Malleus Maleficarum*, I will include occasional reference to Maxwell-Stuart's translation, as it clearly delineates gender in relation to "workers of magic" by using *maleficus* to mean "male worker of harmful magic" and the word "witch" to refer to the female *maleficae*.

A Note on Language

It may seem indisputable that the word "witch" appears within the *Malleus Maleficarum*, but the earliest editions of the text do not use language that is easily translatable to "witch" or "witchcraft." Mackay uses "sorcerer," "sorceress" and "sorcery" in his translation, which would, in later editions of the *Malleus Maleficarum*, be transposed with the words for "witch." Mackay's use of the former relates to the idea of "an elaborated concept of witchcraft" which is dominated by six distinct features:

1. The sorcerer/ess has entered into a pact with the devil
2. S/he has had sexual relations with the devil
3. The practice of aerial flight
4. The aerial flight allows attendance to a ritual led by the devil (where sexual acts were performed)
5. "The practice of maleficent magic"
6. The murder of babies (born or unborn).[13]

This description of witchcraft and what it entails gives a nuanced look into the conceptions around the practice, particularly the relationship between the practitioner and diabolic entity. This chapter will use sorceress and witch interchangeably, though Mackay and scholars such as Broedel and Maxwell-Stuart provide excellent analysis about the nuance of language in various translations.

Scholars also hold various beliefs about who actually authored the *Malleus Maleficarum*. Though both Institoris and Sprenger are listed as the authors of the *Malleus Maleficarum*, most scholars of this history, including Herzig, Broedel and Maxwell-Stuart, agree that it was likely Institoris who authored the text. Broedel's work illustrates that it's possible Sprenger was unaware that his name was even attached to the work.[14] Mackay, on the other hand, sees no reason to believe that Sprenger had nothing to do with the text, as

> only an imbecile would have fabricated a claim to joint authorship in a sworn document that would be included with the forgery and which it would be impossible to keep from coming to the notice of the man who was being falsely associated with the work.[15]

In other words, Institoris had too much authority and clout to have to steal someone's name for credibility's sake alone. Mackay argues that, due to Sprenger's academic background, it is possible that he authored Part One, while the references to Ravensburg and Innsbruck in Parts Two and Three make it more likely that Institoris authored those sections.

The debate around authorship is crucial when looking at histories where those with power and privilege constructed the narrative for those around them. Due to the potential harm that such an artifact could cause, very few people who might have practiced any kind of magic, sorcery, witchcraft or medicinal healing would have been able to keep a detailed record. The remains of grimoires from this time period are few and far between. Primarily only educated white men would have been able to write and publish a book on medicinal healing, as evidenced by the longevity of Nicholas Culpeper's *Complete Herbal: Over 400 Herbs and Their Uses*. Therefore, those tasked with

16 *Witchcraft: Gendered Perspectives*

the authority to hunt witches, such as Institoris and Sprenger, were the ones responsible for constructing the narrative around witchcraft as evil, diabolic, harmful and largely practiced by women. The significance of this debate cannot be understated, as both Institoris and Sprenger, no matter how much each contributed to the *Malleus Maleficarum*, are responsible for the positioning of witches and witchcraft through the lens of evil and as a threat to Christianity, and the association of women with witchcraft, which further emphasized beliefs in the innate jealousy, weakness, lust and overall sinful nature of women. Though this chapter will only use Institoris' name in reference to authorship for the sake of brevity, this is not an indication that one should overlook Sprenger's involvement with the narrative of the *Malleus Maleficarum*.

The *Malleus Maleficarum* and the Question of Misogyny

In 1971, Keith Thomas published *Religion and the Decline of Magic*, a book that has served as one of the foundations of modern scholarship on witchcraft, including the prevailing concept of those accused of witchcraft as primarily women, often widowed and/or elderly and likely to have faced financial and/or food insecurity. Though men were also accused of heresy, as well as younger women considered too weak to resist the devil's allure, the image of the haggard old witch, on the margins of society and a fright to look upon, is as synonymous with witches as broomsticks and cauldrons.

Thomas' extensive research demonstrated that, while early treatises on witchcraft used the language of male or female to describe those who could be heretics, later works often used the pronoun "she" to indicate who was a witch.[16] Reginald Scot's *The Discoverie of Witchcraft* (1584) serves as a prime example of the repeated use of "she" to indicate who had historically been identified and targeted as a witch:

> Item, the behaviour, looks, becks, and countenance of a woman, are sufficient signes, whereby to presume she is a witch: for alwais they looke downe to the ground, and dare not looke a man full in the face . . . it is indifferent to sale in the English toong; She is a witch; or, She is a wise woman.[17]

As this chapter will illustrate, the same reliance on the pronoun "she" to refer to those suspected of witchcraft is prevalent in the *Malleus Maleficarum*.

Thomas' work inspired scholars and activists to investigate histories of the occult, the supernatural and witchcraft, including diving into the deeply problematic and misogynistic arguments in Institoris and Sprenger's *Malleus Maleficarum*. In 1974, Andrea Dworkin published *Woman Hating*, and, using the Summers translation, lambasted the text for its unabashed misogyny. She quotes Summers' translation on women,

> To conclude: All witchcraft comes from carnal lust, which is in women insatiable. See Proverbs xxx: there are three things that are never satisfied,

yea, a fourth thing which says not, it is enough; that is, the mouth of the womb

and argues that this perspective on women showed that

> we are dealing with an existential terror of women, of the "mouth of the womb," stemming from a primal anxiety about male potency, tied to a desire for self (phallic) control; men have deep-rooted castration fears which are expressed as a horror of the womb. These terrors form the substrata of a myth of feminine evil which in turn justified several centuries of gynocide.[18]

Critics of Dworkin and this perspective are not necessarily in disagreement with the assertion that the attacks on women were rooted in patriarchal religious and social systems. Both Herzig and Mackay argue that even "the tract's title, *Malleus Maleficarum* (The Hammer of [Female] Witches)[,] certainly conveys its author's presumption that witchcraft is essentially a female crime."[19] However, both Herzig and Mackay, in their respective works, argue that such a viewpoint ignores the nuance of language and a history which also targeted heretical men and revered holiness in pious women. Herzig argued that,

> the friar who vilified the female sex in the *Malleus* also expressed his admiration for women whose unrestrained impressionability enabled them to attain a mystical union with Christ for which no man could ever aspire. Moreover . . . most of Institoris's writings were actually directed against heretical men.[20]

Mackay, in his introduction to the *Malleus Maleficarum*, further argues that the text isn't technically misogynistic due to the fact that the attacks do not universally apply to all women, "and the work contains references to pious women who resist the allurements of sorcery or fall victim to it."[21] These arguments indicate that, while the text illustrates a prevalence of negative attacks on women, attacks that should not be ignored, scholars must be careful in taking extreme approaches to their characterization of the *Malleus Maleficarum*, as doing so could result in neglecting the nuance of men as targets as well as perpetrators and the role of pious women in this history.

While recognizing that the history of witchcraft – the trials, violence, torture and death – extends far beyond the bounds of affecting elderly widows only, this chapter's approach will be to examine how the authors of the *Malleus Maleficarum* positioned women as weak, sexual and culpable for heretical wrongdoings, denying many of the women they came across the power and/or agency necessary to refute and/or deny these claims. Often, particularly in the second and third parts of the *Malleus Maleficarum*, the authors implored the readers to "trust" them and not ask too many questions about the validity of what they had witnessed but to take their word for it, given their authority as friars and inquisitors. Furthermore, the examination of the work in this chapter will also serve to demonstrate how the literary, political and academic writings of the following centuries were shaped by the narrative of the witch as a woman cast out by society and in league with the devil himself.

Part One of the *Malleus Maleficarum:* Scholastic Reasoning

In the first part of the *Malleus Maleficarum*, the structure is arranged in a question-and-answer format, reminiscent of scholarly works such as Plato's *Republic*, though rather than the dialogue occurring between two named people, Institoris formulates questions in a pre-emptive state, stating the question before anyone specific has the chance to ask it and therefore challenge his authority. Institoris further demonstrates his authority through references from scholastic works, well-known literature and the Bible as credible sources.

The opening of Part One poses the question of "whether claiming that sorcerers exist is such a Catholic proposition that to defend the opposite view steadfastly is altogether heretical."[22] This essentially poses the question of whether witchcraft exists and, if so, how can such a belief in the existence of witchcraft be compatible with the doctrine of the Catholic Church? From the outset, Institoris acknowledged the challenge of arguing for the existence of witchcraft, magic and sorcery when the Catholic Church preached the existence of an all-powerful and omniscient God. Naysayers and skeptics at the time questioned how such evil could be done under God's watch, particularly the idea that this power could cause physical harm to the landscape, animals and other humans. Institoris argued that free will allowed for such power to occur, but it was not the individual witch's power that could cause such harm, but her pact with diabolic forces, namely the devil, which allowed for such atrocities as the Evil force to intervene on her behalf.[23]

Furthermore, Institoris argued that any opposition to the existence of witchcraft was, in and of itself, heresy:

> The first are censured completely for heresy by the *Doctors in the Commentary on Pronouncements*, Bk. 4 in the distinction cited above, especially by St. Thomas. In the "Response" section in Art. 3 [Sent. 4.34.1.3.Co.], he says that this opinion is completely contrary to the authorities of the Saints and is rooted in lack of faith. His reasoning is that since the authority of the Holy Scripture says that demons have power over bodily objects and over the imagination of humans when they are allowed to by God.[24]

Citing numerous sources, Institoris illustrates that the devil and demons are, as a whole, fallen angels and possess a certain amount of otherworldly power.

The witch, therefore, becomes the devil's representative on Earth as the agent of that power. Just as the church is the representative of God on Earth, the witch serves the devil. And it is the church's responsibility to banish the witches in order to weaken the influence of all diabolic power. To state that one, to oppose the existence of witchcraft was heresy and two, the increased threats of witchcraft had wreaked moral, spiritual and physical havoc which could lay siege to all of Christianity unless radical steps be taken, allowed for Institoris to position witchcraft "to an almost limitless number of applications and makes plausible their claim that witches constitute a serious threat to Christendom."[25] This positioning made it difficult for readers to refute any of Institoris' claims, as to deny the existence of witchcraft was heresy, yet to affirm meant agreeing not only with the doctrine of the Catholic Church, but with the actions taken against witchcraft because of the threat it allegedly posed. Avoiding the possibility of heresy meant wholly supporting the church's prescriptions for battling the harmful magic associated with witchcraft. As a papal inquisitor, Institoris positioned himself not only as an authority on witchcraft, but as representative of the Catholic Church.

Throughout the course of Part One of the *Malleus Maleficarum*, the question emerges as to why women are most likely to be sorceresses. Institoris begins his response with the statement that he will not try to prove the contrary, "since experience itself makes such things believable more than do the testimony of words and of trustworthy witnesses."[26] He then says that "some doctors" ascertain that "there are three elements in the world that do not know how to maintain a middle course in terms of goodness or evil . . . a tongue, a churchman, and a woman."[27] Throughout this section of the *Malleus Maleficarum*, Institoris cites a variety of theological and historical sources in order to demonstrate that these three entities, particularly women to whom he devotes the most space, only have the capacity for extremes of absolute piety or evil.

Institoris relies heavily on theological sources in order to argue for the absolute evil of women. He begins:

> The evil of women is discussed in Ecclesiasticus 25[:22–23]: "There is no head worse than the head of a snake, and there is no anger surpassing the anger of a woman. It will be more pleasing to stay with a lion and a serpent than to live with an evil woman." Among many things that follow and precede, he concludes about the evil woman in the same passage, "Every evil is small compared to the evil of a woman" [verse 26]. Hence, Chrysostom says in reference to the passage, "It is beneficial not to marry" [Matt. 19:10]: "What else is a woman but the enemy of friendship, an inescapable punishment, a necessary evil, a natural temptation, a desirable disaster, a danger in the home, a delightful detriment, an evil of nature, painted with nice color? Therefore, if it is a sin to send her away, then since it is appropriate to keep her, now there is truly an obligatory sort of torture in that we are either to commit acts of adultery in sending her away or have daily quarrels" [Unfinished Work on Matthew 38].[28]

The emphasis here on the wickedness of women takes a great deal of liberty regarding the context of the scripture itself. For example, in the conversation around marriage and divorce in Matthew 19:10, the disciples question if marriage is worth the risk if divorce is not an option, wondering if it is "beneficial not to marry." In the *Malleus Maleficarum*, instead of providing the context for the questions of marriage as posed by the disciples, Institoris moves on to words from an unfinished work, allegedly by the apostle Matthew, that paint women not only as evil, but as temptresses that men cannot resist. Through this perspective, it is not a man's fault if he marries an adulteress because she is "inescapable," "necessary," "desirable," "delightful" and "painted with nice color." Once a man marries this woman, only to later find out that she is unfaithful and/or a witch, the husband is stuck in an unenviable position, as to divorce would be a sin against the church, but to stay with her is "torture."

Though Institoris initially claimed that he would not belabor the point of why women were more likely to be sorceresses, he spends a considerable amount of time explaining why women are more susceptible to the devil's craft. This includes a woman's gullibility, a lapse in memory that causes her to forget her piety, quick tempers, the carnal natures of her body, the use of her voice to lie and cajole, and her vanity in order to please men. He concludes this section with the summation that,

> Everything is governed by carnal lusting, which is insatiable in them ... and for this reason they even cavort with demons to satisfy their lust ... Hence, and consequently, it should be called the Heresy not of Sorcerers but of Sorceresses, to name it after the predominant element. Blessed be the Highest One, Who has, down to the present day, preserved the male kind from such disgraceful behavior, and clearly made man privileged since He wished to be born and suffer on our behalf in the guise of a man.[29]

Though the oppression of women was hardly new in the late fifteenth century, the *Malleus Maleficarum* proved instrumental in framing witchcraft as "a gendered crime: for the first time, witches came to be defined as primarily female, and all women were seen as prone to become witches."[30] Institoris' misogyny is unmistakable in the *Malleus Maleficarum*, yet historians are divided on where the friar got these ideas and why they might have developed so strongly that he would write a book so full of vitriol against women.

Part Two of the *Malleus Maleficarum:* The Inquisitor's Experiences with Witches

While Part One relied heavily on theology and academic scholarship as evidence of the existence of witches against skeptics, Part Two of the *Malleus Maleficarum* moves away from this approach in favor of Institoris' own experiences as anecdotal "proof" of the threat posed by the diabolic magic of sorceresses. In the opening to Part Two, Institoris "beseeches" the reader

> in the name of God, not to ask for an explanation of all matters, when suitable likelihood is sufficient if facts that are generally agreed to be true either on the basis of one's own experience from seeing or hearing or on the accounts given by trustworthy witnesses are adduced.[31]

This plea reminds the reader of Institoris' experience as an inquisitor in Ravensburg and Innsbruck and that his narratives are not hearsay, but of "suitable likelihood."

According to Institoris, there were 18 ways in which a witch would enact her sorcery:

1. Sorceresses entice innocent girls to become part of the "faithless"
2. By swearing an allegiance or making a pact with the devil
3. By transporting their body or spirit
4. When the sorceress gives of herself to the devil
5. By practicing acts of sorcery through the Sacraments of the Church
6. Through the obstruction of procreation
7. Using the art of conjuration in order to remove a penis
8. Through the ability to turn humans into animals
9. Through the use of conjuring spells and illusions
10. When the devil acts through the witch by inhabiting her body
11. The infliction of general illnesses
12. The infliction of specific illnesses
13. When midwives who are also sorceresses kill or sacrifice babies for the devil
14. Causing harm to animals
15. The ability to "stir up" hail, rain and lightning storms, particularly to cause damage

16–18. The three ways men and not women engage in witchcraft and sorcery.[32]

The chapter then goes through each of these in order to fully demonstrate how the sorceress might engage in such malice. Institoris also added his own experiences in each of these sections, illustrating further proof through his own eyewitness accounts.

In the first chapter of the second part, entitled "On the different methods by which demons allure and entice the innocent through sorceresses to increase this form of breaking the faith," Institoris speaks of when he and Sprenger had been in the Office of Inquisition, weaving a tale of innocent and desperate women who "had consulted suspected sorceresses because of losses inflicted on cows through the deprivation of milk and on other domestic animals."[33] The sorceresses told the women that, in exchange for the remedies, all they had to do was to make a small "promise to a spirit." Institoris argued that the promise might seem trivial but would lead to the woman's ultimate renunciation of her faith. One such example he gives is

> that when the priest greets the congregation during the solemn rites of the Mass by saying, "The Lord be with you," the woman who still survives because of the protection of the secular arm, always adds in the vernacular, "Kehr' mir die Zunge im Arsche um" ["Twirl your tongue in my ass"].[34]

Still, this method, he argued, was reserved for older women who, instead of possessing lustful desires, are "more greedy for earthly benefits." Younger women, on the other hand, would need to be enticed through "pleasures of the body."[35] When spurned by a lover or left destitute due to an empty promise of marriage, Institoris argued that they would turn to the devil for revenge.

> Young girls are sometimes corrupted by lovers with whom they have shamelessly copulated for the sake of marriage. The girls trust their lovers' promises, and then when they are rejected, they are disappointed in their every expectation and consider themselves to be disgraced in every regard. At this point, they turn to every sort of assistance offered by the Devil.[36]

Institoris then repeatedly points out that this type of instance, the corruption of young women through the pleasures of body and flesh, is so common that he would need far more space to give every instance. His descriptions of such instances include phrases such as "no counting the number," and he even insists that a whole book could be written on what happened in one diocese alone.

One such example Institoris provides is the story of Helena Scheuberin, a woman rumored to be sexually promiscuous and to possess a great deal of magical power. In his recollection, Institoris tells this story:

> There is a place in the diocese of Brixen,[62] and there a young man testified to such a case regarding his wife, who had been affected by sorcery directed against him. "I fell in love with a certain woman during my youth," he said, "and while she continually importuned me to join with her in marriage, I rejected her and took as my wife a woman from another territory. I nonetheless wished to please her for the sake of friendship and invited her to the wedding. She came, and when the other, respectable women were giving presents (offerings), the woman whom I had invited raised her hand and said in the hearing of the other women who were standing around, "There will be few healthy days that will you have after this one." Terrified, my bride asked the by-standers who this woman was who had made such threats to her, since she did not

recognize her, having been brought for marriage, as I've already said, from another territory. The other women stated that she was a lax and promiscuous woman. In any case, the events that she foretold ensued, and in that order – a few days later she was affected by sorcery, so that she lost the use of all her limbs. More than ten years later, the effects of this sorcery can still be seen on her body today.[37]

When Scheuberin was brought before Institoris for questioning, the inquisitor asked a multitude of questions regarding her sexual activity, including her virginity, going so far in this line of inquiry that he "made his fellow commissioners exceedingly uncomfortable."[38] He was subsequently asked to stop the line of questioning due to its irrelevance and inappropriateness and the trial was eventually dismissed due to Institoris' leading questions and procedural errors.[39] Mackay, in a footnote in the translation, also demonstrates that Institoris continued to repeat the husband's assertion of Scheuberin's sorcery as "fact, claiming that Scheuberin had had sexual relations with many men."[40] The story's emphasis on sex, sexuality and promiscuity illustrates Institoris' view of women: holy women were pious and reverent while all other women, particularly those who strayed from the church or were seen as promiscuous or sexual in some capacity, were potential sorceresses.

Part Three of the *Malleus Maleficarum*: Instructions for Accusation, Trial and Punishment

If there was any lingering doubt that Institoris held a firm conviction that women were the most likely to follow the devil and engage in acts of witchcraft and sorcery, the heavy reliance and repeated emphasis on "woman," "she" and "sorceress" in Part Three of the *Malleus Maleficarum* would put those doubts to rest. While the third part acknowledges that men can also be tried for heresy, the use of feminine language and pronouns in the titles of various sections, as well as specific situations and examples of what might happen during accusation and confession, indicate that Institoris' work firmly identified witchcraft as a gendered crime.

The final part of the *Malleus Maleficarum* reads like an instruction manual, giving the dos and don'ts of prosecuting suspected sorceresses: questioning witnesses, how to assess guilt, instruments of torture and divining punishment. The process for the procedural structure of accusation, trial and punishment is laid out methodically and in a manner that appears to be reasonable. Furthermore, on multiple occasions, Institoris reminds the reader that his authority on the subject comes from the bull issued by Pope Innocent III. Though bishops had often been responsible for presiding over local inquisitions, Institoris invoked the papal bull in order to demonstrate the validity of his experience and knowledge, justifying his methods for prosecution and illustrating that his work is that of God. "This bull was delivered to us inquisitors in furtherance of the care that we bestow on the work to the best of our abilities with the help of God."[41] This phrasing not only invokes the papal bull, but illustrates that Institoris, in working with both the Pope and God, uses this as evidence that he is well versed in what needs to be done judicially in order to stamp out the crime of heresy and sorcery. He argues that this must be taken in three parts: "initiating proceedings," "the method of continuing proceedings" and "the method of bringing the proceedings to a conclusion and passing sentence."[42]

It is with the first question, "initiating proceedings," that the use of feminized language becomes an integral part of Institoris' writing. In addressing this first question, Institoris wrote, "The first question is what is the appropriate method for initiating proceedings involving the Faith against sorceresses."[43] It is an interesting choice of language, as, in his introduction to the three parts, Institoris wrote, "The first is what the method of initiating proceedings involving the Faith is if the matter relates to sorceresses."[44] The initial use of the word "if" is missing when Institoris later addresses the question of initiating proceedings. In addition, the words "he" and "men" accompany all mention of authorities, such as the judge or the notary, even referring to theoretical witnesses with the pronoun "he." While there are mentions of the potential accused as "he" from time to time, most of the references to the accused include feminine language and pronouns, while all others are referred to in the masculine.

Institoris had enough forethought to address issues with potential witnesses, including the biases one might have against the accused, longstanding feuds between neighbors and the notion of "mortal enemies." In regard to "mortal enemies," he wrote,

> it is understood that a death has in fact been inflicted among them or one was intended . . . and similar things that are manifestly indicative of the perversity and ill-will of the perpetrator against the victim . . . hence such mortal enemies are excluded by law from giving testimony.

He also includes enmities, though doesn't define what constitutes an "enmity" as he does with "mortal enemy," but concludes that "as for other enmities, especially serious ones, in consideration of the fact that women are in fact easily moved to enmities, although these enmities do not completely debar, nonetheless, they weaken their statements," and goes on to warn men not to immediately dismiss the testimonies of enmities simply because women are "quarrelsome."[45]

The question of how to continue proceedings begins with the heading, "How the proceedings are to be continued (question six) and how the witnesses are to be examined in the presence of four other persons and the two ways in which the denounced woman is to be questioned."[46] Some questions, according to Institoris, were to be asked "without delay," including those about "why the common people feared her . . . whether she knew that she had a bad reputation and that she was hated" and more "in order to reach the foundation of the enmity, because in the end the denounced woman will allege enmity."[47] However, in this case, Institoris argued that the enmity isn't like the notion of "mortal enemy" but one where the enmity "was stirred up in a female fashion" and therefore is admissible, as "it is characteristic of sorceresses to stir up such enmity against themselves either by pointless words or by deeds."[48]

The question of torture and sentencing also draws attention to assumptions about the alleged sorceress' manipulative intentions. Institoris instructs that the denounced woman should be stripped naked (in the company of other respectable women) in order to determine if she is harboring any device for sorcery.[49] Her silence (or lack thereof) must also be taken into account, especially if she shows too much or not enough emotion. As the sorceress "does not have this ability (to shed tears)," it is the job of the authorities to pay careful attention to whether she is emitting genuine tears (which would be a sign of innocence) or false tears. An invocation by a priest or judge ought to be able to make such a determination, though it is possible, he says, for a sorceress to cry through the "Devil's cunning."[50] Inconsistent answers were also a sign of potential guilt, leading to the need for torture through means such as the application of hot irons or consumption of boiling water. According to the accusations, sorceresses had the ability to conjure lightning and hailstorms and fly through the air, and would even murder infants. Therefore, since it was possible that they could be resistant to torture, a lack of response to torture was also to be monitored.

The *Malleus Maleficarum* ends with a detailed account of what to do in the instances of various outcomes: innocence, guilty of a bad reputation only, a woman guilty of a bad reputation who must be exposed to torture, sentencing of a denounced woman with only light suspicion, the means to sentence a woman who is "vehemently suspected" and the method to sentence a woman who is "violently suspected."[51] Depending on the severity of suspicion, sentences ranged from rehabilitation through church members to the possibility of life sentences in prison and execution.

Though the judge in the proceeding would pass the sentence on the accused, the final line of the *Malleus Maleficarum* appears to leave the ultimate judgment to God: "Praise be to God, extermination to heretics, peace to the living, and eternal repose to the dead. Amen."[52] The idea of "extermination" possibly comes from the Fourth Lateran Council who, in 1215, wrote:

> Catholics who take the cross and gird themselves up for the expulsion of heretics shall enjoy the same indulgence, and be strengthened by the same holy privilege, as is granted to those who go to the aid of the holy Land.[53]

In this context, it is easy to take "extermination" to mean killing and the *Malleus Maleficarum* certainly supported the idea of sentencing a heretic (sorceress) to death. However, in the preceding paragraph, the Council Fathers refer to heresy as a crime punishable by excommunication and condemnation, not death. The choice of language in Institoris' final line frames the heretic as deserving of banishment and/or death, but not peace during life or eternal repose in Heaven.

Conclusion: Lasting Impact of the *Malleus Maleficarum*

As Bergin et al. argue in *'The* Malleus Maleficarum' *and the Construction of Witchcraft*, "the book's argument is predicated upon a series of assumptions about the nature of creation, about man's relationship with God and with the devil, and about witchcraft and witches," assumptions that would solidify the idea of sorcery and witchcraft as heretical crimes primarily committed by women.[54] The *Malleus Maleficarum* wasn't simply a single book published by a fanatical and misogynistic friar; it also served as the standard of what it meant to identify, accuse and try someone for the crime of witchcraft. Several treatises, pamphlets and books would go on to refer to the *Malleus Maleficarum* in their own assessments of witchcraft. For example, in his 1624 work *The Triall of Witch-Craft*, the English physician John Cotta wrote, "Some execute their hellish intentions by infernal compositions, drawn out of the bowels of dead and murdered infants; as Johannes Baptist Porta in his book *de Magica naturali*, doth from his own knowledge affirm and thereto the *Malleus Maleficarum*."[55] While not every reference to the *Malleus Maleficarum* over the next two centuries suggested deep belief in Institoris' assertions (in *The Discoverie of Witchcraft*, Reginald Scot outrightly rejected Institoris' belief in witchcraft, referring to it as a phobia), many seemed to echo the standards set forth by the *Malleus Maleficarum*. As discussed in the next chapter, works such as King James VI's *Daemonologie* demonstrated that Scripture warns society of witches who pose a threat not only to the landscape and local populations, but to the monarchy itself.

Notes

1 Scholars such as Bengt Ankarloo, Stuart Clark, Peter Brown, Pomelo Moro and JoAnn Scurlock have written on the history and literature of witchcraft in the periods prior to the *Malleus Maleficarum*. Stories such as *The Golden Ass* by Apuleius, sections of the Old Testament and characters such as Media are all examples of the witch narrative existing prior to the *Malleus Maleficarum*.
2 Also referred to as Institoris (meaning "shopkeeper").
3 Joseph Bergin, Hans Broedel, Penny Roberts and William G. Naphy, eds. *'The* Malleus Maleficarum' *and the Construction of Witchcraft: Theology and Popular Belief* (Manchester: Manchester United Press, 2004), 11–13.
4 Joseph Bergin, Hans Broedel, Penny Roberts and William G. Naphy, eds. *'The* Malleus Maleficarum' *and the Construction of Witchcraft: Theology and Popular Belief* (Manchester: Manchester United Press, 2004), 14; Tamar Herzig, "The Bestselling Demonologist: Heinrich Institoris' *Malleus Maleficarum*," in *The Science of Demons: Early Modern Authors Facing Witchcraft and the Devil*, ed. Jan Michaelson (London: Taylor and Francis, 2020), 54.

5 Joseph Bergin, Hans Broedel, Penny Roberts and William G. Naphy, eds. 'The Malleus Maleficarum' and the Construction of Witchcraft: Theology and Popular Belief (Manchester: Manchester United Press, 2004), 18.
6 Joseph Bergin, Hans Broedel, Penny Roberts and William G. Naphy, eds. 'The Malleus Maleficarum' and the Construction of Witchcraft: Theology and Popular Belief (Manchester: Manchester United Press, 2004), 13.
7 Johannes Dillinger, "Germany – 'the Mother of Witches'," in The Routledge History of Witchcraft, ed. Johannes Dillinger (New York: Routledge, 2020), 95.
8 Johannes Dillinger, "Germany – 'the Mother of Witches'," in The Routledge History of Witchcraft, ed. Johannes Dillinger (New York: Routledge, 2020), 97.
9 Wolfgang Behringer, "Climate Change and Witch Hunting: The Impact of the Little Ice Age on Mentalities," in Climate Variability in Sixteenth-Century Europe and Its Social Dimension, ed. Rudolf Brazdil and Christian Pfister (Rudiger Glaser: Springer Science and Business Media Dordrecht, 1999), 336.
10 Liv Helene Willumsen, The Voices of Women in Witchcraft: Northern Europe (London: Routledge, 2022), 15.
11 Christopher S. Mackay, The Hammer of Witches: A Complete Translation of the Malleus Maleficarum (Cambridge: Cambridge University Press, 2009), 113–114.
12 Joseph Bergin, Hans Broedel, Penny Roberts and William G. Naphy, eds. 'The Malleus Maleficarum' and the Construction of Witchcraft: Theology and Popular Belief (Manchester: Manchester United Press, 2004), 3.
13 Christopher S. Mackay, The Hammer of Witches: A Complete Translation of the Malleus Maleficarum (Cambridge: Cambridge University Press, 2009), 19.
14 Joseph Bergin, Hans Broedel, Penny Roberts and William G. Naphy, eds. 'The Malleus Maleficarum' and the Construction of Witchcraft: Theology and Popular Belief (Manchester: Manchester United Press, 2004), 18, 36.
15 Christopher S. Mackay, The Hammer of Witches: A Complete Translation of the Malleus Maleficarum (Cambridge: Cambridge University Press, 2009), 5.
16 Keith Thomas, Religion and the Decline of Magic: Studies in Popular Beliefs in Sixteenth- and Seventeenth-Century England (London: Weidenfeld and Nicolson, 1971), 436.
17 Reginald Scot, The Discoverie of Witchcraft (London: Elliot Stock, 1886), 20, 88.
18 Andrea Dworkin, Woman Hating: A Radical Look at Sexuality (New York: Penguin Books, 1974), 133–134.
19 Tamar Herzig, "The Bestselling Demonologist: Heinrich Institoris' Malleus Maleficarum," in The Science of Demons: Early Modern Authors Facing Witchcraft and the Devil, ed. Jan Michaelson (London: Taylor and Francis, 2020), 58.
20 Tamar Herzig, "The Bestselling Demonologist: Heinrich Institoris' Malleus Maleficarum," in The Science of Demons: Early Modern Authors Facing Witchcraft and the Devil, ed. Jan Michaelson (London: Taylor and Francis, 2020), 63.
21 Christopher S. Mackay, The Hammer of Witches: A Complete Translation of the Malleus Maleficarum (Cambridge: Cambridge University Press, 2009), 26.
22 Christopher S. Mackay, The Hammer of Witches: A Complete Translation of the Malleus Maleficarum (Cambridge: Cambridge University Press, 2009), 91.
23 Tamar Herzig, "The Bestselling Demonologist: Heinrich Institoris' Malleus Maleficarum," in The Science of Demons: Early Modern Authors Facing Witchcraft and the Devil, ed. Jan Michaelson (London: Taylor and Francis, 2020), 55.
24 Christopher S. Mackay, The Hammer of Witches: A Complete Translation of the Malleus Maleficarum (Cambridge: Cambridge University Press, 2009), 92.
25 Joseph Bergin, Hans Broedel, Penny Roberts and William G. Naphy, eds. 'The Malleus Maleficarum' and the Construction of Witchcraft: Theology and Popular Belief (Manchester: Manchester United Press, 2004), 24.
26 Christopher S. Mackay, The Hammer of Witches: A Complete Translation of the Malleus Maleficarum (Cambridge: Cambridge University Press, 2009), 160.

27 Christopher S. Mackay, *The Hammer of Witches: A Complete Translation of the Malleus Maleficarum* (Cambridge: Cambridge University Press, 2009), 160.
28 Christopher S. Mackay, *The Hammer of Witches: A Complete Translation of the Malleus Maleficarum* (Cambridge: Cambridge University Press, 2009), 162.
29 Christopher S. Mackay, *The Hammer of Witches: A Complete Translation of the Malleus Maleficarum* (Cambridge: Cambridge University Press, 2009), 170.
30 Moira Smith, "The Flying Phallus and the Laughing Inquisitor: Penis Theft in the *Malleus Maleficarum.*" *Journal of Folklore Research* 39, no. 1 (January–April 2002), 87.
31 Christopher S. Mackay, *The Hammer of Witches: A Complete Translation of the Malleus Maleficarum* (Cambridge: Cambridge University Press, 2009), 261.
32 Christopher S. Mackay, *The Hammer of Witches: A Complete Translation of the Malleus Maleficarum* (Cambridge: Cambridge University Press, 2009), 272.
33 Christopher S. Mackay, *The Hammer of Witches: A Complete Translation of the Malleus Maleficarum* (Cambridge: Cambridge University Press, 2009), 275–276.
34 Christopher S. Mackay, *The Hammer of Witches: A Complete Translation of the Malleus Maleficarum* (Cambridge: Cambridge University Press, 2009), 276–277.
35 Christopher S. Mackay, *The Hammer of Witches: A Complete Translation of the Malleus Maleficarum* (Cambridge: Cambridge University Press, 2009), 276–277.
36 Christopher S. Mackay, *The Hammer of Witches: A Complete Translation of the Malleus Maleficarum* (Cambridge: Cambridge University Press, 2009), 278–279.
37 Christopher S. Mackay, *The Hammer of Witches: A Complete Translation of the Malleus Maleficarum* (Cambridge: Cambridge University Press, 2009), 279.
38 Joseph Bergin, Hans Broedel, Penny Roberts and William G. Naphy, eds. *'The Malleus Maleficarum' and the Construction of Witchcraft: Theology and Popular Belief* (Manchester: Manchester United Press, 2004), 2.
39 Joseph Bergin, Hans Broedel, Penny Roberts and William G. Naphy, eds. *'The Malleus Maleficarum' and the Construction of Witchcraft: Theology and Popular Belief* (Manchester: Manchester United Press, 2004), 2–3.
40 Christopher S. Mackay, *The Hammer of Witches: A Complete Translation of the Malleus Maleficarum* (Cambridge: Cambridge University Press, 2009), 279.
41 Christopher S. Mackay, *The Hammer of Witches: A Complete Translation of the Malleus Maleficarum* (Cambridge: Cambridge University Press, 2009), 492.
42 Christopher S. Mackay, *The Hammer of Witches: A Complete Translation of the Malleus Maleficarum* (Cambridge: Cambridge University Press, 2009), 500.
43 Christopher S. Mackay, *The Hammer of Witches: A Complete Translation of the Malleus Maleficarum* (Cambridge: Cambridge University Press, 2009), 503.
44 Christopher S. Mackay, *The Hammer of Witches: A Complete Translation of the Malleus Maleficarum* (Cambridge: Cambridge University Press, 2009), 500.
45 Christopher S. Mackay, *The Hammer of Witches: A Complete Translation of the Malleus Maleficarum* (Cambridge: Cambridge University Press, 2009), 513.
46 Christopher S. Mackay, *The Hammer of Witches: A Complete Translation of the Malleus Maleficarum* (Cambridge: Cambridge University Press, 2009), 513.
47 Christopher S. Mackay, *The Hammer of Witches: A Complete Translation of the Malleus Maleficarum* (Cambridge: Cambridge University Press, 2009), 518.
48 Christopher S. Mackay, *The Hammer of Witches: A Complete Translation of the Malleus Maleficarum* (Cambridge: Cambridge University Press, 2009), 518.
49 Christopher S. Mackay, *The Hammer of Witches: A Complete Translation of the Malleus Maleficarum* (Cambridge: Cambridge University Press, 2009), 546.
50 Christopher S. Mackay, *The Hammer of Witches: A Complete Translation of the Malleus Maleficarum* (Cambridge: Cambridge University Press, 2009), 549–550.
51 Christopher S. Mackay, *The Hammer of Witches: A Complete Translation of the Malleus Maleficarum* (Cambridge: Cambridge University Press, 2009), 576, 579, 583, 587, 590, 595.

52 Christopher S. Mackay, *The Hammer of Witches: A Complete Translation of the Malleus Maleficarum* (Cambridge: Cambridge University Press, 2009), 657.
53 Council Fathers, "Fourth Lateran Council: 1215 Council Fathers," https://www.papalencyclicals.net/councils/ecum12-2.htm, accessed May 6, 2024.
54 Joseph Bergin, Hans Broedel, Penny Roberts and William G. Naphy, eds. *'The Malleus Maleficarum' and the Construction of Witchcraft: Theology and Popular Belief* (Manchester: Manchester United Press, 2004), 34.
55 John Cotta, "The Infallible True and Assured Witch; or the Second Edition of the Tryall of Witch-Craft Shewing the Right and True Methode of the Discoverie with a Confutation of Erroneous Waies. Carefully Reviewed and More Fully Cleared and Augmented," in *Digital Witchcraft Collection*, ed. Cornell University (London: I.L. for Richard Higginbotham, 1624).

2 "Something Wicked This Way Comes"

The Witchhunts of Scotland, England and Salem

Introduction

The witch craze in Europe lasted from the fourteenth to the eighteenth century, with the last known witch execution taking place in Poland in 1783. Few areas of Europe were immune, but Scotland and Germany had the highest concentration of witch trials over the centuries while France and England saw few prosecutions, yet accusations and executions persisted in those countries as well. In total, accusations of witchcraft and subsequent trials occurred across 21 European nations over five centuries.[1] Historians have noted several possible reasons for the upsurge in witchcraft accusations, including the plague, political unrest, religious competition during the Reformation, environmental disasters, economic uncertainty and the changing dynamics of women's roles in society.

This chapter will highlight two cases in Europe and one in Salem, Massachusetts in order to illustrate how the narrative of witches and witchcraft stayed largely in the hands of those with power and privilege. Through King James VI's *Daemonologie*, William Shakespeare's *Macbeth* and Thomas Potts' *The Wonderfull Discoverie of Witches*, this chapter will demonstrate the proliferation of assumptions and stereotypes about witchcraft, particularly the kind of women who not only practice the art, but must be tried for their offenses against God and the court. Though the women discussed in this chapter are merely a tiny fraction of the accused and only represent three geographic regions where witch trials took place, I chose these particular cases due to the similarities between the accused as healers and their connections to broader published and/or performed works. More specifically, through the works of King James VI, Shakespeare and Potts as well as the surviving trial documents themselves, this chapter will emphasize the language used about the accused in each case, including allegations of threat and violence, the use of reputation as evidence and the prominent stressing of the accused's poverty and appearance, particularly in regard to her age and alleged marks that would denote her being a witch.

DOI: 10.4324/9781032717227-3

A Note on Primary Sources

For the purposes of this chapter, all quotes from primary sources will be altered for the sake of readability and will include the modern English spelling of words. In order to be faithful to the author's original text, including spellings and punctuation, this chapter will repeat those quotes in the endnotes as they appear in the original document.

Scotland: North Berwick, 1590–1592

In 1591, *Newes from Scotland* published a dramatic account of the proliferation of witchcraft. The work included the trials and executions of several witches who were charged with treason, among other acts of sorcery. Their treasonous acts included a plot to murder the king, working "to bewitch and drown his Majesty in the sea coming from Denmark, with such other wonderful matters as the like hath not been heard at any time."[2] The pamphlet said that King James VI and his wife, Anne of Denmark, were targets of a murder plot and named witches in North Berwick as responsible not only for the conspiracy to kill the king and his wife at sea, but also for pacts with Satan and performing diabolic rituals. Allegedly, erroneous claims about the happenings in North Berwick revealed several untruths and falsehoods, motivating the anonymous author to publish the pamphlet as a means of getting out the "truth."

Geillis Duncan, a young domestic servant in East Lothian, was the first to be named in the pamphlet and later accused of witchcraft. Duncan's employer, a bailiff named David Seton, "suspected her of witchcraft because she often stayed out late at night."[3] As *Newes from Scotland* touted that the suspected devil worship and murder conspiracies occurred after dark, Seton's "evidence" was enough to bring serious allegations against Duncan. Duncan underwent a series of tortures, including *pilliwinks* (also known as a thumbscrew) "and binding or wrenching her head with a cord or rope, which is a most cruel torment also."[4] Despite the torture she endured, Duncan only elicited a confession after it was found that she had a "Devil's mark," noted in *Newes from Scotland* as proof of her guilt, as "by due examination of witchcraft and Witches in Scotland, it hath lately been found that the devil doth generally mark them with a private mark."[5] In her confession, Duncan implicated Agnes Sampson as a fellow witch.

Known as "The Wise Wife of Keith," Sampson served as a noted healer in East Lothian, learning the craft from her father at an early age.[6] A widow by the 1590s, Sampson lived in poverty and acted as a midwife and healer in order to provide for herself. By the time Duncan had named her as a fellow witch, Sampson had already been suspected and accused of witchcraft several times, including for committing the "un-godly" act of alleviating the pains of childbirth.[7] She had been imprisoned in Haddington for a brief time before she was brought to Edinburgh in late 1590, where she would be questioned on three separate occasions.

The case of Agnes Sampson is a unique one, as King James VI himself was in attendance as an interrogator who issued a command that Sampson undergo a complete examination to find the devil's mark. *Newes from Scotland* reported that:

> this Agnes Sampson had all her hair shaven off, in each part of her body, and her head thrown with a rope according to the custom of that Country, being a pain most grievous, which she continued almost an hour, during which time she would not confess anything until the Devil's mark was found upon her privates, then she immediately confessed whatsoever was demanded of her, and justifying those persons aforesaid to be notorious witches.[8]

Like Duncan, after the discovery of a mark, Sampson confessed to witchcraft and to the crime of trying to murder the king. Her confession consisted of elaborate storytelling, including a coven with over 200 witches as members, and how the devil had instructed that they conduct spells and throw a dead cat into the ocean in order to conjure a storm that would throw King James VI's ship off course.[9] Sampson said she had asked the devil why he bore such hatred against His Majesty, to which he replied that he saw King James VI as his greatest enemy in the world.[10] In her confession she also stated that

> the earl Bothwell hard moved her to inquire what should become of the king, how long he should reign, and what should happen after his death and that the spirit having undertaken to make away the king, after he had failed in performing, and was challenged by her, confessed it was not in his power.[11]

Sampson's formal trial took place on January 27, 1591, where 51 counts were brought against her, including for "sailing with her accomplices out of North Berwick . . . [where] the Devil raised an evil wind . . . and caused the ship to perish" and her confession before King James VI where she described a meeting with the devil who made her and others "keep his commandments, which were to do all the evil they could." Sampson, found guilty on all accounts, was sentenced

> to be taken to the castle of Edinburgh and there bound to a stake and worried [i.e. strangled] while she was dead, and thereafter her body to be burned in ashes and all her moveable goods to be escheat and in brought to our sovereign lord's use.[12]

On January 28, Agnes Sampson became the first of the North Berwick witches to be executed for her crimes.

Torture and the devil's mark are the commonalities we can see between Duncan's and Sampson's confessions, only elicited after they had undergone harrowing violence and extreme pain followed by the "proof" of their witchcraft due to marks on their bodies. It was only under duress that Duncan, the young housemaid, named names and, at her execution, admitted she had done so in the hope that, by giving the interrogators what they wanted, she might be able to save herself from further torture. This was to no avail. After months in prison, Duncan was executed on December 4, 1591.

Sampson's confession goes much further than Duncan's, as she wove a story of a devil's pact, rituals involving dead cats and intimate knowledge of the king's whereabouts and relationship with his wife. Her confession also includes her first encounter with the devil:

> Agnes confesses that after the death of her husband the devil appeared unto her in the night . . . for the sustenation [keeping] of her and her bairns [babies] bidding her be of good cheer . . . promising that if she would serve him she nor they should lack nothing. And being motivated with her poverty and his fair promises of riches and revenge of her enemies, took him for her master and renounced Christ.[13]

It is unclear if Sampson truly believed that she had visited with the devil. It is also unclear why she would not only confess to witchcraft but also reveal her involvement in a detailed plot to murder the king, but it is telling that she only told these stories after undergoing extreme torture. It's also possible that she was led to certain answers by the interrogators, though her intricate knowledge of the convention might have come from what she learned while imprisoned.[14] It's also important to note that she was speaking to King James VI himself. Sampson, an older widow known for being a healer and accused of witchcraft several times before, had His Majesty himself as an interrogator, leaving her in a disadvantaged position in a wildly unbalanced power dynamic.

King James VI's *Daemonologie*, 1597

The trials at North Berwick, particularly the confession of Agnes Sampson, had convinced King James VI that witches were not only real and posed a dangerous threat to society, but also had treasonous intent, determined to remove him from the throne. This inspired his 1597 work *Daemonologie*, which, like the *Malleus Maleficarum*, left a lasting impression of how witches were viewed in the time period. Broken up into three parts, *Daemonologie* borrows from the structure of early theological and philosophical works, posing questions and responses between characters of his own making, Philomathes and Epistemon, who discuss the presence and threat of witchcraft.[15] The use of this kind of structure served as a rebuttal against more skeptical works such as Johann Weyer's *On the Tricks of Demons* (1563) and Reginald Scot's *The Discoverie of Witchcraft* (1584).[16]

Throughout the entirety of *Daemonologie*, King James VI positions witchcraft as a crime largely committed by women. The argument in the first chapter of Part One seeks to demonstrate, as "Proven by the Scripture, that these unlawful arts [of witchcraft] in general, have been and may be put in practice," relying on the biblical story of Saul as explanation of the practice.[17] The second part of the work dedicates a large portion to the description of sorcery and witchcraft as a whole. The third part of *Daemonologie*, like the *Malleus Maleficarum*, gives instructions on the punishment of witches, taking an uncompromising viewpoint on what should happen to those witches found guilty of their alleged crimes.

While the first part of *Daemonologie* focuses on questions of the existence of witches and the practices of witchcraft, the second part moves beyond the possibility of witchcraft to arguments about the connections between women and witchcraft. "Why are there more women of that craft not men? What things are possible to them to effectuate [make something happen] by the power of their master?" only to have Epistemon reply that

> The reason is easy, for as that sex is frailer than man is, so is it easier to be entrapped in these gross snares of the Devil, as was over well proved to be true by the Serpents deceiving of Eve.[18]

Much like the *Malleus Maleficarum* a century before, *Daemonologie* relies on sexist belief systems that position women as frailer, weaker and more gullible and, therefore, more susceptible to the devil's entrapments.

Another form of evidence of the proliferation of witchcraft relies on the information King James VI heard as parts of the confessions given by the North Berwick witches. For example, in one of Sampson's descriptions of magical doings, the interrogators recounted that,

> she confesses that upon a complaint of a woman of the frowardness [person who is difficult to deal with] of her father-in-law and her earnest desire to be quit of him, she made a picture of wax and raised a spirit at a waterside beside a brier bush, desiring her to enchant it to serve for his destruction, and send it to the said-woman to put under his bed sheet or bed head.[19]

In the second book, King James VI wrote that the devil teaches his subject the art of "how to make pictures of wax or clay: That by roasting thereof, the persons that they bear the name of may be continually melted or dried away by continual sickness."[20] The mention of wax here not only refers back to Sampson's confession, but may also connect to King James VI's fear of assassination. In 1578, wax statues in the likeness of Queen Elizabeth and her councilors were found in a stable just outside of London. The statues were considered a "magical attack" against the queen, as the material allowed for a detailed representation of her face and body, but wax also served as an attack due to the way it could easily misshapen the body through heat and manipulation of the figure. As Lynn Maxwell points out,

> wax figures are like political figures not simply because they have similar forms, but also perhaps because they are, metaphorically at least, of the same matter. At the same time, the vulnerability of wax to manipulation, disfiguration, and melting enhances the dangers of magical attacks waged through wax.[21]

It is possible that King James VI was already aware of such magical attacks against political figures, which would help to account for his emphasis on the detail in *Daemonologie*.

Another aspect of *Daemonologie*'s third book is its emphasis on sex and sexual relations, particularly between the devil and witch or other supernatural beings that appear to feed upon sex, such as incubi (male) or succubi (female). King James VI refers to the devil's (or other entities') use of bodies for sex or the stealing of semen as "abuses," noting that incubi often abuse women when they are sleeping after having stolen semen from a dead body. Of important and disturbing note is his comment that "we read of a Monastery of Nuns which were burnt for their being that way abused."[22] This is the only sentence dedicated to this story, so it is unclear what monastery he is referring to and when this happened, yet it would appear that, despite King James VI's acknowledgment that such sexual acts are "abuses," the burning of abused women for being sexually violated by spirits such as incubi was commonplace enough not to warrant more information. This positioning of women as culpable for sexual violations against them not only informs an understanding of the powerlessness of women accused of witchcraft, but also gives insight into broader implications of longstanding societal attitudes about sexual violence perpetrated against women. If nuns – women of God – were not pious enough to escape this punishment, what would that mean for other women, women with reputations for sexual activity or elderly women known for their hostile behavior and attitudes?

Pregnancy and midwifery also play into *Daemonologie*'s emphasis on sexual abuses: "Indeed it is possible to the craft of the Devil to make a woman's belly to swell after he has that way abused her, which he may do ... by herbs as we see beggars daily do."[23] The mention of herbs is significant here, as healers, such as Sampson, would have used herbs as part of their practice, yet King James VI aligns the use of herbs with beggars. Samson, who lived in poverty at the time of her trials, might have been perceived as a beggar and, through King James VI's characterization, completely disregards her significant role as a healer in the community.[24] The dismissal of women like Samson as healers was fairly commonplace, particularly as the use of herbs and reliance on the senses stood as antithetical to the teachings of the Catholic Church. During the Scientific Revolution, as more discoveries emerged about eggs and sperm, the Catholic Church took firm stances against any kind of

Macbeth, 1606

In 1606, shortly after the death of Queen Elizabeth made King James VI of Scotland King James I of England, William Shakespeare's *Macbeth* was performed on stage for the first time.[26] The play, featuring a Scottish man who is prophesied by witches to be king, was heavily influenced by *Daemonologie*, and introduced audiences to the possibilities of what a witch looked and sounded like as well as the idea of witches holding secret meetings after dark. As Richard Wilson argues,

> But it was in the opening of Shakespeare's play that the idea was introduced onto the London stage of witches convening deliberately for their own malign purposes, and with it a new paradigm of witchcraft as conspiracy centered on rituals of the witches' sabbat.[27]

Though Duncan had been accused of witchcraft due to her employer's observation that she often left the home after dark, it was not common knowledge that witches convened in secret or held meetings to enact foul and dark magic.[28] Shakespeare's *Macbeth* would go a long way to solidify that perception of witches among audiences.

Act One opens with a stage direction of thunder and lightning, a clear reference to the association of weather magic and witches, though it is possible that it also refers more specifically to the storm that affected King James I and his wife, Anne. Three witches enter the stage and, in a very short opening scene, are concluding this meeting and preparing for the next one, where they will meet with Macbeth. The first witch asks, "When shall we three meet again? In thunder, lightning or in rain?" which works both as a reference to repeated meetings and their reliance upon storms for their magical dealings.[29] Prior to their exit, merely 12 lines into the first act, references to storms, fog, cats, toads and the number 3 are invoked, demonstrating Shakespeare's familiarity with the signs and symbols associated with witches and witchcraft at the turn of the century.[30]

The earliest editions of the play provide very little information about what the witches are supposed to look like. It is only through the other characters' reactions and dialog that the witches are perceived as ugly and unfeminine. When Macbeth and Banquo come upon the witches in Act One, Scene Three, Banquo remarks,

> How far is't called to Forres? What are these, So withered and so wild in their attire, That look not like th'inhabitants o'the earth, And yet are on't? Live you, or are you aught That man may question? You seem

to understand me, By each at once her choppy finger laying Upon her skinny lips. You should be women, And yet your beards forbid me to interpret That you are so.[31]

Much scholarship has gone into interpreting the gendered portrayal of the witches as spoken by Banquo here. "Withered" likely refers to advanced age, while "wild in their attire" would suggest that they are not finely dressed, possibly insinuating poverty. The "not like th'inhabitants o'the earth" goes a long way to dehumanize the witches, as does "Live you, or are you aught that man may question?" "Choppy" likely refers to their fingers as chapped or rough, while the reference to "beards" questions their femininity and could also potentially refer to their age.

The configuration of the witches as the three "Weird Sisters" also sets up a dynamic connection between the concept of witches and the witch-family. An analysis of the Weird Sisters demonstrates that they are not only companionable (a stark contrast to other sister relationships in Shakespeare's plays) but embody a female power without the need for male companionship. To illustrate this,

> Terry Eagleton uses Julia Kristeva's deconstructive feminism to interpret the witches in *MacBeth*: "They are poets, prophetesses, and devotees of female cult, radical separatists who scorn male power and lay bare the hollow sounds and fury at its heart."[32]

As later demonstrated in Chapter 5, the connection between tightknit family bonds and those who practice witchcraft proliferates storytelling about witchcraft and the magical arts.

England: Pendle, 1612–1634

Just six years after the first stage production of *Macbeth*, the Device family of Lancashire would be caught in an intricate web of witchcraft accusations and trials. England's period of persecution began with the first statute on witchcraft, the Witchcraft Act of 1542, which defined the crime of witchcraft as any invocation, conjuration, enchantment or sorcery done to hurt another, acquire money or oppose Christianity. A total of 500 people were executed for witchcraft between 1542 and the repeal of the statutes in 1736, with an estimated 1,000 people accused of the crime over the near 200-year period.[33] The Pendle witch trials, of which the Devices were included, resulted in 12 accusations, 10 of whom were executed whilst 1 died awaiting trial. The star witness: a 9-year-old girl named Jennet Device.

Though popular retellings of the Pendle witches might say, as supernatural storytelling is wont to do, that the events began on All Hallows' Eve, the actions that set the famous trials into motion started on March 21, 1612. Alizon Device, a local beggar in Lancashire, had gone for a walk through

Trawden Forest, stopped a peddler by the name of John Law and asked him for pins, which he refused.[34] Upon his refusal, Alizon allegedly saw a black dog who acted as her familiar and led to what was described in the records as a "witchcraft-induced illness," in this case, a stroke. Though seemingly innocuous, the request for pins was actually of strong significance in the trial to come, as pins were largely associated with dark magic, featuring in other trial documents in England and elsewhere. John's son, Abraham, brought the story to the attention of Roger Nowell, the local Justice of the Peace. On March 30, Nowell took statements from Alizon, as well as her mother, Elizabeth, and her brother, James. Two days later, on April 2, Nowell "examined Elizabeth Device's mother, the eighty-year-old Elizabeth Southerns (alias 'Old Demdike'), Anne Whittle (alias 'Chattox') and three local witnesses."[35] On April 10, Good Friday, Alizon and the other members of the Device family met at their family home of Malkin Tower to discuss the accusations. Later, 9-year-old Jennet Device would testify that "the meeting was called to give a name to Alizon's familiar and decided that all those who attended, including her family, were witches."[36] News of the meeting, which was confirmed by the Device family, convinced Nowell that "they were confronting a major outbreak of witchcraft." On August 19, Old Demdike died in prison.[37] On August 20, the others were executed.

The story of the Pendle witches begs many questions, namely why would a 9-year-old girl be allowed to give such damning testimony and why, in a time period and location where there were relatively few witchcraft accusations, let alone trials, did 11 people die for the crime? The answer to the first question can be traced directly back to King James VI's *Daemonologie*, which stated that children "are not capable of reason to practice such things" so would not be persuaded by their own involvement in witchcraft.[38] The answer to the second question has its roots in economic hardship and societal attitudes about Christianity, particularly during the Reformation. However, as James Sharpe writes,

> So times were hard in Pendle early in the seventeenth century, and the local religious situation was confused and possibly polarized. What initiated the trials of 1612, however, was a desire by the pedlar John Law and his family to prosecute an incident of *maleficium* and the encouragement given to this prosecution by Roger Nowell.[39]

Alizon's belief in her own powers coupled with Law's untimely stroke make this case take on a more personal undertone rather than the larger social implications of economic and religious conditions.

Thomas Potts, *The Wonderfull Discoverie of Witchcraft*, 1613

Despite the personal nature of the Pendle witch case, the broader narrative of the story, including who penned the records, is an important aspect of the lasting legacy and impact of how witchcraft trials are positioned and retold. It would be easy to dismiss the relevancy of King James VI's *Daemonologie* in the Pendle case, given that the work was 15 years old and the English king had denounced his beliefs in witchcraft by this time. It would also make sense to write off the connection between *Macbeth* and the Pendle witches, given the emphasis on Scottish history in the play and the unlikeliness that the play had been performed for residents in or near Lancashire by 1612. However, when we examine Potts' *The Wonderfull Discoverie of Witchcraft*, it is clear that, as Barbara Ehrenreich has argued, "the witch herself–poor and illiterate–did not leave her story. It was recorded, like all history, by the educated elite, so today we only know the witch through the eyes of her persecutors."[40] Though Potts claimed his account was a factual and objective one, his narrative positions Nowell as a religious and "honest gentleman" while the accused are described as dangerous and malicious figures, making the work much more biased than the author would have his readers believe.[41]

Potts served as a clerk at the Lancaster Assize where nearly all of the Pendle witch trials took place. Two of the trial judges, Sir James Altham and Sir Edward Bromley, tasked Potts with writing a reproduction of the case proceedings and "was carefully crafted to confirm James's *Daemonologie*."[42] In their scholarship on *The Wonderfull Discoverie of Witches*, both Stephen Pomfrey and Marion Gibson demonstrate that Potts' work is significant in that it provides a rare account of witchcraft trials in full detail with insight into the legal and judicial proceedings of the time, yet alongside the storytelling is a bias that calls into question "whether that process can straightforwardly give us access to the actual personalities and events of the early seventeenth century."[43]

Before getting into the proceedings of the trials, Potts implores his readers to have some latitude so that he may "lay open the life and death of this damnable and malicious witch, of so long continuance (old Demdike) of whom our whole business hath such dependance."[44] He goes to great lengths to describe Elizabeth Southerns (often referred to as a witch or "Old Demdike" in the work, but rarely by name) in a way that would encourage any reader to identify her not only as a witch, but as an outcast of society, dangerous and evil. "She was a very old woman, about the age of four score years . . . she dwelt in the Forest of Pendle, a vast place fit for her profession: what she committed in her time, no man knows."[45] He then provides the reader with Southerns' life story: a witch of 50 years who brought up her children and grandchildren to also practice witchcraft, a longtime "agent" of the devil, living to torment anyone who crossed her path. Only after he paints this picture does Potts include what she said in her confession, positioning her as villainous and evil, before he gives detailed accounts of the proceedings. Of the confession, he wrote that she had confessed to meeting the devil on her way home from begging 20 years earlier and that she sold her soul to him "in hope of such gain as was promised by the said Devil."[46] Potts' account of Southerns paints her as an unsympathetic figure willing to sell her soul to the devil for payouts and gains. However, it is important to note that, in her confession, she said that she had been a beggar at the time she met the devil 20 years before, indicating that she had been roughly 60 years old and living in poverty at the time of this "meeting."

Southerns had often been called upon by neighbors to cure sick livestock, but she had lost her eyesight by the time of the trial and her granddaughter, Alizon, would often accompany her to various places in order to help her get around. One of the stories Alizon told in her confession was from the previous Christmas, when a man named Richard Baldwin had ordered them to "get out of my grounds Whores and Witches, I will burne the one of you and hang the other."[47] It had been suspected that Southerns' eldest son, Christopher, was born out of wedlock prior to her marriage to Thomas Ingham (Elizabeth Device's father), so Baldwin's use of "whore" was more than an empty insult and yet another attack on Southerns' character and the legitimacy of the Device family as a whole. Alizon said that she had heard her grandmother curse Baldwin, saying to her demonic spirit, "Revenge thee of him."[48] Within a year, Baldwin's daughter had fallen ill and died.

The question of why Alizon would confess to her own use of witchcraft against John Law and recount when she had been a witness to her grandmother's rituals and curses remains a mystery. Did she believe in her own power? Did she believe that she and her family would be protected by the devil? Did she, like so many accused before her, believe that her life would be spared if she told the judges what she thought they wanted to hear? Was she unaware of the consequences of her confession? These questions remain unanswered because her confessions (as well as the confessions of others involved in the Pendle trials) are filtered and retold by Potts, a clerk who was ordered to tell the story by two of the presiding judges, both of whom examined the manuscript prior to its publication. As Gibson points out, "Potts's *Discoverie* is certainly instructive, for its omissions and imperfections (both deliberate and naive) teach a harsh lesson in blind trust in authority, reliance on official accounts and the infallibility of the written word in history." Potts' work does not provide a detailed account of witchcraft or its legal definition, nor does it give a full account of the procedures therein. What his work does is provide a narrative of the Pendle trials through the lens of his privilege and tells "us what he believed early modern readers wanted to read about witchcraft [and] what his patrons wanted him to produce."[49] Furthermore, if we trace Potts' works to the ones that came before, there are striking parallels between his accounts of witchcraft and what is presented in both *Daemonologie* and the *Malleus Maleficarum*: almost always a woman, the witch is an agent of the devil, who often interfered with the workings of God and Christianity through herbalism and spell work, and was presently involved in or had a history of sexual promiscuity.

Salem: 1692–1693

The discourse on witchcraft did not stay confined within the borders of Europe. Between 1630 and 1642, roughly 20,000 Puritans rejected the notion that the English government could declare any religion to be truth and law and migrated to North America in order to worship God in the way they saw fit. One of the most famous Puritans, John Winthrop, emerged as a leader in Massachusetts Bay Colony and sought to enact his vision of New England as a "city upon a hill," a beacon of excellence, forgiveness, love and charity. He believed that God ordained his people to lead the way to create what he called "the city upon a hill," a place where religion and governance could meet. Those who did not adhere to Christianity were threats to this structure. As Abram C. Van Engen argues, Winthrop's "vision is as inspiring as it is limited. For this sweet sympathy of affections, Winthrop believed, could only arise among those who were converted and regenerated by the power of the Holy Spirit."[50] This emphasis on godliness and holiness within the governance of Puritan society provides a great deal of insight into the mania and panic of the Salem witch trials.

Prior to the famous cases of witchcraft in Salem, Massachusetts in 1692 and 1693, Cotton Mather, a Protestant minister out of Boston, delivered and published a series of sermons on the proliferation of witchcraft in the colonies, including *Memorable Providences, Relating to Witchcrafts and Possessions, Clearly Manifesting, Not Only That There are Witches, but That Good Men (as Well as Others) May Possibly Have Their Lives Shortened*. This work became standard reading in Puritan New England after its publication in 1689. The book, *Memorable Providences*, was purported to be found in the home of Samuel Parris, the minister who had begun to proselytize on the presence of Satan in the world and in whose home Tituba, discussed in the paragraphs below, was a slave. Inspired by an accusation of witchcraft against an Irish washerwoman a year earlier, Mather's *Memorable Providences* not only illustrates a strong belief in witchcraft prior to the Salem trials, but also that knowledge of what had happened in Europe had reached the shores of the colonies.

> It was not long before one of her Sisters, and two of her Brothers, were seized, in Order one after another with Affects' like those that molested her. Within a few weeks, they were all four tortured every where in a manners very grievous, that it would have broke an heart of stone to have seen their Agonies. Skilful Physicians were consulted for their Help, and particularly our worthy and prudent Friend Dr. Thomas Oakes,' who found himself so affronted by the Dist'empers of the children, that he concluded nothing but an hellish Witchcraft could be the Original of these Maladies.[51]

Mather then goes on to describe how the children had been tormented simultaneously, their necks, hands and backs feeling sprains at any given time as a result of the witchcraft allegedly at play.

In autumn of 1691, several local teenage girls began to experience "fits," including contortions and impulsive screaming, and flinched at spirits that "pinched" them. This happened first in the household of Rev. Samuel Parris and later in the home of Thomas Putnam. Found to be "under an evil hand," the girls revealed that they had received fortunes from Tituba, an African-Caribbean slave in the Parris household.[52] By February 1692, three women – Tituba, Sarah Goode (a beggar) and Sarah Osborne (a nearly bedridden widow) – had been accused of witchcraft. In March 1692, all three women were brought into the meeting house upon accusation, but each was interrogated separately. Both Goode and Osborne were purported to have visited the girls as spirits or specters. Goode repeatedly denied any wrongdoing, saying that she had been "falsely accused" and eventually said that it was Osborne who had tormented the children, not her. Osborne had long been housebound and in weak health for many years prior to her arrest. Like Goode, she repeatedly denied any wrongdoing. She did admit to hearing a voice tell her to stop attending Sabbath meetings (sermons), but she continued to go anyway until her health prevented her from doing so. However, the question of her not continuing to attend was enough evidence that Satan might have been afoot in Osborne's life after all. Both Goode and Osborne were tried and hung.

Like Goode and Osborne, Tituba, at first, denied any wrongdoing in her testimony. However, she admitted to seeing "a man that told me: serve him. And I told him no, I would not do such a thing."[53] She then launched into a confession of seeing Goode and Osborne hurt the children and that the devil had told her he'd "kill the children" if she did not serve him, telling stories of seeing black dogs, cats as familiars and black silk robes worn by fellow witches. In her confession, Tituba stated, "Goode good and Goode Osburn told that they did hurt Mr Currens child and would have had me hurt him two, but I did not." When asked about Osborne's "familiar," she responded,

> Yellow dog, she had a thing with a head like a woman with 2 legges, and wings. Abigail Williams that lives with her Uncle Parris said that she did see the same creature, and it turned into the shape of Goode Osborn.

Tituba also claimed to have seen a wolf with Goode.[54] Tituba later revealed she lied in her confession to save her life.

By October 1692, Mather published another work on witchcraft, *The Wonders of the Invisible World*, which, in a similar manner to works before it, laid out what "presumptions" might encourage investigators to look into a case of witchcraft and ways to find proof after a confession.[55] Mather's work also included accounts of what had already transpired, including an account of Tituba's story. After a few paragraphs describing the merits of Parris' character, Mather writes of Tituba:

> The first complain'd of, was the said *Indian* Woman, named *Tituba*, she confessed that the *Devil* urged her to sign a Book, which he presented

to her, and also to work Mischief to the Children, &c. She was afterwards Committed to Prison, and lay there till Sold for her Fees. The account she since gives of it is, that her Master did beat her and otherways abuse her, to make her confess and accuse (such as he call'd) her Sister-Witches, and that whatsoever she said by way of confessing or accusing others, was the effect of such usage; her Master refused to pay her Fees, unless she would stand to what she had said."[56]

As seen with King James VI's *Daemonologie*, Shakespeare's *Macbeth* and Potts' *The Wonderfull Discoverie of Witches*, the narratives and descriptions of accused witches came through the words of white men with power and influence. The story of Tituba is no exception, with little of her story recorded or kept outside of the records of her testimony and supposed confession. However, unlike the white women accused, comments are made on Tituba's race in the records. Ezekiel Cheever, a court clerk, referred to her as an "Indian woman" in his record on March 1, 1692, while Joseph Putnam notes her in his personal records as "indyen."[57] As Veta Smith Tucker points out, "The fusion of African and Indian identity that occupied the early colonial mind and congealed in their perception of Tituba may have been based on empirical (visual) evidence that eyewitnesses considered obvious and, therefore, unnecessary to record."[58] In several of the records, she is often referred to as "the Indian" or "Indian woman."

Conclusion

The "witch craze," "mania" or "hysteria" was hardly as chaotic as these phrases might suggest. From 1561 to 1727, under the Scottish Witchcraft Act (1563–1736) witchcraft persecutions soared through Scotland, where a total of 3,837 people were suspected of witchcraft and 3,413 were accused, roughly 84 percent of whom were women. Court records, documents and treatises were laid out methodically and in a manner that appears to be not only reasonable, but factual. This was a methodical process, driving the methods of torture and execution for three centuries. As will be discussed in Chapter 3, the move into the Enlightenment, with further emphasis on logic, reason and scientific advancement, would see a shift in attitudes toward and about witchcraft.

Notes

1 Peter T. Leeson and Jacob W. Russ, "Witch Trials," *The Economic Journal* 128 (August 2018), 2067.
2 Anonymous, *Newes from Scotland, Declaring the Damnable Life of Doctor Fian a Notable Sorcerer, Who Was Burned at Edenbrought in Lanuarie Last* (London: University of Glasgow, 1591), 11. Original quote: "to bewitch and drowne his Maieftie in the fea coming from Denmarke, with fuch other wonderfull matters as the like hath not bin heard at anie time."

44 Witchcraft: Gendered Perspectives

3 Liv Helene Willumsen, *The Voices of Women in Witchcraft: Northern Europe. Routledge Studies in the History of Witchcraft, Demonology, and Magic* (London: Routledge, 2022), 144.
4 Anonymous, *Newes from Scotland, Declaring the Damnable Life of Doctor Fian a Notable Sorcerer, Who Was Burned at Edenbrought in Lanuarie Last* (London: University of Glasgow, 1591), 11. Original quote: "and binding or wrinching her head with a cord or roape, which is a most cruell torment also."
5 Anonymous, *Newes from Scotland, Declaring the Damnable Life of Doctor Fian a Notable Sorcerer, Who Was Burned at Edenbrought in Lanuarie Last* (London: University of Glasgow, 1591), 14. Original quote: "by due examination of witchcraft and Witches in Scotland, it hath lately beene founde that the diuell doth generally marke them with a privie marke."
6 Nicola A. Ring, "Healers and Midwives Accused of Witchcraft (1563–1736) – What Secondary Analysis of the Scottish Survey of Witchcraft Can Contribute to the Teaching of Nursing and Midwifery History," *Nurse Education Today* 133 (2024), 3.
7 Nicola A. Ring, "Healers and Midwives Accused of Witchcraft (1563–1736) – What Secondary Analysis of the Scottish Survey of Witchcraft Can Contribute to the Teaching of Nursing and Midwifery History," *Nurse Education Today* 133 (2024), 5.
8 Anonymous, *Newes from Scotland, Declaring the Damnable Life of Doctor Fian a Notable Sorcerer, Who Was Burned at Edenbrought in Lanuarie Last* (London: University of Glasgow, 1591), 14. Original quote: "this *Agnis Sampson* had all her haire shauen of, in each parte of her bodie, and her head thrawen with a rope according to the custome of that Countrye, beeing a paine most greeuous, which she continued almost an hower, during which time she would not confesse any thing vntill the Diuels marke was found vpon her priuities, then she immediatlye confessed whatsoeuer was demaunded of her, and iustifying those persons aforesaid to be notorious witches."
9 Anonymous, "Confession of Agnes Sampson, One of the 'North Berwick' Witches," in *The National Archives*, January 29, 1590.
10 Anonymous, *Newes from Scotland, Declaring the Damnable Life of Doctor Fian a Notable Sorcerer, Who Was Burned at Edenbrought in Lanuarie Last* (London: University of Glasgow, 1591), 16.
11 James Spottiswood, *The History of the Church of Scotland, Beginning the Year of Our Lord 203 and Continuing to the End of the Reign of King James VI Vol. 2* (Edinburgh: Spottiswood Society, 1874), 411. The Earl of Bothwell mentioned in the confession was considered a rival by King James VI.
12 Brian P. Levack, *The Witchcraft Sourcebook 2nd Edition* (London: Routledge, 2015), 252–253.
13 Anonymous, "Confession of Agnes Sampson, One of the 'North Berwick' Witches," in *The National Archives*, January 29, 1590, 2.
14 Liv Helene Willumsen, *The Voices of Women in Witchcraft: Northern Europe. Routledge Studies in the History of Witchcraft, Demonology, and Magic* (London: Routledge, 2022), 155.
15 Both names, Philomathes and Epistemon, invoke ancient Greek words (philomath and episteme) rooted in knowledge, science and learning.
16 Brian P. Levack, *The Witchcraft Sourcebook 2nd Edition* (London: Routledge, 2015), 158.
17 King James VI of Scotland, *Daemonologies, in Forme of a Dialogue, Divided into Three Bookes* (Edinburgh: Robert Walden-Grave, 1597), 39. Original quote: "Proven by the Scripture, that thefe unlawfulll artes in genre, haue bene and may be put in practife."
18 King James VI of Scotland, *Daemonologies, in Forme of a Dialogue, Divided into Three Bookes* (Edinburgh: Robert Walden-Grave, 1597), 42, 43–44. Original

quotes: "Why are there are more women of that craft nor men? What things are possible to them fo effectuate by the power of their mafter?" "The reafon is eafie, for as that fexe is frailer than man is, fo is eafier to be intrapped in thefe groffe frames of the Deuill, as was over well proved to be true, by the Serpents deceiving of Eva at the beginning."

19 "A Witch's Confession." "Confession of Agnes Samson," Catalog # SP 52/47, Folder #14i, Early Modern Witch Trials, National Archives, UK, 2. https://www.nationalarchives.gov.uk/education/resources/early-modern-witch-trials/a-witchs-confession/.

20 King James VI of Scotland, *Daemonologies, in Forme of a Dialogue, Divided into Three Bookes* (Edinburgh: Robert Walden-Grave, 1597), 44. Original quote: "how to make Pictures of waxe or clay: That by rofting thereof, the perfones that they beare the name of, may be continuallie melted or dryed awaie by continuall fickneffe."

21 Lynn Maxwell, "Wax Magic and *The Duchess of Malfi*," *Journal for Early Modern Cultural Studies* 14, no. 3 (Summer 2014), 34.

22 King James VI of Scotland, *Daemonologies, in Forme of a Dialogue, Divided into Three Bookes* (Edinburgh: Robert Walden-Grave, 1597), 67. Original quote: "we reade of a Monafterie of Nunnes which were burnt for their being that way abufed."

23 King James VI of Scotland, *Daemonologies, in Forme of a Dialogue, Divided into Three Bookes* (Edinburgh: Robert Walden-Grave, 1597), 68. Original quote: "Indeed it is poffible to the craft of the Deuill to make a woman's bellie to fwel after he hath that way abufed her, which he may do . . . by herbes, as we fee beggars daily doe."

24 Several works, such as *The Trotula* (twelfth century) and *An Illustrated Old English Herbal* (eleventh century), identify various herbs and plants as significant in fertility. They mention herbs and plants such as pennyroyal, laurel, marsh mallow, clove and others for increased fertility.

25 John M. Riddle, *Eve's Herbs: A History of Contraception and Abortion in the West* (Cambridge: Harvard University Press, 1997), 155.

26 William Shakespeare, *Macbeth*, third edn (London: The Arden Shakespeare, 2015), 13. There are some debates around when *Macbeth* was first performed, but 1606 is a largely accepted date.

27 Richard Wilson, "The Pilot's Thumb: *Macbeth* and the Jesuits," in *The Lancashire Witches: Histories and Stories*, ed. Robert Poole (Manchester: Manchester University Press, 2002), 126.

28 Richard Wilson, "The Pilot's Thumb: *Macbeth* and the Jesuits," in *The Lancashire Witches: Histories and Stories*, ed. Robert Poole (Manchester: Manchester University Press, 2002), 127.

29 William Shakespeare, *Macbeth*, third edn (London: The Arden Shakespeare, 2015), 1.1.1–2.

30 It is hotly debated just how much support for King James VI the play is supposed to demonstrate. Aspects of the play's plot allow for more complexity and nuance in this regard. Clark and Mason give more details on this debate in the introduction to the Arden Shakespeare's *Macbeth*, third edn.

31 William Shakespeare, *Macbeth*, third edn (London: The Arden Shakespeare, 2015), 1.3.39–47.

32 Marianne Novy, *Shakespeare and Feminist Theory* (London: Bloomsbury Arden Shakespeare, 2017), 126–127.

33 Liv Helene Willumsen, *The Voices of Women in Witchcraft: Northern Europe. Routledge Studies in the History of Witchcraft, Demonology, and Magic* (London: Routledge, 2022), 183–184.

34 Marion Gibson, "Thomas Pott's 'Dusty Memory': Reconstructing Justice in *The Wonderfull Discoverie of Witches*," in *The Lancashire Witches: Histories*

and Stories, ed. Robert Poole (Manchester: Manchester United Press, 2002), 48. The trial records give three different accounts of this encounter. The first says that she made him lame because he would not sell her any pins, the second that she had begged for pins and he refused her and the third that he had tried to give her some even though she didn't have any money, but she made him lame anyway.
35 James Sharpe, "Introduction: The Lancashire Witches in Historical Context," in *The Lancashire Witches: Histories and Stories*, ed. Robert Poole (Manchester: Manchester University Press, 2002), 2.
36 Marnie Camping-Harris, "The Pendle Witches: How a Nine-Year Old Girl Sentenced Her Family to Death," *Retrospect Journal* (October 2022), https://retrospectjournal.com/2022/10/23/the-pendle-witches-how-a-nine-year-old-girl-sentenced-her-family-to-death/.
37 James Sharpe, "Introduction: The Lancashire Witches in Historical Context," in *The Lancashire Witches: Histories and Stories*, ed. Robert Poole (Manchester: Manchester University Press, 2002), 3.
38 King James VI of Scotland, *Daemonologies, in Forme of a Dialogue, Divided into Three Bookes* (Edinburgh: Robert Walden-Grave, 1597), 78. Original quote: "are not that capable of reafon as to practife fuch things."
39 James Sharpe, "Introduction: The Lancashire Witches in Historical Context," in *The Lancashire Witches: Histories and Stories*, ed. Robert Poole (Manchester: Manchester University Press, 2002), 8.
40 Barbara Ehrenreich, *Witches, Midwives, and Nurses 2nd Edition: A History of Women Healers* (New York: Feminist Press, 2010), 21.
41 Thomas Potts, *The Wonderfull Discoverie of Witches* (Manchester: Charles Sims and Co., 1745), 108–109.
42 Stephen Pomfrey, "Potts, Plots, and Politics: James I *Daemonologie* and *The Wonderfull Discoverie of Witches*," in *The Lancashire Witches: Histories and Stories*, ed. Robert Poole (Manchester: Manchester University Press, 2002), 27.
43 Marion Gibson, "Thomas Pott's 'Dusty Memory': Reconstructing Justice in *The Wonderfull Discoverie of Witches*," in *The Lancashire Witches: Histories and Stories*, ed. Robert Poole (Manchester: Manchester United Press, 2002), 43.
44 Thomas Potts, *The Wonderfull Discoverie of Witches* (Manchester: Charles Sims and Co., 1745), 108. Original quote: "lay open the life and death of this damnable and malicious witch, of fo long continuance (old Demdike) of whom our whole bufineffe hath such dependence."
45 Thomas Potts, *The Wonderfull Discoverie of Witches* (Manchester: Charles Sims and Co., 1745), 108. Original quote: "She was a very old woman, about the age of Foruefscore years. . . . Shee dwelt in the Forrest of Pendle, a vafte place, fitte for her profefsion: what fhee committed in her time, no man knows."
46 Thomas Potts, *The Wonderfull Discoverie of Witches* (Manchester: Charles Sims and Co., 1745), 110. Original quote: "in hope of fuch gaine as was promised by the fayd Deuill."
47 Thomas Potts, *The Wonderfull Discoverie of Witches* (Manchester: Charles Sims and Co., 1745), 111.
48 Thomas Potts, *The Wonderfull Discoverie of Witches* (Manchester: Charles Sims and Co., 1745), 116.
49 Marion Gibson, "Thomas Pott's 'Dusty Memory': Reconstructing Justice in *The Wonderfull Discoverie of Witches*," in *The Lancashire Witches: Histories and Stories*, ed. Robert Poole (Manchester: Manchester United Press, 2002), 52.
50 Abram C. Van Engen, *City On a Hill: A History of American Exceptionalism* (New Haven: Yale University Press, 2020), 29–30.

51 Cotton Mather, "Memorable Providences, Relating to Witchcrafts and Possessions" (1689), http://law2.umkc.edu/faculty/projects/ftrials/salem/ASA_MATH.HTM, accessed May 30, 2024
52 Robert W. Thurston, "The Salem Witch Hunt," in *The Routledge History of Witchcraft*, ed. Johannes Dillinger (New York: Routledge, 2020), 198.
53 Marilynne K. Roach, *The Salem Witch Trials: A Day-by-Day Chronicle of a Community Under Siege* (Lanham, MD: Taylor Trade Publishing, 2003), 28.
54 Marilynne K. Roach, *The Salem Witch Trials: A Day-by-Day Chronicle of a Community Under Siege* (Lanham, MD: Taylor Trade Publishing, 2003), 29–30.
55 Robert W. Thurston, "The Salem Witch Hunt," in *The Routledge History of Witchcraft*, ed. Johannes Dillinger (New York: Routledge, 2020), 200.
56 Cotton Mather, "Memorable Providences, Relating to Witchcrafts and Possessions" (1692). "More wonders of the invisible world, or, The wonders of the invisible world display'd in five parts . . .: to which is added a postscript relating to a book intitled, The life of Sir William Phips/collected by Robert Calef, merchant of Boston in New England." In the digital collection *Early English Books Online*, https://name.umdl.umich.edu/A32160.0001.001. University of Michigan Library Digital Collections, accessed January 9, 2025, 91.
57 Veta Smith Tucker, "Purloined Identity: The Racial Metamorphosis of Tituba of Salem Village," *Journal of Black Studies* 30, no. 4 (March 2000), 626.
58 Veta Smith Tucker, "Purloined Identity: The Racial Metamorphosis of Tituba of Salem Village," *Journal of Black Studies* 30, no. 4 (March 2000), 631.

3 "Garmented in Light"
Reimaginings of the Witch Through Nineteenth-Century Poetry

Introduction

By the start of the eighteenth century, legal proceedings and court cases brought against witches in Europe had begun to sharply decline, though the criminalization of witchcraft would persist in some areas as late as 1782 with the execution of a witch in Switzerland. Reasons for this decline are widely varied, but one key factor is the rise of what Brian Levack refers to as "judicial scepticism," the idea that those who were in control of the legal proceedings behind witchcraft trials did not believe that all who were convicted were actually guilty of any crime, nor did they approve of the use of torture as a means of extracting the truth. These judges, magistrates and inquisitors sought for more standard practices for procedure.[1] Statutes such as the Witchcraft Act of 1735, which made it a crime to accuse anyone of practicing magic and revoked previous Witchcraft Acts, created a culture of incredulity and skepticism about the existence of witchcraft and magic, particularly amongst the elite and ruling classes. Beliefs in magic and witchcraft did not end with the trials, however. In both the Romantic and Early Modern eras, countless poets, novelists and artists sought to reimagine the portrayal of witches. This chapter will explore several literary works from the nineteenth century in order to demonstrate the artistic and literary perception and reclamation of the witch for popular consumption. Works analyzed in this chapter will include Percy Bysshe Shelley's "The Witch of Atlas" (from where the chapter title comes), Mary Coleridge's "The Witch" and Emily Dickinson's "The Murmur of a Bee" as examples of poetry that incorporated the supernatural into their work. In addition to examination of the works themselves, this chapter will examine popular and critical reception of the pieces.

Enlightenment and Romanticism

In 1736, Parliament passed the Witchcraft Act which repealed the statutes enacted by King James I in 1606. At first glance, this move appears to align with the accepted knowledge about the Age of Enlightenment, a period from the late seventeenth to late eighteenth century known for its emphasis on reason and the pursuit of scientific progress. In his famous 1784 essay "What is

DOI: 10.4324/9781032717227-4

Enlightenment?," Immanuel Kant argued that "Enlightenment is mankind's exit from its self-incurred immaturity. Immaturity is the inability to make use of one's own understanding without the guidance of another."[2] Enlightenment meant stepping out of the shadows of ignorance and blind belief, and instead relying on one's intellect and desire for knowledge to interrogate life's questions for oneself.

Looking at the Enlightenment era, it appears obvious that cases in witchcraft would rapidly decline. The era's emphasis on science, philosophy and the pursuit of knowledge makes it seem as though people "knew better" and weren't as gullible or quick to believe outlandish ideas as they had been in previous centuries. However, it is too simplistic a view to say that people living during the Enlightenment era eschewed all belief in witchcraft, magic and the supernatural in favor of science, medicine and rationalist thought. As Owen Davies and Willem de Blécourt argue, the Enlightenment should "be seen as a period of subtler renegotiation between cultures, and a period when the relationship between private and public beliefs became more problematic and discrete, and therefore more difficult for the historian to detect."[3] In other words, a decline in documented trials and executions does not necessarily equal a decline in personal belief and/or practice, but demonstrates a shift in the relevancy of practice in relation to the larger social, religious and political dynamics in a particular region.[4] Though judicial proceedings regarding witchcraft might have been at an end, belief and its effects on everyday life certainly were not.

The Romantics of the late eighteenth and early nineteenth centuries reflect this assessment of Davies, Michael Hunter and other scholars of this era of witchcraft. The Romantic era, which followed the Enlightenment and lasted roughly from 1780–1850, challenged the perspectives of their predecessors, seeing such thinkers as too single-minded and objective. Romantic thinkers emphasized the complexity of human nature and utilized various modes of expression, such as art, music, drama, poetry and literature, to express individual thought and emotional experience. Romantic era literature demonstrated a fascination with the supernatural, focusing on themes of magic and spirituality as well as invoking figures such as fairies and witches as embodiments of the natural world. As Maria del Pilar Bravo writes, "English Romanticism was peculiarly characterized by its conception of creation as an artist's natural gift or faculty. This implied that each painter, writer, sculptor, etc. was able to construct his own world by means of his own imagination."[5] Romantic literature invoked the supernatural and folklore as ways to construct a unique and individual reality that could both reflect the world they knew and go beyond its limitations.

Changing Narrative of the Witch

In addition to poetry, fairy tales and dramas, scholars of the nineteenth century also focused on the witch, primarily with the idea of looking at the history of the witch trials through a deeply critical lens. These works examined the various political, feminist, religious, economic and legal frameworks of the witch trials in both Europe and colonial America, investigating a landscape of misinformation, marginalization and injustice in their respective histories. Though this chapter is limited to select poems from the nineteenth century, it is important to recognize that the reimagining and rewriting of the witch narrative was not limited to poets or a few select Romantic writers but was part of a growing mass of scholars and artists who sought to challenge the historical narratives.

In 1841, Charles Mackay published *Memoirs of Extraordinary Popular Delusions* (later renamed *Extraordinary Popular Delusions and the Madness of Crowds*), which examines the idea of crowd psychology, where the psychology of the masses is different than that of the individual, leaving the individual to follow the idea of the crowd over their own logic or reasoning. Mackay explored several different historical "manias" in his work, including "the witch mania."

> Europe, for a period of two centuries and a half, brooded upon the idea, not only that parted spirits walked the earth to meddle in the affairs of men, but that men had power to summon evil spirits to their aid to work woe upon their fellows. An epidemic terror seized upon the nations . . . Every calamity that befell him he attributed to a witch. If a storm arose and blew down his barn, it was witchcraft; if his cattle died of a murrain . . . they were not visitations of Providence, but the works of some neighbouring hag, whose wretchedness or insanity caused the ignorant to raise their finger and point at her as a witch. . . . Thousands upon thousands of unhappy persons fell victims to this cruel and absurd delusion.[6]

Mackay's use of words like "ignorant," "cruel" and "absurd" in his introduction to the chapter illustrates a definitively critical and oppositional position to the justification for witch trials in Europe a few centuries earlier. Rather than believe that the calamities were the providence of God's will, meaning God allowed for bad things to happen to them, Mackay argued that people preferred to lay blame on some outside force. Furthermore, he blames belief in the devil and "evil spirits" on man's fervent desire for immortality in some form, the belief that there is more to existence than this one human lifetime. In the case of the witch trials, the desire to believe in some form of immortality or live in denial of calamity as part of God's will led to the torture and death of thousands.

Later in the chapter, Mackay references the case of Geillis Duncan and Agnes Sampson, referring to King James VI's mania and prejudice against witches growing as he "advanced with his manhood," and the trials of Duncan and Sampson as "extraordinary" due to "the number of victims, the absurdity of the evidence, and the real villainy of some of the persons implicated."[7] As

Mackay observed (as have other scholars), the similarities between Duncan's and Sampson's confessions, as well as Dr Fian's, are remarkable, particularly given that all three admitted to plotting against the king in the hope of ending his reign. According to Mackay, "James was highly flattered at the idea that the devil should have said that he was the greatest enemy he ever had" and might have even relished in hearing the stories told in the confessions, as they reinforced the power and significance he held on the throne.[8] Though it was clear that, at times, the stories became too much for King James VI, his influence over the outcomes of the trials was undeniable. The guilt or innocence of the accused was incomparable to the threat against his life, leading to the deaths of all those who stood trial.

Mackay continues the chapter in much the same fashion, recounting various cases and condemning those who exhibited too much power and let things get out of hand, resulting in the loss of thousands of lives. He ends the chapter with a hope that those times are long past and that the superstitions of men like King James VI would be the exception rather than the rule. Yet he warned that just because the "witch mania" had long ended did not mean that it could not return. As Mackay argued,

> The poisonous tree that once overshadowed the land may be cut down by the sturdy efforts of sages and philosophers; the sun may shine clearly upon spots where venomous things once nestled in security and shade; but still the entangled roots are stretched beneath the surface, and may be found by those who dig.[9]

Notes on Poetry Selections

The selection of poems featured in this chapter is only a fraction of the poetry, fiction, drama, song and fairy tales that could have been chosen for this section on Romantic era literature and the supernatural. Works such as Charlotte Brontë's *Jane Eyre*, Mary Shelley's *Frankenstein*, Emily Brontë's *Wuthering Heights* and Charles Dickens' *Great Expectations* all feature otherworldly characters and themes that center on death and ghostly or reanimated figures. Sir Walter Scott's *The Lady of the Lake* and William Allingham's "The Fairies" examine the duality within the lore and mythology of their respective figures. In 1812, Wilhelm and Jacob Grimm published their first volume of fairy tales and would later go on to write about some of the most villainous witches in literary history, including the child-eating witch in *Hansel and Gretel* and the perpetually jealous and cruel witch in *Snow White*. The latter half of the nineteenth century saw the publication of fantastical works such as Lewis Carroll's *Alice's Adventures in Wonderland* and George MacDonald's *The Princess and the Goblin*. Countless scholars of the Romantic and Victorian periods have researched, analyzed and theorized on the historical and cultural significance of each of these works, including the supernatural and fantastical as vehicles to provide commentary on, among other topics, Christianity, the role of women and classism in the authors' respective societies.

However, the three poems selected for this chapter carry important themes about witches that serve as a historical bridge between the outright misogyny and stereotyping in works such as the *Malleus Maleficarum* and the rise of witchcraft as an embodiment of empowering feminist, spiritual and/or ecological narratives of the twentieth and twenty-first centuries. Those themes include: the witch as deeply intertwined with nature and the environment; the beauty and allure of the "wild" woman; criticism of society's unjust perspectives on women, particularly those perceived as witches; and the continued narratives of the witch who practices sorcery and dark magic, yet with a more nuanced and complex examination of the witch herself.

The poetry discussed in the remainder of this chapter reflects a growing desire among artists and writers to restructure the narrative around the portrayal and use of the word "witch." Though Shelley and his Romantic era contemporaries do not allude to the witch trials in most of their works, Shelley's "The Witch of Atlas" does reframe the witch, demonstrating a more complex and nuanced character than the "hag" narratives such as exist in *Macbeth*.

Similar to Mackay, both Coleridge and Dickinson are critical of the traditional narratives of the witch that leave women as no more than beings of "wretchedness" or "insanity." In each of their poems, the narrator sees the magic and enchantment associated with witchcraft but positions the witch as more emotionally complex and consciously evolved than the traditional views of witches and witchcraft have previously allowed.

Percy Bysshe Shelley, "The Witch of Atlas"

Percy Bysshe Shelley wrote "The Witch of Atlas" in 1820, just two years before his death by drowning at the age of 30. His 30 years were rife with bullying, self-doubt, nightmares, anxiety over his health, financial stress and bouts of deep depression. Many of these issues he had in common with his wife, Mary Shelley née Godwin. Year after year, each experienced an unusual amount of death, including the premature deaths of several of their children and the suicides of Mary's half-sister, Frances, and his estranged wife, Harriet. In 1820, at the behest of their physician, the Shelleys, alongside Mary's stepsister, Claire, moved to a village just outside the town of Pisa, Italy, in order to be in a more agreeable climate that promised fewer stressors. By August of that year, Percy's emotional and physical health seemed much improved, which Mary stated was a "rare and substantial enjoyment." Despite this noted improvement, Percy still could not find literary success, having been rejected by various magazines and losing out on the opportunity for his work to be performed on the London stage.[10]

On August 12, Percy took himself for a hike up Monte San Pellegrino, a trip which would inspire "The Witch of Atlas." The capricious and otherworldly poem of 72 stanzas, published after his death, has long been criticized for its lack of narrative clarity and groundedness in the human condition.[11] Mary, herself distressed by Percy's lack of critical reception and success, criticized the poem, as it appeared that Percy was "discarding human interest and passion, to revel in the fantastic ideas that his imagination suggested."[12] Upon her criticism, Percy added six stanzas, each eight lines long, to the beginning of the poem, calling her out for being "critic-bitten," and cried out, "O let me not believe that anything of mine is fit to live!"[13] Mary's critique and Percy's biting response made it clear that a sharp tension had infiltrated the happier and more adjusted times experienced earlier in the year.

"The Witch of Atlas" has a mythological unnamed witch as the central character, though the poet appears to be the narrator, rather than the witch in question. Throughout the work, though she eventually leaves her cave and travels the world, the witch prefers to be away from the company of others, despite her fascination with humankind. "At first she lived alone in this wild home, her and her own thoughts were each a minister" (lines 209–210) demonstrates her preference for solitude in her cave away from all the subjects, human and otherworldly, that would gladly befriend or serve her. Later in the poem, the witch creates a child, presumed to be a hermaphrodite, as the child is referred to as a "sexless thing," out of "fire and snow together, tempering the repugnant mass with liquid love" (lines 321–323).[14] Rather than have sexual contact with another, the witch uses her "strange art" to create a child. William Crisman argues that this "aloofness" is not the result of any snobbery or sense of superiority, but is rooted in the witch's childhood experiences, particularly the loss of her mother in the earlier stanzas. "Her inclination to think of sexual relations as 'repugnant' bestiality seems only natural, since her mother 'dissolved away' at her father's touch."[15]

The final dozen or so stanzas see the witch, both fascinated by humankind but desiring to remain distant, visit humans as they sleep.

> A pleasure sweet doubtless it was to see
> Mortals subdued in all the shapes of sleep.
> Here lay two sister twins in infancy;
> There, a lone youth who in his dreams did weep;
> Within, two lovers linkèd innocently
> In their loose locks which over both did creep
> Like ivy from one stem; – and there lay calm
> Old age with snow-bright hair and folded palm.[16]

Her joy at witnessing humans as they sleep, free from pain and anguish, is soon tempered by the reality that not all humans are quite so beautiful and innocent in their waking hours. As she continues to examine all the humans, whether in "tortured" sleep or innocent rest, the witch recognizes "the naked beauty of the soul lay bare, And often through a rude and worn disguise She saw the inner form most bright and fair" (lines 571–573). She chose to give the most beautiful humans "a strange panacea in a crystal bowl" (line 594), which promised they'd live "thenceforward as if some control, mightier than life, were in them" (lines 596–597) and that death, when it came, would be like a gentle and unencumbered sleep for all eternity. For those she deemed less beautiful, "she would write strange dreams" (line 617) that would disturb those who experienced the nightmare. For example, "the miser in such dreams would rise and shake into a beggar's lap" (lines 622–623) and "the king would dress an ape up in his crown and robes" (lines 633–634).[17] Even the administrations of the panacea or the strange dreams demonstrate that the witch does not desire real contact with the human world, and it's debatable whether these choices are merely part of her fancy rather than actions actually taken. As Crisman argues, the poem's fancifulness or comedic elements are "built from psychologically serious material."[18] Shelley's emotional and physical health, as well as his experiences with death and catastrophe, can easily be interpreted through the seemingly airy tone of "The Witch of Atlas."

The "witch" portrayed in this work is a far cry from the evil and diabolic figure described in works like the *Malleus Maleficarum* or *Daemonologie*, nor is she the shrewd and shriveled hag featured in Shakespeare's *Macbeth*. She is a much more complex character in Shelley's work, both beautiful and ethereal, yet feels loss and fear due to the psychological ramifications of her mother's dissolution.

> Her mother was one of the Atlantides:
> The all-beholding Sun had ne'er beholden
> In his wide voyage o'er continents and seas
> So fair a creature, as she lay enfolden
> In the warm shadow of her loveliness; –
> He kissed her with his beams, and made all golden
> The chamber of gray rock in which she lay –
> She, in that dream of joy, dissolved away.[19]

Though the witch's psychological scarring is reminiscent of Shelley's own experiences with death and depression, Harold Bloom argued that this poem is not so much an allegory as serving as a

> mythopoeic fantasy . . . [the witch] being garmented only by the light from her own beauty, a light that darkens the poet's eyes . . . Before they can behold her unshadowed beauty, she weaves a veil to protect them from the ill consequences of too direct a confrontation.[20]

Through this lens, Shelley is creating his own myth about the witch, beautiful and powerful, born from the sun, with enough magic and light to cover the earth, so much so that it could harm humans to look directly at the light as they could become blinded by her offerings. As Diane Purkiss writes, "the witch is a figure of beauty explicitly linked with a lost preindustrial past of intuition and imagination; this fits with Shelley's flirtations with a Romanticised paganism."[21] This perspective turns the witch from sinister evil doer shrouded in darkness to a sublime bringer of light and beauty.

It is important to note that the witch, herself, does not have agency within the poem. The poet is the narrator and it is through the poet's eyes that we learn of her birth, see her magic wielded and gain insight into her feelings. Shelley's inclusion of women in his various works suggests a more equitable perspective than many of his male contemporaries of the time and it is clear that his literary relationship with Mary, though contentious, served as a significant motivator for his work. As Nora Crook argues, however, it is debatable whether Shelley's "views on the 'relationship between the sexes' was theoretical only, or had been acted out, for good or ill."[22] After all, his relationships with women throughout his lifetime were hardly equitable or harmonious. In 1814, the then 22-year-old Shelley had left his wife, Harriet, and their 1-year-old daughter to elope with the 16-year-old Mary Godwin. Though attempts have been made by scholars and biographers to separate the poet from the art, Shelley's treatment of Harriet and his response to Mary's criticism cannot be overlooked in any analysis of women or female-identified figures in his work.[23] The complexity of Shelley's behavior, mental health, childhood experiences and treatment of his wives requires a more nuanced examination than positioned here. With that understanding in mind, for the purposes of this chapter, "The Witch of Atlas" stands as an example of Romantic-era poetry where the narrative of the witch and witch mythology was undergoing a rapid change.

Mary Coleridge, "The Witch"

Mary Coleridge was born in London in 1861, the daughter of Arthur Duke Coleridge, a law clerk at the Assize in the Midland Circuit and the great-great-grandniece of the famed Romantic poet Samuel Taylor Coleridge. Her lineage included writers and artists across a variety of disciplines, including her aunt, Sara Coleridge, a famed editor, and both of her parents, who were accomplished singers. A lifelong student of literature and poetry, Mary Coleridge admired the works of Shakespeare and Sir Walter Scott, infusing her own work with lyricism and a dramatic edge. Throughout her life, she had a front-row seat to the most cutting-edge scholastic and artistic works of the day: Henrik Ibsen, W.B. Yeats, Leo Tolstoy, Charles Darwin and William James, among others. Coleridge never married, choosing instead to dedicate her life to her passions of writing, education and intellectual curiosity.[24] She engaged in a number of different forms and genres, including historical novels, ballads and romance, yet kept her poetry largely secretive due to the nature of her famed ancestor's poetry, "protective of her celebrity poet and distant relative's legacy."[25]

"The Witch," a ballad of three stanzas each containing eight lines, consists of a narrator, the witch herself, looking for a respite from her dread and weariness in the first two stanzas. In the first eight lines, the witch pleads to be let in "through the door" in order to find shelter from the biting cold and snow.

> I have walked a great while over the snow,
> And I am not tall nor strong.
> My clothes are wet, and my teeth are set,
> And the way was hard and long.
> I have wandered over the fruitful earth,
> But I never came here before.
> Oh, lift me over the threshold, and let me in at the door![26]

Her weariness is felt from the outset, trudging through snow "a great while," and the line "my teeth are set" might be an indication of gritting her teeth against the cold and wind of winter. She follows the same pattern in the second stanza, ending with the lines "I am but a little maiden still, My little white feet are sore. Oh, lift me over the threshold, and let me in at the door!" The witch in these two stanzas demonstrates the duality of both dread and desire within her, the exhaustion of the long, arduous journey, hoping that the door will be opened for her when she arrives.[27]

The speaker in the third stanza appears to shift to another voice, the person on the other side of the door. Some scholars have argued that this voice is that of a male, most notably Samuel Taylor Coleridge, and the narrator of the first two stanzas has been on her journey in order to find acceptance in the male-dominated world of poetry and literature.

> Her voice was the voice that women have,
> Who plead for their heart's desire.
> She came – she came – and the quivering flame
> Sunk and died in the fire.
> It never was lit again on my hearth
> Since I hurried across the floor,
> To lift her over the threshold, and let her in at the door.[28]

This stanza, however, can also be read as the witch speaking, holding herself up as a mirror of the witch in the first two stanzas. Heather Braun argues that Coleridge often wrote about mirrors and looking-glasses as destructive to the power and strength of women in society. Braun writes that, "For Coleridge, mirrors represent a weakening of this power and mystique, an act of self-reflection that keeps the supposed femme fatale rooted in her own image and forced to contemplate the truth or absence of her intent to harm."[29] The witch, seeing herself reflected in the woman on the other side of the door "and the quivering flame[,] sunk and died in the fire." The witch had lost herself once she crossed the threshold.

The ambivalent meaning and varied interpretations of the poem allow for greater nuance for the narrative of the witch. Is Coleridge suggesting that toil and challenge are more rewarding than safety and warmth? Or does the witch collapse because she encounters the domestic image of herself, the woman society says she ought to be? Or is it, as some scholars have suggested, the witch asking for a place at the table, to be accepted by the men who once rejected her? However one may interpret the poem, Coleridge's brevity and ambiguity as a poet allow the subject of "The Witch" to experience emotional depth without fitting herself neatly into any of the labels or categories set for her in society. She is not the evil and diabolic witch of the previous centuries, nor is she the beautiful yet unpredictable seductress of earlier Romantic works. The audience is unsure what makes her weary or why she has had to trudge through snow. Even the fire did not protect her. More broadly, the poem itself transcends the suggestion that it is preoccupied with her literary lineage or with feminist and social ideologies of her time. Braun states that poems such as "The Witch"

> take us beyond concerns with her poetic lineage or her involvement in advancing social movements. Among the recurring themes of her poetry is a keen interest in the mutation of both form and perspective over time: she alternates between a nostalgic need to freeze time and an eagerness to infuse familiar forms with new ideas.[30]

The ballad form of "The Witch" is familiar in its structure, yet the narrative of the witch herself, with the emphasis on her internal conflict, the struggle with both desire and dread, and the loss and gains of herself on the journey, opens the door for a new cultural conception of what it means to be a witch.

Emily Dickinson, "The Murmur of a Bee"

Born in Massachusetts in 1830, Emily Dickinson lived the majority of her life under the strict thumb of her father, Edward Dickinson, a well-known lawyer and politician, who suffered bankruptcy in 1833. Though he was eventually able to regain property and achieve success, Edward Dickinson's preoccupation became one of order, status and image, concealing much of what lay within, most notably "a history of debt and financial embarrassment."[31] Her father's dominance and control over Emily's and her other sisters' lives, led her to live her life as much inside her head as in the natural world around her. Though the causes are not entirely clear, around 1854, Dickinson began to alienate herself almost entirely from society, choosing to write letters to those to whom she remained close, and stayed tied to her home and garden.[32]

Dickinson began gardening at an early age, having learned the basics of soil and maintenance from her mother, who had brought roses to the Amherst Homestead in 1828, tending to them with her daughters through their childhood. Dickinson's love for nature and gardening followed her into her adult years and she took classes in Botany from Amherst Academy and Mount Holyoke Female Seminary, even creating a herbarium of flowers complete with their Latin names.[33] Flowers, bees, birds and the seasons feature prominently in her nearly 2,000 poems, demonstrating an intricate knowledge of the natural sciences as well as serving as symbols of Dickinson's perceptions of society, gender, faith and her inner world.

"The Murmur of a Bee" is three stanzas, each five lines, and illustrates this interplay between nature, faith and Dickinson's inner world. Judith Farr argues that the bee appears as "prototypes of God the Father or as types of the eager lover," primarily serving as a testament to themes of faith/faithlessness or sexuality in Dickinson's poetry.[34] In "The Murmur of a Bee," Dickinson uses the bee as a journey toward God, though not the God concerned with rules, mandates and piety, but one who is an "Artist" and has created such beauty that encapsulates the senses.

> The Murmur of a Bee
> A Witchcraft–yieldeth me–
> If any ask me why–
> 'Twere easier to die–
> Than tell–[35]

The witchcraft in this sense is about the power to awaken those senses and bring her closer to God. As Rosemary McTier explains,

> If Dickinson finds comfort and renewed faith in the awe that nature inspires, it is because God intended her to find it there ... She "yield[s]" to the voice of the bee, 'A Witchcraft' ... that has the power to awaken Spring.[36]

Dickinson's use of the word "witchcraft" here is a far cry from the idea of a diabolic power that seeks to harm humanity and turn it further from God and the church. Instead, God is the "Artist" who possesses such witchcraft, such power, that can enchant and compel her spirit.

> The Red upon the Hill
> Taketh away my will–
> If anybody sneer–
> Take care–for God is here–
> That's all.
>
> The Breaking of the Day
> Addeth to my Degree–
> If any ask me how–
> Artist–who drew me so–
> Must tell![37]

Though she does not know how or why such a profound transformation can occur, she is comforted by the sense of beauty: "She is only certain of God's presence, 'for God is here' and only he, the 'Artist–who drew [her] so' can 'tell' or explain why nature transforms her or why she is able to be transformed."[38] It is in nature that Dickinson finds her sense of awe and of self as well as her relationship with her faith. Though scholars have argued that her poems suggest a rejection of God and Christianity, it is more likely that Dickinson resisted the doctrines of her Calvinist upbringing, instead finding the divine in that which God created.

Though the use of the word "witchcraft" in "The Murmur of a Bee" relates to the beauty and power of God and nature and may seem tangential to the concept of "witch" in Shelley's and Coleridge's works, it is not Dickinson's only reference to witchcraft and magic in her poetry. "Witchcraft has not a pedigree" and "Witchcraft was hung, in History" allude to the origin and history of witchcraft, connecting both to the idea of what is a part of our everyday lives and what will follow us to death. Paul Crumbley argues that Dickinson's use of "witchcraft" in the latter title "rescues witchcraft from the margins . . . Rather than rejecting history altogether, Dickinson privileges conduct deemed unnatural by the official record as a way of illuminating an alternative account of human events immediately applicable to the present moment."[39] This suggests that Dickinson was not only familiar with the dark history of witchcraft accusations and oppression, but deliberately incorporated the word into her poetry in order to give it new meaning. The "witchcraft" in "The Murmur of a Bee" does not drive the speaker into darkness and away from God, as had been suggested by the literature in previous centuries, but rather brings her closer to sources of light, such as "the Breaking of Day" and the divine, "God is here."

Conclusion

The works discussed in this chapter have amongst them a common theme of the internal landscape of the witch herself. In Shelley, her psychological underpinnings and suppressed traumas affected her well-being and sense of self, often causing her to retreat to her inner world rather than face the ridicule and cruelty of the outside world. The witches in both Shelley and Coleridge experience an inner turmoil that results in them finding respite in their cave or home as a means of self-protection from harm, though whether the witch is truly protected or exposed to further pain is up for interpretation. Even Mackay, in his *Extraordinary Popular Delusions and the Madness of Crowds*, reflects on the accused witch's decisions to confess as a direct reaction to the fear and irrationality that dominated society around her, choosing to confess out of a sense of safety and protection rather than any sense of guilt or wrongdoing. Though some, like Agnes Sampson, may have actually wanted to see harm come to King James VI and even participated in spells or rituals to see that demise come to pass, Mackay argues that each was driven to confess due to the nightmarish tortures they endured.

Dickinson, on the other hand, embodies the witch as a state of mind, an altered consciousness that can transcend the noise of the human world.

Dickinson's narrator likens their sensory experiences in nature to witchcraft, an enchantment that captures their senses and imagination, leading them toward faith in a God that can create such beauty. In this way, each of the narrators of the poems has a heightened sense of awareness and sensitivity to the world around them. Shelley's narrator recognizes the beauty and light of the witch of Atlas, while Coleridge's narrator sees that the witch she encounters is taking a great risk by living independently, enduring the harsher aspects of the natural world before retreating to the speaker's home. The imagery of nature in each poem – the sun and light in Shelley, the winter imagery in Coleridge and the bee in Dickinson – encapsulates the idea of the witch and witchcraft as existing outside the boundaries of societal norms or expectations.

Not all literary incorporations of the witch in the nineteenth century took such an approach. Grimms' Fairy Tales reinforced the "witch as diabolic and evil" in several of their stories. The dual nature of the witch also emerges in various works. In several pieces of literature from the time period, the witch is both alluring and untamed, which makes her all the more beautiful, yet the same thing that makes her so enchanting is also what makes her dangerous. John Keats' "La Belle Dame Sans Merci" (translated to "The Beautiful Merciless Lady") sees the main character, a dying knight, experience a beautiful love with a fairy woman, only to wake up alone, having been told he'd been "enthralled" as he slept. Even Shelley, in his final stanza of "The Witch of Atlas," promises to tell more of her exploits, as

> These were the pranks she played among the cities
> Of mortal men, and what she did to Sprites
> And Gods, entangling them in her sweet ditties
> To do her will, and show their subtle sleights,
> I will declare another time; for it is
> A tale more fit for the weird winter nights
> Than for these garish summer days, when we
> Scarcely believe much more than we can see.[40]

The witch of the earlier stanzas has become one who plays "pranks" on "Sprites and Gods, entangling them" with her song "to do her will." In several works throughout the century, the witch is as much mischief maker and seductress as she is beautiful and nuanced.

What we can glean from these literary references of witchcraft is that the narrative of what it meant to be a witch had undergone a radical transformation from earlier incarnations of "the wickedness of woman" in the *Malleus Maleficarum* and the bearded meddling hags of *Macbeth*. As the nineteenth century ended and the twentieth century rapidly approached, the narrative of the witch would continue on this path of transformation. The twentieth century would not only see the dawn of the witch as a cultural mainstay at Halloween and as a staple in entertainment media, but also witness witchcraft become an integral focus of environmental, feminist and religious movements.

Notes

1. Brian Levack, "General Reasons for Decline in Prosecutions," in *Witchcraft and Magic in Europe: The Eighteenth and Nineteenth Centuries*, ed. Bengt Ankarloo and Stuart Clark (Philadelphia: University of Pennsylvania Press, 1999), 7.
2. Immanuel Kant, "An Answer to the Question: What is Enlightenment?" 1784, https://enlightenment.commons.gc.cuny.edu/files/2016/12/Kant-What-is-Enlightenment.pdf, accessed June 18, 2024.
3. Owen Davies and Willem de Blécourt, *Beyond the Witch Trials: Witchcraft and Magic in Enlightenment Europe* (Manchester: Manchester University Press, 2004), 1.
4. For more on the nuanced relationship between the Enlightenment and the decline of witchcraft, see Owen Davies and Willem de Blécourt as well as other works by Owen Davies, Michael Hunter and Marijke Hofstra.
5. Maria del Pilar Bravo, "Literary Creation and the Supernatural in English Romanticism," *GIST Education and Learning Research Journal* 1 (2007), 139.
6. Charles Mackay, *Extraordinary Popular Delusions and the Madness of Crowds* (Boston: L.C. Page and Company, 1932), 462–463.
7. Charles Mackay, *Extraordinary Popular Delusions and the Madness of Crowds* (Boston: L.C. Page and Company, 1932), 494–495.
8. Charles Mackay, *Extraordinary Popular Delusions and the Madness of Crowds* (Boston: L.C. Page and Company, 1932), 496.
9. Charles Mackay, *Extraordinary Popular Delusions and the Madness of Crowds* (Boston: L.C. Page and Company, 1932), 563.
10. Miranda Seymour, *Mary Shelley* (New York: Grove Press, 2000), 247–248.
11. William Crisman, "Psychological Realism and Narrative Manner in Shelley's 'Alastor' and 'The Witch of Atlas'," *Keats–Shelley Journal* 35 (1986), 126–127.
12. Miranda Seymour, *Mary Shelley* (New York: Grove Press, 2000), 248.
13. Percy Bysshe Shelley, "The Witch of Atlas," https://knarf.english.upenn.edu/PShelley/witch.html, accessed June 14, 2023.
14. Percy Bysshe Shelley, "The Witch of Atlas," https://knarf.english.upenn.edu/PShelley/witch.html, accessed June 14, 2023.
15. William Crisman, "Psychological Realism and Narrative Manner in Shelley's 'Alastor' and 'The Witch of Atlas'," *Keats–Shelley Journal* 35 (1986), 131–132.
16. Percy Bysshe Shelley, "The Witch of Atlas," https://knarf.english.upenn.edu/PShelley/witch.html, accessed June 14, 2023, lines 529–537.
17. Percy Bysshe Shelley, "The Witch of Atlas," https://knarf.english.upenn.edu/PShelley/witch.html, accessed June 14, 2023, lines 529–537.
18. William Crisman, "Psychological Realism and Narrative Manner in Shelley's 'Alastor' and 'The Witch of Atlas'," *Keats–Shelley Journal* 35 (1986), 139.
19. Percy Bysshe Shelley, "The Witch of Atlas," https://knarf.english.upenn.edu/PShelley/witch.html, accessed June 14, 2023, lines 57–64.
20. Harold Bloom, "The Witch of Atlas," in *Modern Judgements*, ed. R.B. Woodings (London: Palgrave, 1968), 94.
21. Diane Purkiss, *The Witch in History: Early Modern and Twentieth-Century Representation* (London: Routledge, 1996), 7.
22. Nora Crook, "Shelley and Women," in *The Oxford Handbook of Percy Bysshe Shelley*, ed. Michael O'Neill (Oxford: Oxford University Press, 2012), 66.

23 Nora Crook, "Shelley and Women," in *The Oxford Handbook of Percy Bysshe Shelley*, ed. Michael O'Neill (Oxford: Oxford University Press, 2012), 70–76.
24 Simon Avery, *Selected Poems of Mary Coleridge* (Exeter: Shearsman Books, 2010), 11–13.
25 Heather L. Braun, "'Set the Crystal Surface Free!': Mary E. Coleridge and the Self-Conscious Femme Fatale," *Women's Writing* 14, no. 3 (2007), 498.
26 Simon Avery, *Selected Poems of Mary Coleridge* (Exeter: Shearsman Books, 2010), 36.
27 Heather L. Braun, "'Set the Crystal Surface Free!': Mary E. Coleridge and the Self-Conscious Femme Fatale," *Women's Writing* 14, no. 3 (2007), 501.
28 Simon Avery, *Selected Poems of Mary Coleridge* (Exeter: Shearsman Books, 2010), 36.
29 Heather L. Braun, "'Set the Crystal Surface Free!': Mary E. Coleridge and the Self-Conscious Femme Fatale," *Women's Writing* 14, no. 3 (2007), 503.
30 Heather L. Braun, "'Set the Crystal Surface Free!': Mary E. Coleridge and the Self-Conscious Femme Fatale," *Women's Writing* 14, no. 3 (2007), 506.
31 Domhnall Mitchell, *Emily Dickinson: Monarch of Perception* (Amherst: University of Massachusetts Press, 2000), 48.
32 William C. Spengeman, *Nineteenth-Century American Poetry* (London: Penguin Books, 1996), 352.
33 Anonymous, "Emily Dickinson and Gardening," https://www.emilydickinsonmuseum.org/emily-dickinson/biography/special-topics/emily-dickinson-and-gardening/, accessed August 14, 2024.
34 Judith Farr, *The Passion of Emily Dickinson* (Cambridge: Harvard University Press, 1992), 226.
35 Emily Dickinson, *The Complete Poems of Emily Dickinson*, ed. Thomas H. Johnson (Boston: Little Brown and Company, 1960), 73.
36 Rosemary J. McTier, "'An Insect View of Its Plain': Nature and Insects in Thoreau, Dickinson, and Muir" (PhD Dissertation, Duquesne University, 2009), 134.
37 Emily Dickinson, *The Complete Poems of Emily Dickinson*, ed. Thomas H. Johnson (Boston: Little Brown and Company, 1960), 73.
38 Rosemary J. McTier, "'An Insect View of Its Plain': Nature and Insects in Thoreau, Dickinson, and Muir" (PhD Dissertation, Duquesne University, 2009), 135.
39 Paul Crumbley, "Dickinson's Use of Spiritualism: 'Nature' of Democratic Belief," in *A Companion to Emily Dickinson*, ed. Martha Nell Smith and Mary Loeffelholz (Malden, MA: Blackwell Publishing, 2008), 241.
40 Percy Bysshe Shelley, "The Witch of Atlas," https://knarf.english.upenn.edu/PShelley/witch.html, accessed June 14, 2023, lines 665–672.

4 "An Ye Harm None"
The Rise of Wicca in the Twentieth Century

Introduction

The many origins and influences of the Rede are just one example of the ways in which paganism, Wicca and witchcraft have come to take on religious, social and political interpretations in the twentieth century. Much of what modern audiences associate with Wicca – moon rituals, the Wheel of the Year celebrations, Goddess worship and more – is thought to be part of an "Old Religion" that predates Christianity. In reality, the "Father of modern Wicca," Gerald Gardner pulled from a variety of sources and experiences, including his work as an archaeologist in Malaysia, a scholar of tribal animism, his membership in the Order of Woodcraft Chivalry, as well as works by Charles Godfrey Leland, Aleister Crowley, Margaret Murray and others, in order to put together what he would eventually call Wicca. As scholars such as Ronald Hutton have demonstrated, Gardner borrowed and adapted heavily from these sources, at times even plagiarizing and co-opting various works and practices to develop a cohesive religion that appeared rooted in ancient cultures.[1]

Though sometimes seen as a huckster, other times media-hungry, Gardner's influence on modern paganism is undeniable. This chapter begins with Gardner not because he is considered the "founder" of Wicca, but in order to start with the historical moment of more widespread attention given to Wicca/paganism, demonstrating its rapid rise in the second half of the twentieth century. As Hutton and others have demonstrated, Gardner did not invent Wicca nor did he rediscover a lost and ancient religion. As this and subsequent chapters will demonstrate, modern paganism, Wicca and witchcraft have emerged in Western society as part of the religious, cultural, social and political landscape. This chapter is not a how-to regarding specific practices and rituals, but an examination of how modern Pagan and Wicca culture emerged through the lens of a few foundational players and their written works, including Gardner and Valiente in England and Starhawk in the United States. This chapter will also examine how the history of witchcraft influenced the feminist movement of the 1970s, merging the history of oppression and violence with the symbols most commonly associated with the witch.

DOI: 10.4324/9781032717227-5

A Brief History of Witchcraft in the Nineteenth and Early Twentieth Centuries

It would be all too easy to look at the witch trials and persecution of witches as a horrifying period in the past, something that happened "back then," dismissing the orchestrating agents as gullible, power-hungry or "of a different era." The previous chapter even appears to support this, as poets, novelists, dramatists and other artists of the nineteenth and early twentieth centuries favored, even revered, the imagery and history of the supernatural, particularly the witch. However, the narrative of the witch in art and literature did not echo private sentiments and lingering prejudices against those who practiced any form of magic or witchcraft. Over the last several decades, historians have been looking carefully at instances of persecution and accusation long after the mid-eighteenth century, noting that, even though court records and law books no longer contained detailed records of anti-witchcraft campaigns and trials, judicial records detailing abuses, harassment, manslaughter and murder point to instances where "people continued to take the law into their own hands with regard to dealing with witches, and this led to what have been called 'witch trials in reverse.'"[2] Historian Owen Davies points to the case of Mary Nicholas as an example. In Abergavenny, Wales in 1827, a riotous group dragged Nicholas, an elderly woman in her nineties, to the farm of one of the perpetrators, William Watkins, a farmer who believed she had been responsible for the death of his cattle. Watkins and three others, a constable and two servants, forced her to kneel before his colt to bless it, and then proceeded to draw blood from her hand, as they believed that a witch would not be hurt by such an action. The four men then "proceeded to strip the upper part of her person for the purpose of finding a supposed mark where she suckled imps" but instead found a wart on her head, proceeding to "cut off her hair" and "duck her" as further methods to prove she was a witch. Watkins and his three accomplices were later found guilty of assault.[3]

However, such a gruesome event proved to be the exception, not the rule, in a century that saw the witch narrative move between notions of devil worship, enchanting literary figure, subject of historical and archaeological scholarship, and the central force in alternative spiritual, esoteric and/or religious practices. At the same time Coleridge and Dickinson were writing poetry that captured the mystery and beauty of witches and their history, noted folklorists, archaeologists and historians such as Leland and Murray had begun writing about groups of witches with roots in ancient cultures and mythologies. Leland's *Aradia, or the Gospel of Witches* presents itself as a sacred text of ancient witchcraft. An expatriate to Italy, Leland met a young woman named Maddalena, who assisted him in the research and gathering of folklore. On January 1, 1897, Maddalena was purported to have given Leland a sacred text written in her own hand. After receiving the text, Leland said he never saw or heard from Maddalena again and interpreted the text based on his understanding of witchcraft through the lens of the

"Gospel." Believing it to be derived primarily from oral traditions and narratives, Leland read of the Goddess Diana and her daughter Aradia, known as "the female Messiah." In his own work, *Aradia, or the Gospel of Witches*, he wrote that Maddalena's "little book sets forth how the latter was born, came down to earth, established witches and witchcraft, and then returned to heaven," essentially the origin story of how witches came to be.[4] Though this is Leland's telling of his interactions with the Italian folk-witch, scholars today are not convinced of this as a definitive truth. Historians such as Linda J. Jencson argue that even if Maddalena had sent him such a sacred text, it isn't likely that his interpretations are derived from her beliefs, but instead they "are clearly his own, not those of any actual Tuscan *strege* individual, let alone any kind of traditional community."[5]

Murray also wrote about the history and potential origins of witchcraft in two different works: *The Witch Cult in Western Europe* and *The God of Witches*. A noted Egyptologist, feminist and suffragist, Murray often challenged the systemic misogyny in academic settings. Her foray into witchcraft began with the desire to find supporting evidence that those targeted in the witch trials were practicing an ancient form of witchcraft and were persecuted for this belief. She originally came across the idea in London during World War I, which set her on a course of examining as many court records, pamphlets and testimonies as she could access, claiming to have "omitted the opinions of the authors, and have examined only the recorded facts" as part of her research.[6] Utilizing records that were published in the nineteenth century across mostly Scotland but also England and parts of Europe, Murray attempted to "give an impression of a fairly uniform pagan religion" whose deity was a Horned God.[7] Scholars such as Hutton and Jencson have long since criticized Murray's overuse of quotations from the records, arguing that her lack of interrogation of the sources weakened her thesis, as did

> her excessive synthesis of unrelated imagery as symptomatic of folk-loristic's early, unscientific obsession with finding "ur-forms," the supposed single-source origin, and "pure" original version once believed to lie behind every later custom, narrative, or folk belief.[8]

To her contemporaries, it was clear that Murray had no interest in moving on from this outdated methodology and continued to double down on her belief that her findings showcased a single origin of the witchcraft religion.[9] In 1931, she published *The God of Witches* for a more mainstream audience and continued to give lectures on the subject for decades to come.

The significance of Leland's and Murray's respective works is undeniable, laying the groundwork for Gardner's interpretation of the "Old Religion" (a term both Leland and Murray used) and fundamental practices used in his establishment of Wicca. However, as scholars have noted, their work is suspect and ripe for extensive critique, including, among other issues, accusations of bias, deceit and cultural appropriation. Both Leland and Murray utilized primary sources and took them at face value, interpreting them in ways that made sense in regard to their own ideas and opinions. For example, though the words of Maddalena are included in *Aradia, or the Gospel of Witches*, they are selected and written through the lens of an outsider, a white male English academic who was not a folk-witch himself, but one who sought to understand the practices through research and observation.

However, to dismiss Leland or Murray outright would also be problematic. As Paul Cowdell points out, the criticism, ridicule and even vilification of figures such as Murray do not detract from the fact that her work held public and widespread appeal. Even into her nineties, Murray continued to hold fast to her beliefs and ignored the academic criticism and debate of her works. Cowdell notes that, "By the 1950s, she engaged less and less with disputes over that work . . . Her aloofness from the debate regarding her own pronouncements . . . lent her only a greater silent weight that would raise her status even further among acolytes."[10] In other words, the "acolytes" who had come to regard her work as part of their burgeoning spiritual community regarded her refusal to engage with critics as reason for steadfast belief. Even if her legacy began to be "dismantled" after her death, her beliefs remained in the minds of many of those practitioners who had initially been persuaded by Murray's ideas.

Leland and Murray were hardly the only two influential figures in public discourse around witchcraft and alternative spirituality. One such figure, Crowley, stands as somewhat of an antithesis to what Gardner's Wicca would eventually become. Crowley, a Ceremonial Magician and later Satanist who decried himself the Beast 666, famously adopted the creed, "Do what thou wilt shall be the whole of the law," which appears to have been the inspiration for the Wiccan Rede, "an ye harm none, do what ye will."[11] In addition to his colorful personality, indulgence in sex and drugs, and noted misogyny, scholars have also drawn attention to the number of ways Crowley differed from Gardner's later pronouncements, particularly Crowley's lack of interest in organized or systemic religious practice.[12]

Like Leland and Murray, it would be easy to dismiss Crowley based on cursory research into his reputation both during his life and after his death. As Hutton demonstrates, though, more nuanced research into Crowley reveals a man uninterested in Christian notions of good and evil, so his moniker of "Beast 666 symbolized a divine, human, and animal self conjoined in harmony" rather than a deep-seated belief in the fallen angel of Lucifer or a propensity toward evil-doing or hell-raising.[13] Crowley's writings seem to have decentered Satan as a primary figure, leaving the development of Satanism as a religion in the hands of other writers in the early twentieth century.[14] Though there appears to be some influence of Crowley on Gardner, the former's apparent disinterest in any sort of organized religion as well as his well-known misogyny made it clear that he could not have influenced some of the most significant aspects of Wicca, particularly the emphasis on the Goddess.[15]

Each of these three figures – Leland, Murray and Crowley – is far too complex to be given full weight in this chapter, and the above paragraphs have only begun to scratch the surface of their respective controversies and legacies. What unites all three for the purposes of this chapter is their obvious influence on Gardner's development of Wicca, as is noted in his own published and unpublished works, leaving a lasting impression on the perspectives and viewpoints of Wicca in the second half of the twentieth century.

Gerald Gardner, Doreen Valiente and Modern Wicca

The legacy of Gardner is one fraught with controversy and contradiction. Both vilified for his charlatanic proclamations and lauded for his dedication to bringing the Goddess and witchcraft out of the shadows, Gardner has, both during his lifetime and after his death, been wrapped in enigma. Born on June 13, 1884 in Lancashire, UK, to a wealthy timber family, Gardner spent his childhood suffering from asthma and a few physicians convinced his parents that warmer climates could help him tremendously. He traveled to, among other places, Madeira, with his nurse, Josephine McCombie, who met and married while Gardner was in her care. McCombie's groom owned a tea plantation and convinced Gardner's parents to allow the three of them to live together in order to help his health. As a young man, Gardner answered an advertisement to work in the fields of Borneo, eventually moving on to Singapore and Malaysia before returning to England in 1916.[16]

Gardner's autobiographical accounts, through interviews as well as his writings, demonstrate a stark contrast to what would have been possible. For example, he would later claim he earned two PhD degrees (one from the University of Singapore and one from Toulouse in France) as well as an MA, but these proved to be fabrications after Valiente had done a little research into his educational background. She noted that the University of Singapore had not existed at the time that Gardner had claimed to earn the degree (1934) and that Toulouse had never heard of him.[17] He'd become quite interested in religious practices while serving as a Customs Officer in Malaysia and placed particular attention on the Sakis, a local tribe of people who lived in the forest and participated in rituals such as dancing around a fire and throwing plants into the flames.[18] Like Leland, it is clear that some of the customs of Gardner's "Old Religion" had roots in a culture to which he was an outsider.

Another baffling mystery is that of "Old Dorothy." Two years after retiring in 1936, Gardner moved to New Forest in order to protect his collection of artifacts in case of war.[19] It was there he met Dorothy Clutterbuck ("Old Dorothy") who he claimed was the leader of a coven of witches who practiced the "Old Religion." His story goes that she initiated him into her coven in 1939 and had "realised that I had stumbled upon something interesting; but I was half-initiated before the word, 'Wica' which they used hit me like a thunderbolt, and I knew where I was, and that the Old Religion still existed."[20] The experience left him electrified and he fervently desired to bring the witch's traditions and cultures to the outside world. They forbade it, fearing persecution, but did allow him to portray some of their rituals in the form of a novel, *High Magic's Aid* (1946).

The legend of "Old Dorothy" is a contentious one among scholars and, for many, her existence remained in dispute. Though her existence was proven to be real, as noted by Valiente and others as well as later scholars such as Hutton, her role as the leader of a witch coven remains difficult to reconcile. Hutton's own research into Clutterbuck's diaries revealed "a simple, kindly, conventional, and pious" woman who clearly committed her life to her Christian faith.[21] Hutton surmises that Gardner had known of Clutterbuck and used her name as his coven's initiator either to experience a "private delight" that someone so pious could be associated with witchcraft or as a way to protect the identity of the New Forest Coven's real leader.[22]

One of the greatest controversies of Gardner's life was his repeated desire to bring Wicca to a wider public. Once England repealed the last of its witchcraft secrecy statutes in 1951, making it easier for witches and Wiccans to practice more openly, Gardner brought news of his rediscovery of the "Old Religion" to the national press, including through a series of stories for the *Sunday Pictorial* (later to be renamed the *Sunday Mirror*) in the summer of the same year. In an article titled "Calling All Covens," Gardner invited various witches and practitioners to join in with rituals and ceremonies. The author, Allen Andrews, described Gardner as "The witch-doctor–doctor of philosophy from Singapore and a doctor of literature from Toulouse . . . [with] twinkling eyes" who declares that being a witch is "great fun!"[23]

Mere months later, articles in the *Sunday Pictorial* were far less kind and welcoming to the idea of local witches and boisterous covens. Sensationalist stories of black magic, ritual nudity and sacrifice flooded the newspaper, relying on ideas such as devil worship as fodder for how to portray the dealings of people like Gardner. Despite the increasing negative headlines and stereotypical portrayals of witchcraft as devil worship, Gardner continued to engage in newspaper, radio and TV interviews in order to promote Wicca. Many within his coven, including Valiente, begged Gardner to stop doing any press, insisting that he was doing far more harm than good for the religion. Valiente and many others believed that putting the story in the hands of the press would damage the religion, whereas controlling the narrative through the publication of their own books would go a long way to bring people into the fold. Gardner would hear none of it.[24]

In June 1955, the *Sunday Pictorial* published an article with the headline "No Witchcraft is Fun," an obvious callback to Gardner's initial interview with the paper, and included "This man's whitewash is dangerous" in bold underlined letters above the title. The author, Peter Hawkins, warned his readers of the blood rituals, nude dancing, prayers to a Horned God and "stimulation through wine, music, and drumming." Hawkins said that the true danger lay in Gardner's books, particularly *Witchcraft Today*, a work intended to detail the rituals of witchcraft and the "Old Religion" for a wider audience. Hawkins wrote,

> There is no doubt at all that there are satanic devil-worshippers in Britain who are ever ready to provide this type of sexual perversion to capture the men and women they hope to make their slaves. That is why I believe that [Gardner's] books in the wrong hands can be dangerous. **AND THERE IS NO WAY OF STOPPING THEM FROM GETTING INTO THE WRONG HANDS.**[25]

One of the most complex elements of Gardner's legacy, particularly as pertains to this book, is his views on women. From the outset, it appears that Gardner held women and the concept of the feminine in exceptionally high regard. In his work *Witchcraft Today*, published in 1954, Gardner provides a historical/mythological account of the Goddess, writing that "the matriarchal period has been tentatively dated from the middle of the ninth to the middle of the seventh millennium BC, during which time caves, trees, the moon and stars all seem to have been reverenced as female emblems."[26] As the mythological history went, "primitive man" feared the strangeness of rebirth where they might be in a life with unfamiliar people or in a time and location that would be difficult to navigate. They asked the Goddess to bless them with reincarnation among friends and family, to which the Goddess obliged.

> The goddess of the witch cult is obviously the Great Mother, the giver of life, incarnate love. She rules spring, pleasure, feasting, and all the delights. She was identified at a later time with other goddesses and has a special affinity for the moon.[27]

Though he also described the importance of the Horned God, ruler of death and magic, Gardner emphasized that the feminine rituals and prayers from the "Old Religion" should be respected, making it no question that the Goddess should be a primary deity in Wicca.

Gardner also insisted that women hold positions such as High Priestess and be treated with respect and reverence in accordance with the Goddess. The High Priestesses could be seen as the Goddess' representatives on Earth, ones who could call to the Great Mother in ceremony and ritual. Aware that some of the "pageantry" in the "Old Religion" could appear to observers as Wicca merely Christianity in disguise, Gardner argued that the prioritization of the feminine was one of the ways that Wicca could be set apart from the church. Over ritualistic ceremonies, "the priestess usually presides. Candles are used, one to read the book by and others set around the circle. This does not in any way resemble the practice of any other religious sect I know."[28] Gardner echoes this sentiment in his follow-up book *The Meaning of Witchcraft*, published in 1959, where he outlines various rituals relating to moon cycles and the Wheel of the Year. For example, during Yule, or the Winter Solstice, Gardner describes how

> the priestess, or female leader of the coven, stands behind a cauldron in which a fire is ignited, while the rest dance round her sunwise, with burning torches. They call it the Dance of the Wheel, or Yule, and its purpose is to cause the sun to be reborn.[29]

In this ritual, the rebirth of the sun, often symbolized as male or masculine, is called upon by women, or a feminine presence, standing in stark contrast to Christian traditions that, particularly during the time Gardner was writing, offered few opportunities for leadership to women within the church.

One of the most famous High Priestesses to come out of Gardner's coven was Valiente. If Gardner was considered the "Father" of modern Wicca, Valiente would be its "Mother." Born Doreen Dominy on January 4, 1922 to a middle-class Christian family, Valiente began working with magic in her teens, having found books on the subject at her local library. Her parents, unhappy with her interest in spell craft, sent her to a convent school which she had "walked out of . . . at the age of fifteen, and flatly refused to return."[30] By 1943, she had met Casimiro Valiente,

> a refugee from the Spanish Civil War, who had gone on to fight with the Free French forces against Hitler . . . In spite of his war record, he was regarded as a foreigner and therefore a lower form of life. So was I, for having married him.[31]

The bigotry toward Casimiro gave Valiente insight into what "it is like to be on the receiving end of racism," and she spent a great deal of time in her writings considering witchcraft through a lens of inclusivity.[32]

In fall of 1952, Valiente read an article in the *Illustrated* titled "Witchcraft in Britain," detailing the Sabbats of Halloween, Candlemas (later called Imbolc), May Eve (Beltane) and Lammas. In the article, she read of one of Gardner's most well-told stories, the raising of a cone of power on August 1, 1940 in order to prevent Hitler crossing into Britain. The stories left her intrigued and she immediately wrote a letter to the article's author who sent it to Gardner. After being invited to join the coven, she traveled to Stonehenge with him and his friend, Dafo, one of the original founders of the theater in Christchurch where Gardner had been introduced to local witches. Soon she had become a High Priestess within the coven, well respected and instrumental in the production and creation of various rituals, spells and chants which are now well known within Wiccan circles.

She described that Gardner had, like he did with all initiates, given her a copy of his novel *High Magic's Aid*, a fictionalized account of the rituals and celebrations of practicing covens. She said that he did so because he "wanted to see what effects his description of a witch initiation had upon them. If they were upset by ritual nudity and ritual flagellation, matters would proceed no further."³³ Valiente argued that the media had presented witchcraft as one of "luring" young women into deviant sexual practices, but Gardner wanted to be upfront with potential initiates, letting them decide whether or not the ritual practices of nudity and flagellation would be something they wanted to welcome into their lives. To Valiente, this meant that consent was part of the initiates' experience, though it is unclear if they had the opportunity to be part of the coven without participating in rituals of nudity and flagellation. Valiente described the flagellation as something she didn't like at the beginning of her time in the coven, but she "came to accept it for one good reason – it worked. It genuinely raised power and enabled one to have flashes of clairvoyant vision. The flagellation was not intended to cause pain, but merely to stimulate."³⁴ Gardner had incorporated these elements of nudity, sex, sexuality and flagellation into the practices of his coven because, he had claimed, it was one of the ancient ways of gaining true sight.

Valiente's greatest contributions came from working with Gardner on his "Ye Bok of Ye Art Magical," later to be known as *The Gardnerian Book of Shadows*, published in 1953. Gardner had begun working on "Ye Bok" himself and had created a litany of rituals, spells, celebrations and histories all seen as part of the "Old Religion." Within its pages were passages copied from a variety of sources, including biblical scripture and other grimoires, books by Crowley and the Waite-Smith tarot pack.³⁵ Though "Ye Bok" was clearly not entirely composed of ancient documents of a long-lost religion, Valiente believed that it had the potential to be a powerful work. However, Valiente had uncovered some evidence to suggest that Crowley had had a hand in writing some of the rituals and chants, and was perhaps even paid to do so.³⁶ She warned Gardner that he'd never succeed at "reviving the Old Religion" or even gaining acceptance of it due to the association between his work and Crowley.³⁷ Gardner reacted defensively and told Valiente that if she could do better, she should go ahead and do so. She did exactly that, rewriting the *Book of Shadows* to cut out Crowley's words (and inherent misogyny) in order "to bring it back to what I felt was . . . our own words."³⁸ Inspired by Leland's *Aradia, or the Gospel of Witches*, Valiente rewrote what has become known as "the Charge":

Mother darkness and divine
Mine the scourge and mine the kiss
Five-point star of life and bliss
Here I charge thee in this sign.

Bow before my spirit bright
Aphrodite, Arianrhod,
Lover of the Horned God
Queen of witchery and night.

Diana, Brigid, Melusine,
Am I named of old by men;

Artemis and Cerridwen
Hell's dark mistress, Heaven's Queen.

Ye who ask me of a boon,
Meet me in some hidden shade
Lead my dance in greenwood glade,
By the light of the full moon.

Dance about my altar stone,
Work my holy magistry,
Ye who are fain of sorcery,
I bring ye secrets yet unknown

No more shall ye know slavery,
Who tread my round the Sabbat night.
Come all ye naked to the rite
In sign that ye are truly free.

Keep ye my mysteries in mirth,
Heart joined to heart and lip to lip.
Five are the points of fellowship
That bring ye ecstasy on earth.

No other law but love I know,
By naught but love may I be known;
And all that liveth is my own,
From me they come, to me they go.[39]

Valiente's interpretation of "the Charge" highlighted the promise of the Goddess, to guide, teach and nurture her followers, leading them on their spiritual journey. Valiente did not invent "the Charge," nor did she claim that these words were hers alone. By her own volition, Valiente's work was heavily inspired by Leland's *Aradia, or the Gospel of Witches*. A side-by-side analysis would demonstrate this very clearly, and, at times, she used his phrasing word for word. However, one of her primary goals in her rewrite of "the Charge" was not to lay claim to any poetic originality of her own, but to remove any connection to Crowley. Wicca held the Goddess as the central deity who has "no other law but love," so it would not only benefit "the Charge" but the reception of Wicca at large to disassociate itself from a well-known misogynist and bigot like Crowley, particularly given his proclamations about Satanism.[40] Valiente knew that careful use of language and a cognizant awareness of public perception would matter in regard to how they should bring Wicca to a mainstream audience. Despite any of Gardner's stories about Crowley (of which there are several and which, at times, contradict one another), Hutton argues "that there is no apparent reference to the witch religion in Crowley's published works but *none* in his unpublished works – which are numerous – either."[41] Whether or not Gardner had told the truth about his experiences with or knowledge of Crowley, or if Crowley indeed had any connection with witchcraft in any sense, Valiente believed that he did and her concern was that any association with a self-proclaimed Satanist who declared that he "did not want to be bossed around by women" would be dangerous to their cause.[42]

In the mid-1950s, Valiente had become particularly concerned with public perception of witchcraft through the media. Though the Witchcraft Act of 1735 had officially been repealed in England in 1951, associations of devil worship, violence and sexual deviance with witchcraft remained an integral part of mainstream narratives, and Valiente feared that Gardner's continued interviews with the press would only serve to reinforce these narratives rather than encourage more people to explore Wicca as part of their spiritual practice. As has been noted, her fears were not unfounded.

Shortly before the publication of Hawkins' article in the *Sunday Pictorial*, a woman in Birmingham, claiming to be a former witch, confessed to acts of dark magic and told stories of Satanic meetings "involving the sacrifice of chickens and drinking of their blood," coming forward in such a public way "in the hope of saving others."[43] Hawkins had reached out to Gardner, who granted an interview, only to be later referred to as a "whitewasher of witchcraft."[44] Valiente told Gardner that he had been set up and that continued talk with the press would only further endanger their practice and hope of bringing Wicca to a broader audience. As more and more headlines continued to associate witchcraft with words like "black magic" and "murder," Valiente and others became increasingly afraid that the Witchcraft Act would be reinstated, and they would be the targets of persecution themselves.[45]

Two factions formed within the coven, one pro-publicity and the other anti-publicity, the latter of which Valiente spearheaded alongside a few other prominent members of the coven. They attempted to dissuade Gardner from further press and instead persuaded him to use print that they could control, such as their published books, to inform the public and debunk myths purported by sensationalistic media. "We pointed out to Gerald pretty forcibly that we had had enough of these continual outbursts of silly publicity seeking on his part, which were only adding fuel to the fire of the national press witch-hunt." Gardner, encouraged by others who had caught the "publicity bug," ignored their protests and, as Valiente writes, acted out of "sheer big-headedness." Frustrated by Gardner's desire to ignore the potential threats associated with speaking to the press, Valiente and others in the anti-publicity camp composed a set of 13 rules titled "Proposed Rules for the Craft," intended to maintain a level of secrecy that had originally been a part of Gardner's Wiccan practice, a "secrecy to which we had all been solemnly sworn when we were initiated – a fact which some people now seemed to remember or forget just as they pleased."[46] They presented the proposition to Gardner in the hopes that he would listen to reason and remember the significance of the secrecy they had sworn to in the first place.

Gardner's rebuttal came in the form of another "ancient" text, "The Laws of the Craft," which he said had existed prior to their "Proposed Rules for the Craft." Valiente claims no one had seen the document before that moment. The document was "couched in mock-archaic language and ornamented with awesome threats . . . and invocations of 'the Curse of the Goddess' upon anyone who dared transgress them." One section in particular angered Valiente, in which it was written that

> The Gods love the brethren of Wicca as a man loveth a woman, by mastering her [and] the greatest virtue of a High Priestess be that she recognize that youth is necessary to the representative of the Goddess. So she will gracefully retire in favour of a younger woman, should the coven so decide in council.[47]

The threat was clear: Valiente owed her power and influence within the coven to Gardner, who could strip her of the role of High Priestess should he choose, particularly given her age (though only in her thirties by this point) and refusal to acquiesce to his whims and desires.

The final straw came when Valiente caught Gardner in a lie about speaking to the press. This was not the first lie she had caught him in; she knew he had lied about receiving advanced degrees at Singapore and Toulouse and had countless times seen the contradictions in his claims about where his Wiccan source information came from. This particular lie wasn't about manipulating information to make it seem more "archaic" or to present himself as a man of credentials in order to make the "Old Religion" seem more streamlined and credible. This lie served only his desire for further media attention. As part of a compromise between them, Gardner had promised to clear any press interviews and stories with them first before agreeing to participate. When she saw that he had done an interview without making good on his promise, Gardner claimed that his publisher, Riders (who had published *Witchcraft Today*), had set up the interview for him and that he had no choice but to agree. When Valiente contacted Riders herself, they said they had done no such thing. By 1957, Valiente had split ways with Gardner and his coven.[48]

The question of Gardner's legacy is clearly fraught. All at once he is an alternative spiritual crusader, perpetrator of cultural appropriation, intelligent, charismatic, fraudulent and media-hungry. Yet, as Hutton writes, "what seems to be established beyond doubt is the central role of Gerald Gardner in developing and propagating the religion," responsible for the emergence and development of modern Wicca and paganism.[49] His compilation of sources and careful attention to detail in his "Ye Bok of Ye Art Magical" contributed to common practices in Wicca today, such as specific moon rituals and celebrations around the Wheel of the Year. What cannot be ignored, however, is that Gardner clearly used his status as founder and his privilege as a white educated, wealthy male in order to get his way, particularly in regard to his threats against Valiente in the mid-1950s. The Goddess may have been worshiped, and women might have the opportunity to rise to a rank such as High Priestess, but, as Valiente has pointed out in her published works, early iterations of Wicca were far from feminist. Women could not be initiated into a coven without a male to guide them (and the inverse was also true) and, like other parts of society, Wicca demonized the concept of homosexuality and openly criticized women who could not have or did not want children.[50] As the Western feminist movement emerged in the 1960s and 1970s, Wicca and paganism would find their way into more activist and political circles.

American Feminism and Witchcraft

In 1963, less than a year before Gardner's death, Betty Friedan published *The Feminine Mystique*, the then radical text that dared speak aloud the truth of many women's experiences: they were unfulfilled in their roles as wife and mother. Though this work has (rightly) been critiqued for its focus on white middle-class women, it nonetheless sparked an already burgeoning conversation in the United States about the expectations of women in postwar society. Friedan's work did not simply emerge out of thin air, but had been the result of a long line of questioning and challenging of these traditional roles by activists and writers alike. Historian Kate Weigand described this practice of activism through writing as a renewed effort to build a feminist movement during the "hostile years" of the postwar era. Borrowing from feminists in the 1910s, these writers used economics, work and labor (both paid and unpaid) to examine the normalization of women's oppression and the impetus for liberation.[51] One such woman, Communist Party leader Mary Inman, examined the "woman question" in her work *In Woman's Defense* (1940), in which she argued that "housework, like factory work, is productive labor" and went on to suggest that housewives should be organized.[52] Friedan, staff member and writer for the *UE News* in the late 1940s, emphasized the desire of women to continue to work once the war was over. By 1948, she "took a consistently radical stance on issues" such as racism, discrimination and, most notably, "the woman problem."[53] Like Inman, Friedan was also concerned with the demands made of housewives; she argued that women who stayed at home had the difficult job of caring for their family "with a limited amount of money to spend and a constant number of mouths to feed," leaving them with the constant pressure of caring for the home and family with little to no respect in broader society for the energy, skill and time put into their work.[54]

Marriage and motherhood were not the only trappings of gender criticized by feminist writers and activists in the mid-twentieth century. Critiques of virtuous sexuality and the myth of virginity, sexist language in the workplace and the glass ceiling, lack of opportunities in the military, higher education, politics and religious institutions were all part of the growing landscape of the second-wave feminist movement. Yet, the road to openly critiquing these ideas and values proved challenging, particularly through the immediate Cold War years of the 1950s. The anti-communist culture in the 1950s took the position that traditional roles for men and women would uphold American values and protect the country from unwanted infiltration.

By the mid-1960s, feminist activists had had enough and sought to have their voices heard. Feminists criticized societal ideas around feminine standards of behavior, rejecting ideas of purity, innocence, quiet and maternity as innate in all women. This included the right to sexuality and sexual experience, rejection of diet culture, freedom of expression through clothing, rejection of sexual objectification, the right to not have children, the right to single parenthood and more. Some, like Friedan, published best-selling books to speak of their own and others' experiences. Many took to the streets to protest or organize groups at the workplace or on college campuses. Imagery and symbolism became increasingly crucial within the social movements of the time, including the feminist movement, for a sense of "collective identity" which Suzanne Staggenborg refers to as "the sense of shared experiences and values that connects individuals to movements."[55] What would the feminist movement look like? What would identify it? In some feminist circles, the reclamation of the imagery and narrative of the witch became the symbol of empowerment, resistance and counter-hegemonic ideology that could help create this collective identity.

The radical feminist group W.I.T.C.H. (whose name changed with the social action or protest it undertook, such as Women's International Terrorist Conspiracy from Hell or Women Inner-viewing Their Collective History) became the most prominent force to utilize the imagery of witch. It was founded in 1968 by radical feminists, including Peggy Dobbins, who had recently gone to court for sprinkling Toni Home permanent solution (used for home perms, etc.) on the floor as the 1968 Miss America received her crown. Dobbins and her counterparts, inspired by other radical groups such as the Redstockings and black activists such as Stokely Carmichael, decided that the imagery of the witch would be an excellent way to take words that had historically been used as pejoratives and turn them into affirmations. The members of W.I.T.C.H. spent 1968 and 1969 dancing wildly, "hexing" various companies and donning black hats, staging protests at AT&T, Wall Street and the Democratic National Convention. According to Dobbins, "embracing the iconography and archetype of the witch was an exercise in 'suspension of disbelief' in trivial superstitions they could mockingly embrace to stand negative stereotypes and caricatures of feminists on their heads." Though the witch iconography was largely symbolic, the group emphasized traditions such as midwifery and herbal medicine that had fallen out of professional favor due to patriarchal standards of practice.[56]

W.I.T.C.H. and other prominent feminist activists of the time had begun to investigate the historical narrative of witches, and declare that the injustices and oppressions against witches and those who had been accused had led to an erasure of powerful women. W.I.T.C.H. had argued that "witchcraft had been the religion of all Europe before Christianity" and that the "suppression" of this religion by the "ruling elite" was "also a war against feminism." Radical feminists such as Mary Daly and Andrea Dworkin echoed this argument, stating that "witch trials had represented the suppression of the Old Religion and the control of women, who might now regain their old power by identifying as witches," lambasting works such as the *Malleus Maleficarum* for their role in what Dworkin had deemed "gynocide."[57] Barbara Ehrenreich and Deirdre English also published *Witches, Midwives, and Nurses*, where they argued that many of the women who had been accused and persecuted were healers and midwives. Like Dworkin, Ehrenreich and English criticized works such as the *Malleus Maleficarum* as deeply misogynist, masking as Christian piety in order to justify their crimes against women healers and midwives.

Though Wicca had come to the United States by the time of W.I.T.C.H.'s emergence and obvious overlaps existed between the two, the gap between witch iconography in Western feminism and the spiritual practices of Wicca remained particularly wide. As Hutton has argued in *The Triumph of the Moon*,

> the use of the witch made by W.I.T.C.H., Daly, and Dworkin had . . . no necessary religious dimension at all, and moreover depended upon the concept that witchcraft was something inherent in all women, or at least something to which all liberated women could relate.[58]

The concept of any experience or identity as being "inherent in all women" was and still is a common critique of the most well-known feminist movements of the time period. Scholars such as bell hooks have argued that the second wave's failure to acknowledge the intersectional experiences of women of color, those who are economically insecure and lesbian women led to rifts within the movement. The emphasis on greater inclusivity and diversity within witchcraft will be addressed more fully in the final chapter of this book.

By the 1970s, more writers had attempted to discuss Wicca through new lenses of social movements, academia and politics. For example, Margot Adler, a journalist and correspondent, published *Drawing Down the Moon*, which addressed the development of Wicca as a "symbolic form," where many American witches, Adler included, began "to accept the Old Religion more as metaphor than reality."[59] However, the book that allowed for the strongest interaction between Western feminist politics and the spiritual beliefs of Wicca was Starhawk's *The Spiral Dance*. Released the same day as *Drawing Down the Moon*, Starhawk's work, according to historian Hutton, "replaced *Witchcraft Today* as the model text for would-be witches."[60] Though *The Spiral Dance* rehashes much of what was contained in her earlier works, such as emphasis on the misogyny of the *Malleus Maleficarum*, the incomprehensible loss of life to executions, the Catholic Inquisition and the trials at Salem, Starhawk's work addresses the systemic powerlessness of women and how a religion with a Goddess at its center could inspire

> women to see ourselves as divine, our bodies as sacred . . . Through the Goddess, we can discover our strengths, enlighten our minds, own our bodies, and celebrate our emotions. We can move beyond narrow, constricting roles and become whole.[61]

This echoed much of what the feminist movement had broadly spoken of, the idea of moving beyond the constriction of traditional roles in order to find empowerment within the body, mind and spirit.

Starhawk also acknowledged the concerns of feminists about Goddess worship.

> The rise of Goddess religion makes some politically oriented feminists uneasy. They fear it will sidetrack energy away from action to bring about social change. . . . The symbol of the Goddess conveys the spiritual power both to challenge systems of oppression and to create new, life-oriented cultures.[62]

To her, Pagan spirituality and feminism were intrinsically linked. The idea of "the personal is political" came through in *The Spiral Dance*, as did the idea of reclamation and empowerment. Starhawk, though aware of Gardnerian Wicca, did not proclaim herself to be Wiccan but, instead, in 1980, founded the organization the Reclaiming Collective, which sought to bring together spirituality and issues of social justice, "a community of people looking to unify spirit and politics."[63] The Reclaiming Collective now has online resources and dozens of chapters around the United States, and continues to hold classes and workshops on feminist spirituality and issues connected to social justice and the environment.

Conclusion

With its central focus on the Goddess, reverence for nature and positions such as High Priestess that elevated positions for women, Wicca would appear to have been feminist in its leaning from the outset. Far more accurate is that the inception of Wicca came from the research of Gardner, a well-connected, well-educated white man of means and opportunity, who, more than once, used his privilege to elevate his status and credentials, at times lying, deceiving or misdirecting in order to present the image of Wicca as an "ancient religion." His commitment to this narrative has left a legacy that is difficult for scholars to unravel and it is crucial to look more closely at those who were a part of his coven in the early days, such as Valiente, and examine how Wicca became intertwined with politics and social movements. As with many other religions, Wicca has not remained static since the mid-twentieth century, with many who practice witchcraft or paganism choosing not to identify as Wiccan. The practices of paganism, Wicca and other forms of witchcraft have morphed over time to be more inclusive and justice oriented, something that will be discussed in Chapter 6.

Notes

1. Ronald Hutton, *The Triumph of the Moon: A History of Modern Pagan Witchcraft* (Oxford: Oxford University Press, 1999), 239.
2. Owen Davies, "Witchcraft Accusations," in *The Routledge History of Witchcraft*, ed. Johannes Dillinger (London: Routledge, 2021), 290.
3. Anonymous, "Extraordinary Assault," *Birmingham Journal* (April 14, 1827), www.britishnewspaperarchive.co.uk, accessed September 12, 2024.
4. Charles Godfrey Leland, *Aradia, or the Gospel of Witches* (London: D. Nutt Publisher, 1899), viii.
5. Linda J. Jencson, "Wicca," in *The Routledge History of Witchcraft*, ed. Johannes Dillinger (London: Routledge, 2021), 321.
6. Margaret Murray, *The Witch Cult in Western Europe: A Study of Anthropology* (Oxford: Clarendon Press, 1921), 11.
7. Ronald Hutton, *The Triumph of the Moon: A History of Modern Pagan Witchcraft* (Oxford: Oxford University Press, 1999), 195.
8. Linda J. Jencson, "Wicca," in *The Routledge History of Witchcraft*, ed. Johannes Dillinger (London: Routledge, 2021), 321.
9. Paul Cowdell, "Margaret Murray: Who *Didn't* Believe Her and Why," *TFH: The Journal of Folklore and History* 39/40 (2023), 9.
10. Paul Cowdell, "Margaret Murray: Who *Didn't* Believe Her and Why," *TFH: The Journal of Folklore and History* 39/40 (2023), 7.
11. Linda J. Jencson, "Wicca," in *The Routledge History of Witchcraft*, ed. Johannes Dillinger (London: Routledge, 2021), 325.
12. Ronald Hutton, *The Triumph of the Moon: A History of Modern Pagan Witchcraft* (Oxford: Oxford University Press, 1999), 172–175.
13. Ronald Hutton, *The Triumph of the Moon: A History of Modern Pagan Witchcraft* (Oxford: Oxford University Press, 1999), 175.
14. Per Faxneld, "Disciples of Hell: The History of Satanism," in *The Routledge History of Witchcraft*, ed. Johannes Dillinger (London: Taylor and Francis, 2021), 338.
15. Linda J. Jencson, "Wicca," in *The Routledge History of Witchcraft*, ed. Johannes Dillinger (London: Routledge, 2021), 324.
16. Michael Howard, *Modern Wicca: A History from Gerald Gardner to the Present* (Woodbury, MN: Llewellyn Publications, 2010), 9–13.
17. Michael Howard, *Modern Wicca: A History from Gerald Gardner to the Present* (Woodbury, MN: Llewellyn Publications, 2010), 11.
18. Michael Howard, *Modern Wicca: A History from Gerald Gardner to the Present* (Woodbury, MN: Llewellyn Publications, 2010), 14.
19. Ronald Hutton, *The Triumph of the Moon: A History of Modern Pagan Witchcraft* (Oxford: Oxford University Press, 1999), 206.
20. Gerald Brousseau Gardner, *The Meaning of Witchcraft* (New York: Magickal Childe Publishing Inc, 1984), 11.
21. Ronald Hutton, *The Triumph of the Moon: A History of Modern Pagan Witchcraft* (Oxford: Oxford University Press, 1999), 211.

80 *Witchcraft: Gendered Perspectives*

22 Ronald Hutton, *The Triumph of the Moon: A History of Modern Pagan Witchcraft* (Oxford: Oxford University Press, 1999), 212.
23 Allen Andrews, "Calling All Covens," *Sunday Pictorial*, July 29, 1951, 6.
24 Ronald Hutton, *The Triumph of the Moon: A History of Modern Pagan Witchcraft* (Oxford: Oxford University Press, 1999), 248–249.
25 Peter Hawkins, "No Witchcraft is Fun," *Sunday Pictorial*, June 12, 1955, 7. The bold capitalized sentence is original to the article.
26 Gerald Brousseau Gardner, *Witchcraft Today* (New York: Magickal Childe Publishing Inc, 1982), 31–32. The spelling of "reverenced" is original to Gardner's text.
27 Gerald Brousseau Gardner, *Witchcraft Today* (New York: Magickal Childe Publishing Inc, 1982), 42.
28 Gerald Brousseau Gardner, *Witchcraft Today* (New York: Magickal Childe Publishing Inc, 1982), 23.
29 Gerald Brousseau Gardner, *The Meaning of Witchcraft* (New York: Magickal Childe Publishing Inc, 1984), 56.
30 Doreen Valiente, *The Rebirth of Witchcraft* (London: Robert Hale, 1989), 41.
31 Doreen Valiente, *The Rebirth of Witchcraft* (London: Robert Hale, 1989), 36.
32 Doreen Valiente, *The Rebirth of Witchcraft* (London: Robert Hale, 1989), 37.
33 Doreen Valiente, *The Rebirth of Witchcraft* (London: Robert Hale, 1989), 39.
34 Doreen Valiente, *The Rebirth of Witchcraft* (London: Robert Hale, 1989), 59.
35 Ronald Hutton, *The Triumph of the Moon: A History of Modern Pagan Witchcraft* (Oxford: Oxford University Press, 1999), 227.
36 Doreen Valiente, *The Rebirth of Witchcraft* (London: Robert Hale, 1989), 57–59.
37 Doreen Valiente, *The Rebirth of Witchcraft* (London: Robert Hale, 1989), 60.
38 Doreen Valiente, *The Rebirth of Witchcraft* (London: Robert Hale, 1989), 61.
39 Doreen Valiente, *The Rebirth of Witchcraft* (London: Robert Hale, 1989), 61–62. Some in the coven critiqued the original poem, finding some of the word choices (like "magistry") incomprehensible and having difficulty pronouncing some of the names of the Goddesses. Valiente rewrote the poem in prose form, which was published in two books, *The Witches' Bible* (originally titled *Eight Sabbats for Witches*) and *The Witches' Way*, both by Janet and Stewart Farrar, and her version of "the Charge" remains the one most commonly used today in Wiccan practice.
40 Doreen Valiente, *The Rebirth of Witchcraft* (London: Robert Hale, 1989), 62.
41 Ronald Hutton, *The Triumph of the Moon: A History of Modern Pagan Witchcraft* (Oxford: Oxford University Press, 1999), 42.
42 Doreen Valiente, *The Rebirth of Witchcraft* (London: Robert Hale, 1989), 45.
43 Doreen Valiente, *The Rebirth of Witchcraft* (London: Robert Hale, 1989), 66.
44 Peter Hawkins, "No Witchcraft is Fun," *Sunday Pictorial*, June 12, 1955, 7.
45 Doreen Valiente, *The Rebirth of Witchcraft* (London: Robert Hale, 1989), 68.
46 Doreen Valiente, *The Rebirth of Witchcraft* (London: Robert Hale, 1989), 69.
47 Doreen Valiente, *The Rebirth of Witchcraft* (London: Robert Hale, 1989), 70.
48 Doreen Valiente, *The Rebirth of Witchcraft* (London: Robert Hale, 1989), 71–72.
49 Ronald Hutton, *The Triumph of the Moon: A History of Modern Pagan Witchcraft* (Oxford: Oxford University Press, 1999), 239.
50 Doreen Valiente, *The Rebirth of Witchcraft* (London: Robert Hale, 1989), 182.
51 Kate Weigand, *Red Feminism: American Communism and the Making of Women's Liberation* (Baltimore: Johns Hopkins University Press, 2002), 2.
52 Kate Weigand, *Red Feminism: American Communism and the Making of Women's Liberation* (Baltimore: Johns Hopkins University Press, 2002), 54.
53 Daniel Horowitz, *Betty Friedan and the Making of the 'Feminine Mystique': The American Left, the Cold War and Modern Feminism* (Amherst: University of Massachusetts Press, 2000), 137, 144.

54 Daniel Horowitz, *Betty Friedan and the Making of the 'Feminine Mystique': The American Left, the Cold War and Modern Feminism* (Amherst: University of Massachusetts Press, 2000), 138.
55 Suzanne Staggenborg, *Social Movements 2nd Edition* (Oxford: Oxford University Press, 2016), 25.
56 Peggy Dobbins, "W.I.T.C.H. Zora Burden's Introduction to Interview with Peggy for Zora's Collection of Verbatim Interviews with *Women of the Underground Resistance*," 2020, http://peggydobbins.net/womensmovement/witchzorarepeggy.html.
57 Ronald Hutton, *The Triumph of the Moon: A History of Modern Pagan Witchcraft* (Oxford: Oxford University Press, 1999), 341.
58 Ronald Hutton, *The Triumph of the Moon: A History of Modern Pagan Witchcraft* (Oxford: Oxford University Press, 1999), 345.
59 Ronald Hutton, *The Triumph of the Moon: A History of Modern Pagan Witchcraft* (Oxford: Oxford University Press, 1999), 369.
60 Ronald Hutton, *The Triumph of the Moon: A History of Modern Pagan Witchcraft* (Oxford: Oxford University Press, 1999), 345.
61 Starhawk, *The Spiral Dance: A Rebirth of the Ancient Religion of the Great Goddess 20th Anniversary Edition* (San Francisco: HarperSanFrancisco), 1999, 33.
62 Starhawk, *The Spiral Dance: A Rebirth of the Ancient Religion of the Great Goddess 20th Anniversary Edition* (San Francisco: HarperSanFrancisco), 1999, 35.
63 Starhawk, "Reclaiming, a Tradition, a Community," Reclaiming Collective, WordPress, www.reclaimingcollective.wordpress.com, accessed October 3, 2024.

5 "Normal is Not Necessarily a Virtue"

TV and Movie Witches of the Twentieth and Twenty-First Centuries

Introduction

As young girls, the recently orphaned Sally and Gillian Owens moved in with their aunts, Frances and Jet, two women well known in the community for their long string of lovers, eccentricity and, most of all, the fact that they are witches. When a desperate woman appears at the door begging the aunts to cast a spell on a man to make him fall in love with her, the girls witness the lovelorn woman prick a bird with a needle, a sacrifice in the name of her desire. Sally, clearly upset by what she has witnessed, repeats, "I hope I never fall in love" several times before her sister, Gillian, whispers, "I can't wait to fall in love." Their desires as girls shape their adult realities. Sally's greatest wish as an adult is to have a "normal life," to which her aunt Frances replies, "My darling girl, when are you going to realize that normal isn't necessarily a virtue? It rather denotes a lack of courage." As it turns out, that is the day she notices Michael, a handsome fruit vendor, and it is she, not Gillian, who grows up to fall in love. Once she and Michael get married and have two beautiful daughters, Sally writes to Gillian to tell her that it's their

> third anniversary and all I have to show for it are two beautiful little girls and a husband I just can't stop kissing. . . . I wish you could see us, no more stones being thrown, no taunts cried out, everything is so blissfully normal. Life is perfect.[1]

Gillian, on the other hand, runs away with her boyfriend as a teen, only to bounce from town to town, leaving her own string of broken hearts behind her.

There are several themes and motifs that a chapter on the imagery and representation of witches in films and television could focus on: the emphasis on witch sisters, the prevalence of aunts who raise the orphaned witch, a positioning of witches as "good" or "bad," the evil witch searching for eternal beauty or youth and many others. While those themes will be touched upon throughout this chapter, the primary focus will be on the witch characters'

DOI: 10.4324/9781032717227-6

relationship to the concept of "normal." In the case of Sally, being normal meant altering her identity as witch, an identity that she was born into, for the sake of avoiding the ridicule and stigmatization of being a witch in her community. Being "normal" for her – a young, pretty, middle-class cisgender white woman – meant domesticity, marriage and motherhood. It was only *after* she met these criteria for "normal" that the stones stopped being thrown and the taunts cried out.

The characters selected for this chapter represent ways to explore how popular culture has shaped the witch as someone who either yearns for a "normal" life or rejects traditional and historical definitions of various identities. Often, characters like Sally, who long for a "normal" life, believe that their only course is rejection either of their identity in order to be accepted by society, or by society in order to embrace their identity. Not all witch characters eschew their witchcraft in favor of domestic "bliss." Witches such as Wanda Maximoff (*WandaVision*) and Piper Halliwell (*Charmed*) practiced witchcraft in secret but still longed for a "normal" domestic life. Conversely, some witch characters such as Agatha Harkness (*WandaVision* and *Agatha All Along*), Willow Rosenberg (*Buffy the Vampire Slayer*) and Nancy Downs (*The Craft*) sacrifice any concept of "normal," embracing their witchy-ness and all the control and power that comes with harnessing the magic, their behavior morphing into an addiction or obsession. Often, the moral of these narratives is that embracing one's identity as witch requires both an acceptance of the painful history and egregious stereotyping against their community, and a "coming out" to society.

The Concept of "Other"

As Sally longed for normalcy, her desire came from a distinct place of recognizing herself and a long line of Owens witches being treated as "Other." In the opening scene of *Practical Magic*, Aunt Frances (Stockard Channing), through voiceover, tells young Sally and Gillian about their ancestor, Maria. The scene shows Maria with a noose around her neck, awaiting execution.

> For more than 200 years, we Owens women have been blamed for everything that has ever gone wrong in this town ... It all began with your ancestor, Maria. She was a witch, the first in our family, and you, my darlings, are the most recent in a long and distinguished line.[2]

Though Frances notes Maria's identity as witch and the fact that she was sexually promiscuous with the married men in town were likely factors in their ancestor's attempted execution, she believes that "they feared her because she had a gift, a power that has been passed on." She used her power to escape from her hanging, only to be banished, pregnant and alone on a nearby island. Frances concludes the story by telling the girls that, if the other children hate them, it's only because "we're different." The difference emphasized in the scene with Maria comes through costuming and physicality. In the scene, Maria stands in stark contrast to the Puritan bystanders witnessing her execution. While the onlookers wear traditional black and white garb, hair mostly covered, Maria has long, loose dark hair, wears a white slip dress and has bare feet, an indication that she does not belong among the righteous and pious women before her.

The term "Other" is predicated upon the idea that there is a "normal," that there is a collective group of people that make up "us" and those who do not conform make up "them." As sociologist Zuleyka Zevallos writes:

> Ideas of similarity and difference are central to the way in which we achieve a sense of identity and social belonging. Identities have some element of exclusivity. Just as when we formally join a club or an organisation, social membership depends upon fulfilling a set of criteria. It just so happens that such criteria are socially-constructed (that is, created by societies and social groups). As such "we" cannot belong to any group unless "they" (other people) do *not* belong to "our" group. Sociologists set out to study how societies manage collective ideas about who gets to belong to "our group" and which types of people are seen as different – the outsiders of society.[3]

The criteria for "belonging" can change over time and will vary between identities, but the overarching message is that to not belong will result in some form of suffering and ostracization. From her aunt's story of their ancestor, Maria, young Sally learned not only that to be different was not worth it, but that it would ultimately lead to loneliness and despair. As an adult, she strove for "normal" to avoid Maria's fate. "Normal" meant belonging, behaving in the ways of the status quo, including marriage to a handsome and hardworking man, finding joy in her children and presenting herself as demure, pretty and, most importantly, unproblematic.

Sally's desire for a "normal" life clearly aligns with what Susan Faludi has deemed a "backlash" against women in the 1980s and 1990s. Media outlets, statistical data and popular culture all seemed to point to the same issue, that women were overwhelmed by the burdens of the professional workplace and responsibilities of home life, "suffering 'burnout'" and experiencing an "infertility epidemic" that made them fearful they may never marry or have children, and succumbing to hysteria amid the stresses of their professional lives.[4] In June 1986, *Newsweek* published "Too Late for Prince Charming?" with the now infamous claim that women were more likely to be killed by a terrorist than get married over the age of 40.[5] Feminism's encouragement of women's aspirations for a career and success outside the home had marred their chances of achieving what they should truly want: a family. Professional women in television and films of the 1980s were largely "scorned, humiliated, and punished for the dual sins of being ambitious and female."[6] Though the 1990s saw the rise of "Girl Power," "Riot Grrrls" and "Girls

Kick Ass" mentality in pop culture – *Buffy the Vampire Slayer* (both film and TV show), *The Powerpuff Girls*, etc. – female characters over a certain age often had romantic relationships, marriage and family in mind.

Just What Do We Mean By "Normal"? Film Theory and Analysis

The idea of "normal" is deeply subjective and it is hotly contested in academic circles as to the usefulness of the word "normal." For the sake of this chapter, "normal" will be viewed through a cinematic lens, using film and television theories in conjunction with character and storytelling archetypes to ascertain what is considered "normal" within the mediums. Feminist film and television scholars have studied these mediums and, based on repeated tropes, behaviors, storylines and situations, have formed categories for female and female-coded characters that illustrate what might be meant by "normal." Though the theories described here are only a fraction of what exists within feminist film analysis, they will serve this chapter's purpose of examining the repeated theme of power imbalance and normal/other in films and television centered on witches.

Laura Mulvey was among the premier theorists in feminist film analysis and her concept of "the male gaze" provides a foundation for analysis. In her 1975 essay "Visual Pleasure and Narrative Cinema," Mulvey described the male gaze in film as a space of objectification and fantasy, where the (presumably heterosexual) male spectator not only has the freedom to look at the female depicted on the screen but can "set an illusion" that he has control and possession over her in that "natural space."[7] This reduces women to sexual objects and props. In the rare case when women deviate from the norm, they are ultimately punished for not adhering to proper women's standards, such as when they challenge male authority or otherwise threaten the emasculation of the male protagonist. Mulvey recognized that the construction of what it meant to be an acceptable "woman" in films had been primarily put together by male writers, directors, casting agents and producers. She argues that,

> traditionally, the woman displayed has functioned on two levels: as erotic object for the characters within the screen story, and as erotic object for the spectator within the auditorium, with a shifting tension between the looks on either side of the screen.[8]

The female character is, therefore, a passive participant in the film, intended to be a spectacle of beauty without being a threat to the male protagonist.

This does not mean that films were not made to address the issues or concerns of women. However, those "women's films" reduced the issues faced by female characters to ones of marriage, motherhood and appearance. These characters often abide by the codes of middle-class propriety, are dependent upon marriage and motherhood for purpose and fulfillment and are willing to sacrifice major aspects of their lives for the sake of their husband and children. As Molly Haskell argues, "central to the woman's film is the notion of middle-classness, not just as an economic status but as a state of mind and a relatively rigid moral code."[9] Acceptance in society meant following codes of femininity as part of a moral imperative: one was seen as "good" (a good wife or good mother) for following these codes, while the opposite ("bad") would be attributed to the character if they did not follow certain standards of modesty, demurity and familial attention.

The institution of motherhood has long been associated with nurturing, self-sacrifice and the greater good. Abigail Adams and the republican motherhood, the Gold Star Mothers who would nobly grieve for their sons lost at war and the ever patient and polished June Cleaver, all serve as representations of what theorist Ann Kaplan refers to as the "Good Mother." Because of these cultural representations and ideologies around motherhood, producers know how to encode the message of who is meeting, exceeding and failing at "motherhood." On their end, the consumer knows the "Good Mother" when they see her. They decode the messages sent about the mother on the screen. When she meets certain criteria, is "totally invested in husband and children, she lives only through them, and is marginal to the narrative," audiences recognize the signs of "Good Mother." Conversely, if the mother is "sadistic, hurtful, and jealous . . . and demanding of her own life," she is, as Kaplan continues to note, the "Bad Mother or Witch." "The Heroic Mother" is akin to the "Good Mother" but is "more central to the action," while the "Silly, Weak, or Vain Mother" is ridiculed by her husband, children and friends. Audiences easily recognize these facets of the mother archetype on screen and, whether consciously or not, decode the encoded message of what makes a Good, Bad, Heroic or Silly Mother.

Kaplan further notes that these delineations are problematic in that consumers are not only receiving messages about what makes a good mother or a mother who fails to live up to societal expectations, but also one narrative about the broad institution of motherhood. As she argues, the job of the film (and we can also apply this principle to television) "is to reinscribe the Mother in the position patriarchy desires for her and, in so doing, teach the female audience the dangers of stepping out of the given position."[10] Audiences recognize the good and bad facets of motherhood, producers encode messages about motherhood into their product, audiences consume the information again through another plotline or scenario, and it goes back around and around. Stuart Hall refers to the acceptance of the message as the "dominant-hegemonic position," in which the viewer is "operating inside the dominant code."[11] In simplest terms, the encoded message has reached the consumer, who has successfully decoded the message and accepted it as the dominant social hegemonic position.

Barbara Creed, one of the first theorists to explore the representation of "Bad Mother" in depth, wrote "Horror and the Monstrous Feminine: An Imaginary Abjection" to investigate the repeated pattern of evil mothers in horror films. Creed dissects and builds upon Julia Kristeva's notion of "abjection," a term signifying "that which does not 'respect borders, positions, rules,' that which 'disturbs identity, system, order.'"[12] Creed uses the human body's waste (feces, urine, vomit) as the first form of abjection with the corpse, with its wasting and rotting flesh, absent of a soul, as the ultimate abject object. The second form of abjection comes with the construction of that which is monstrous on the border of that which is human. Examples include Jekyll and Hyde or Linda Blair in *The Exorcist*. The third form of abjection, to which the majority of her article is dedicated, is that of the maternal figure as abject. Creed argues that the mother as monstrous is a fusion of the first two forms of abjection, as the mother–child relationship is predicated upon the joining of the two bodies during pregnancy and results in bodily wastes which cannot be separated from the relationship.[13] After all, the mother expels bodily fluid during the birthing process and is largely responsible for the clean-up of her child's excretions.

Though this emphasis on the body and its wastes is enough to create disgust in an audience, it is the disturbed and blurred boundaries between mother and child that create the greatest abjection. When the mother cannot let go of her child, is oppressive, possessive and/or neglectful, the understanding of who or what a "mother" is becomes irrevocably disturbed. The audience cannot identify with or find sympathy for such a character, and she is relegated to monstrous. As Creed argues, "it is the gestating, all-devouring womb of the archaic mother that generates the horror . . . [she] is a force that threatens to reincorporate what it once gave birth to."[14] The audience cannot identify with such an all-consuming action, as it perverts and corrupts all that is pure about motherhood: nurture, love, attention and care.

This presents the idea of "woman" and other female-coded characters through a repeated moral lens: to be seen as "good" (whether by other characters or the audience), one must adhere to standards of femininity. The "good" woman is pretty, attractive and innocently sexy, but not so much so that she threatens the male protagonist's sense of self-control or moral value. She is demure and modest while still maintaining her attractiveness, which is also commensurate with her age. She devotes her time and energy to serving her husband and children, but not to the point of being smothering, needy or overbearing. When she violates these codes, she becomes, for the audience, a target for ridicule and mockery or steps over the line into a territory of immoral and/or monstrous.

These theories are not without critique. One of the primary critiques of Mulvey's theory of the "male gaze" is the erasure of identities and agency from its analysis, seeming to disregard the experiences of audience members of various genders, races, sexualities, ages, etc. to fit the notion of the "male gaze." The limited viewpoint of the "male gaze" demonstrates a flaw in feminist discourse from the 1970s, elevating the situation of white heterosexual cisgender women over "Other." Feminist scholar bell hooks recognized this in her work "The Oppositional Gaze," taking Mulvey's notion of the "male gaze" and adapting it to bring women of color into a conversation that had previously excluded them.[15] hooks argued that erasure and absence have long been part of the gaze, and deconstructed the male gaze by positing the black woman as outside the binary.

> Black female spectators, who refused to identify with white womanhood, who would not take on the phallocentric gaze of desire and possession, created a critical space where the binary opposition Mulvey posits of "woman as image, man as bearer of the look" was continually deconstructed.[16]

hooks' work allows further insight into how spectators who do not identify as white cisgender heterosexual men find pleasure and/or meaning within a film. Furthermore, the "woman's film," particularly in the early to mid-twentieth century, centered on conflicts related to the white middle-class woman only.

The concept of "normal" for the witch characters exemplified by the Owens sisters in *Practical Magic* is predicated upon the privileged positions of white, middle-class, cisgender and heterosexual identities as well as standards of beauty, domesticity and femininity. All the characters who seek to be "normal," such as Sally Owens, attempt to hide, even deny, their witchy power in favor of privileged acceptability. Those who rebel against the standards of "normal" are coded in films and television as "bad," "evil" and "villainous," sometimes even "slutty" or "promiscuous," meant to morally signal a "bad" character. A prime example includes the ostracization of all four characters in the 1996 film *The Craft*. More recent films and television shows, such as *Agatha All Along* (2024), have sought to deconstruct those labels, examining the complexity of the witchy character among various genders, sexualities, ages, races and other identities, including how they interact with each other within white heteronormative and patriarchal institutions.

For the Sake of "Normal"

While Sally Owens spent a great deal of time denying her witch identity, other witches in film and television continued to use their powers in secret. Like Sally, they longed for the "normal" of domesticity, marriage and motherhood. Unlike Sally, they did not eschew their witch identities entirely but only used their powers behind closed doors, operating publicly under a facade of "normalcy" so that neighbors, friends and members of their social circles would not find out their true identity of witch or discover the extent of their power. The quest for normal and the need to hide one's identity are two of the most repeated themes within film and television shows about witches, leading to a moral characterization of the witch as either good or bad, dating back to Glinda, the Good Witch of the North, and the unnamed Wicked Witch of the West in *The Wizard of Oz*. However, as Patti LuPone's character, Lilia Calderu, says in the second episode of *Agatha All Along*, "That is extremely reductive. We are not a monolith. And, you know I blame Halloween. Do you see any pointy hats in here? Any green skin? Any brooms? No, sir."[17] As the majority of the witches in these films and television shows know, to reveal one's true identity is to be labeled as "bad," "evil" or "wicked."

Though several witchy characters, at one point or another, yearn for a "normal life," no amount of self-denial or resistance to their authenticity changes the reality of their identity or their need for or reliance upon their powers. For some, revealing their true identity is not an option. Unlike Sally, who was born into a witchy lineage well known by the community, many witch characters are bound by secrecy due to a curse put upon the family, threats from demons and other monstrous creatures or rejection/persecution by people surrounding them. *Sabrina the Teenage Witch*'s Sabrina Spellman (Melissa Joan Hart) balances being a witch with the ordinary pitfalls of being a teenager, knowing that revealing her identity will make life harder for her through high school, risking alienating her crush (later boyfriend Harvey, played by Nate Richert) and her classmates. The Halliwell sisters (*Charmed*) are the latest in a long line of powerful witches known as the Charmed Ones; keeping their identities secret is doubly important, as entities such as "The Source" seek to destroy the magical bond they have as sisters. The middle sister, Piper (Holly Marie Combs), initially worries about the potential evil of being a witch, wishing to be "normal" again.[18] *WandaVision*'s Wanda Maximoff (Elizabeth Olsen), destroyed by grief at the loss of her love, Vision (Paul Bettany), enacts a spell that entraps a town into believing they exist in a perfect community called Westview, based upon sitcom tropes from the 1950s to the 2000s, including a conjured version of Vision and two children to round out her image of a perfect family. This spell is so powerful that to use more magic risks crumbling the perfect "normal" life she has created for herself. Knowing that the agency Sentient Weapon Observation Response Division, or SWORD, is outside of Westview, Wanda must use her witchy powers in order to keep her version of normal. As she says in the fifth episode, "On a Very Special Episode," to a drone representing SWORD, "I have what I want and no one will ever take it from me ever again."[19]

Despite repeated attempts by various witch characters to conceal their powers and identity from those around them, the self-denial is never successful. As Sandra Bullock says of her character, Sally Owens, "she wants nothing more than to conform, to be like everyone else, to be accepted and it's still not happening ... she's not going to be accepted whether she conforms or not," simply because everyone knows that she is "different."[20] Toward the end of the film, when Gillian (Nicole Kidman) is possessed by the spirit of her deceased abusive boyfriend, Sally is left with no choice but to use her magic. Under the direction of her aunts Jet (Dianne Wiest) and Frances (Stockard Channing), Sally uses her connections through the PTA to enlist non-magical women to form an impromptu coven. Each brings a broom from their home, and several comment that they either have some connection to a sense of unexplained magic or an experience with an ex who will not leave them alone. Laying out their brooms on the floor to create a circle, the women hold hands around the enclosed Gillian, repeating the chant "Di te perdant, Te maledico" (roughly meaning "In God's will, destroy you") in order to send Jimmy's (Goran Visnjic) spirit back to the grave.

Though *Practical Magic* did not do well at the box office and Janet Maslin of *The New York Times* referred to it as "a bouncy, bubble-brained movie with the look of a shelter magazine ... a domesticated story in which magic is for dealing with menfolk," the film has gained popularity in recent decades, hailed as a feminist film with a strong focus on sisterhood.[21] Other film enthusiasts see it as feminist due to its nearly all-female cast of characters that rely on themselves as a source of power, empowering "women to join forces and smash the patriarchy."[22] Whether one sees the film as a "bubble-brained" or empowered feminism, *Practical Magic* characters succeed in finding acceptance in their community, which eventually views the sisters as normal women who just happen to be witches.

Too Different to Be Normal

For too many television and film witches, their differences already made them targets of oppression and discrimination. Normal was never going to be a possibility. As with many marginalized populations, these characters already have historical prejudices stacked against them. In addition to stereotypes about their identities as witches (ugly, evil, worship of the devil, etc.), the other identity markers of those characters intersected with their witchy-ness, making it more challenging for them to blend in and be normal. These prejudices, as well as tragedies and trauma, often led "bad" witches to embrace their witchy powers. For example, from the outset, the four teenage girls in the 1996 film *The Craft* are outcasts in their school. The use of magic and witchcraft is not only their pathway to normal but to power over their oppressors. Sarah Bailey (Robin Tunney), a troubled student who experiences hallucinations and suicide ideation, is forced to move to a new house with her father and stepmother and begin at a new school. There she befriends Bonnie Harper (Neve Campbell), who is ridiculed for burn scars she incurred from a car accident, Nancy Downs (Fairuza Balk), who lives in a trailer park with an abusive stepfather and is referred to as "white trash" by her classmates, and Rochelle Zimmerman (Rachel True), a black student who experiences racist-fueled bullying from the popular white girls at the school. For each of these characters, the idea that they could just "be normal" or embody the privileged identities of the beautiful, wealthy and popular white girls at their Catholic prep school proved impossible. Their differences were simply too visible and/or known for them to pass as the privileged "normal."

Rather than attempt to hide amongst their peers or find acceptance in the futile quest for "normal," the girls hone their connections to witchcraft, engaging in spell work and turning to the God Manon to bolster their burgeoning power. When Sarah joins the group of three, a magical spark is united among the four, bringing together the four points of North, South, East and West. Upon this realization, Rochelle says that "he [Manon] will really listen to us," and Sarah asks if the other three worship the devil. Nancy explains that Manon is "god and the devil, it's everything, it's the trees, it's the ground, it's the rocks, it's the moon, it's everything."[23] The four later decide to perform a spell to call on Manon to give them the power to make their lives better. Rochelle asks to take in the ability to not hate those who hate her, Sarah asks to take in the power to love herself and to be loved by a popular boy at school who once spread rumors about her, Bonnie asks to be beautiful both inside and out, and Nancy rounds out the spell by asking to take in "all the power of Manon." All at once, their lives improve dramatically, but not without violating the Wiccan Rede, "an ye harm none." Nancy's abusive stepfather (John Kapelos) dies of a heart attack, Rochelle's racist bully, Laura (Christine Taylor), loses massive clumps of hair, and Sarah's crush, Chris (Skeet Ulrich), becomes obsessed with her, humiliating himself in the process. They are warned by the metaphysical shopkeeper to be mindful of the "Rule of Three," where the outcome of a spell will come back to the caster threefold. Ignoring the warning, the four then decide to "invoke the power of the spirit" to continue their journey to obtain more power. At the height of the spell, Nancy is struck by lightning, believing herself to be blessed by the power of Manon. Her power elevates her above any desire for "normal" or "acceptance," instead taking revenge on Chris, killing him as she was able to kill her stepfather.

Across several movies and television shows about witches, the "bad" witch is always the one who abuses her power, particularly for the sake of personal gain and to harm others. She is often portrayed in all-black attire (in contrast to the shades of white, pastel or rainbow colors worn by the "good" witches), and is far less compassionate, nurturing and/or domestic than her "good" counterparts. Those witches, such as Nancy Downs, who are categorized as "bad" witches also fail to meet the standards of defined womanhood. They hunger for power, act with aggression and violence, and sacrifice their relationships, eschewing compassion and reason in favor of control and domination. As Willem de Blécourt argues, "Historically, and within a patriarchal order in the most general sense of the word, witches were understood as women deemed to harm others by their non-womanhood."[24] Sally Owens embraces womanhood to avoid the taunts, ridicules and stones thrown at her. Those witches who reject traditional notions of womanhood become the ones to cast the stones.

However, this narrative fails to examine the nuance of tragedy and oppression that regularly serves as the backstory for the "bad" witch. The Wicked Witch of the West (Margaret Hamilton) in *The Wizard of Oz* wants revenge on Dorothy for dropping a house on her sister. *Buffy the Vampire Slayer*'s Willow Rosenberg (Alyson Hannigan) gives in to the dark magic of her power after the brutal murder of her girlfriend, Tara (Amber Benson). Maleficent (Angelina Jolie) becomes evil after King Stefan literally ripped off her wings while she slept. The Sanderson sisters (Bette Midler, Kathy Najimy and Sarah Jessica Parker) were orphaned as children and the local reverend threatened to separate them from each other if they didn't obey his commands. Not only did Nancy Downs experience abuse at the hands of her stepfather, as well as witness her mother's abuse, she also became the subject of bullying after Chris spread rumors that she gave him an STI after they had had sex. While Rochelle and Bonnie didn't go as far as Nancy did, they went along with the plans for power and vengeance, as each had been on the receiving end of unspeakable cruelty. Each of these witches turned to dark magic after experiences of death, oppression and/or misogyny, leading them to use their power to harm others in much the same way they themselves had been harmed.

Spotting the "Bad" Witch

No movie has done more to solidify the image of the "bad" witch than *The Wizard of Oz*. With her green skin, exaggerated nose, growling voice and black dress and hat, the Wicked Witch of the West set the tone not only for the future of witch villains in film and television, but also Halloween costumes and decor, video games such as *Stardew Valley* and *Baldur's Gate 3* and quite literally the inspiration for Gregory Maguire's novel turned musical, *Wicked*. As a matter of fact, the Wicked Witch's appearance became so synonymous with fear and terror that Margaret Hamilton went to great lengths to assure children that she was only pretending to be that scary, even appearing on a 1975 episode of *Mister Rogers' Neighborhood* to showcase to children and adults alike that it was only a costume.[25] Though none of the witches in this chapter, outside of the Wicked Witch, have green skin, they often reject standard codes of feminine beauty, portrayed as undesirable due to their lack of femininity and/or rebellious attire and aesthetic. For example, *The Craft*'s Nancy embodies the Goth aesthetic – ghostly white skin, dark pupils, straight jet-black hair and black clothing with harsh lines and an abundance of buttons and/or metal – that has become the tell-tale sign that a cinematic witch will be the "bad" one.

However, it is not just the costuming and makeup that denote who the evil witch in a film will be, but who exists around her for contrast. In Munchkinland, the Wicked Witch (who, over the rainbow, lacked a given name) stood next to the beautiful blonde sparkling Glinda, whose pink gown made her look more like a princess than the standard image of a witch. Nancy looked more rebellious in her goth attire when next to Sarah, with her brown hair and more conventional aesthetic. In the case of *Buffy the Vampire Slayer*'s Willow Rosenberg, not only did she stand in juxtaposition with the blonde heroine, Buffy, but "Dark Willow" also saw herself in contrast to the cute and nerdy bookworm she had been in previous seasons. Her normally red hair turned black, she traded in her corduroy overalls for black billowing-sleeved shirts and leather pants, and the veins under her skin became more prominent, appearing as dark scars across her cheeks and forehead. As Blécourt describes, "Willow turns from being posh Sarah into being goth Nancy and has to spend the opening episodes of season seven battling with the effects of her addiction."[26] The contrast between the "good" witch (feminine, compassionate, posh) and the "bad" witch (aggressive, addicted to power, goth) is coded in costuming and makeup, reminiscent of the witches in *Macbeth* who were clear outsiders to the feminine norm.

Another facet of what constitutes a "good" or "bad" witch relies upon where they land on Kaplan's scale of "Good Mother" or "Bad Mother, or Witch." Several witches in films and television are mothers to babies and young children, while others are thrust into a maternal role due to situations beyond their control. While Piper Halliwell gives birth to her first child, Wyatt, in the fifth season of *Charmed*, her eldest sister, Prue (Shannen Doherty) had to act as a guardian toward her two younger sisters with the absence of their father and the death of their mother. Both would be considered on the side of "good" mothers because they display characteristics of self-sacrifice and nurturing. The same can be said of Molly Weasley (Julie Walters) in the *Harry Potter* series, who fusses over Harry like he was one of her own sons, giving him fourth helpings of everything and knitting him sweaters for Christmas. Unlike Prue or Piper, however, Molly was rarely given any semblance of power or authority outside of her role as mother. As Aisling Walsh writes for *The Mary Sue*, "The Order of the Phoenix has only three women members, and they are never seen making decisions, with Molly Weasley portrayed as little more than a surrogate mother."[27] Even Molly's takedown of Bellatrix Lestrange in *Harry Potter and the Deathly Hallows Part 2* came from the fierce need to protect her daughter, Ginny (Bonnie Wright). As she yells, "Stay away from my daughter, you bitch!" Molly whips out her wand and appears to cast the Killing curse against the Dark Witch.[28] It's also worth noting that Molly and Bellatrix contrast with one another in appearance, with the former having a kindly face and red hair, costumed in multi-colored aprons, and the latter clad all in black, with pale skin and wild hair, providing context for the "good" and "bad" witch even for the *Harry Potter* novice.

Initially, both Wanda Maximoff (*WandaVision*) and Agatha Harkness (*WandaVision* and *Agatha All Along* played by Kathryn Hahn) demonstrate the "good" and "bad" mother/witch dichotomy. While neither is the quintessential "Good Mother," Wanda's motivations for using her powers to create the Westview hex came from her grief not only in losing Vision but also losing the potential to have a family with her love. Throughout the series, Wanda provides a loving home for her family and participates in community activities, exchanging pleasantries with their neighbors, especially her wacky next-door neighbor, Agnes (who later is revealed to be Agatha). Agnes/Agatha's wacky antics shine through when she is a part of Wanda's family dynamic, as surrogate aunt, baby-sitter, "friend who tells it like it is," etc. In episode seven, "Breaking the Fourth Wall," the contrast between Wanda and Agnes/Agatha sharpens, illustrating that Wanda is a mother who struggles with work/life balance, but admits to faltering. In a tongue-in-cheek tone,

Wanda looks at the camera (similar to early 2010s mockumentary sitcoms) and states, "Look, we've all been there, right? Letting our fear and anger get the best of us, intentionally expanding the border of the false world we created." Agnes/Agatha, on the other hand, tells Wanda's kids that she doesn't bite, but then the scene pans to her "interview" and she says, "I did actually bite a kid once."[29] By the end of the season, the contrast grows wider with the reveal that Wanda struggled to keep the illusion of Westview alive, largely due to Agnes/Agatha sabotaging her efforts along the way. The final showdown between Wanda and Agatha demonstrates familiar contrasts in appearance – Wanda as the one closer to "good" remains in her humble jeans and hoodie, while Agatha, the "bad" witch, is clad in black with accents of purple, with wild hair, black hands and dark makeup. Once Wanda, as the Scarlet Witch, perseveres over Agatha, she makes the decision to sacrifice her stronghold over Westview, which requires letting go of Vision and her children, Billy and Tommy. As Carolyn Framke of *Variety* wrote,

> Watching Wanda say goodbye to her sons, who she knew were about to disappear along with the fantasy town she got lost in, was devastating. Letting Vision and Wanda have their most honest, loving conversation to date as a crimson wave of magic loomed ominously in the near distance was an absolute gut punch.[30]

Her sacrifice propelled Wanda into the role of "Good Mother" and the show sets up her grief as a justifiable, or at least an understandable, reason for using her power, letting her exist in the realm of "good" witch. *WandaVision*'s follow-up show, *Agatha All Along*, explored Agatha's relationship with her own mother and opened her backstory as a mother who had lost her son. When one of the other witches in the show's coven posited that Agatha had given up her son for the sake of power, audiences could easily take that assertion at face value. After all, in *WandaVision*, Agatha had already been positioned as a "bad" witch, as well as irresponsible around children. This was only reinforced when Lilia (Patti LuPone) decried Agatha for fulfilling damaging stereotypes: "Witches like you are the reason people think we poison apples, and steal children, and eat babies," to which Agatha replies, "Babies are delicious."[31]

Queering Witchy Television and Cinema

Agatha's position as an outsider seeking to obtain more power for herself sets up another aspect of her identity in *Agatha All Along*, that of a non-straight person. Though her sexual identity isn't explicitly stated, it is clear that she once had a relationship with Rio (Aubrey Plaza) and, in response to the Teen's (Joe Locke) search for answers, Agatha replies, "You want a straight answer? Ask a straight person."[32] Agatha spent the entirety of *WandaVision* bearing witness to Wanda, the Scarlet Witch, utilizing her tremendous power to create a family life for herself. In the penultimate episode, Agatha, while choking both Billy and Tommy with a magical hold, remarks to Wanda, "You have no idea how dangerous you are. You're supposed to be a myth, a being capable of spontaneous creation, and here you are, using it to make breakfast for dinner."[33] Agatha's reference to "breakfast for dinner" illustrates her belief that Wanda doesn't deserve her power, wasting it in order to fit into the hetero-normative dynamic of marriage, parenting and gendered divisions of labor. Though Agatha might be positioned as the "bad" witch at the end of *WandaVision*, the reveal of Agatha's queer identity in *Agatha All Along* as well as her own connections to motherhood allow her character to have more complexity and nuance through her misdeeds.

Though the show clearly states that Agatha is queer, albeit without going too in depth into her past with Rio, the emphasis on her sexuality is downplayed until the final episodes. Instead, the show's claim of being the Marvel Cinematic Universe's "gayest show ever" comes largely from its casting of queer actors (Joe Locke and Sasheer Zamata) as well as aspects of "camp" and "drag" in its cultural references. The build-up caused fans to worry that the Marvel Cinematic Universe had queer-baited (or used gay culture to entice) their audience only to fail in their representation of queer characters. Mey Rude, of *Out* magazine, exclaimed, "Who's kissing other girls? It was Agatha all along!"[34] Kathryn Hahn, who portrayed Agatha in *WandaVision* and *Agatha All Along*, stated that her character's queer identity was "a natural progression. Of course, she's [queer]. Of course she loves everyone. She's attracted to who she's attracted to. And of course she would never define herself as one or the other."[35] Just as Lilia's character found herself unwilling to be pigeonholed by stereotypical representations of witch, Agatha's sexual identity cannot be tied down to a specific label or definition.

Agatha is just the latest in a long line of queer witches in film and television. *Buffy the Vampire Slayer*'s Willow Rosenberg and her girlfriend, Tara Benson, made history as one of the first out lesbian couples on television. The 2018 reboot of *Charmed* featured the Vera sisters, the middle of whom, Mel (Melonie Diaz), is an openly lesbian Latinx witch who engages in several relationships over its four-season run. Netflix's *The Chilling Adventures of Sabrina* has two queer witch characters: Prudence (Tati Gabrielle), a queer biracial witch and the mean girl turned fan favorite who starts to date Ambrose (Chance Perdomo), a black pansexual warlock. The show also cast nonbinary actor Lachlan Watson as Sabrina's friend, Susie. Though not a witch, Susie's queer journey is partly guided by the ghost of one of their ancestors, adding more overlap to the show's queer and supernatural themes. Disney's *The Owl House* introduced Luz (Sarah Nicole-Robles), a 14-year-old Dominican-American girl who gets sucked into the Demon Realm where she meets Eda (Wendie Malick), a mischievous witch who reluctantly agrees to mentor Luz in the ways of witchcraft. In the first season, Luz comes out as bisexual, after kissing Amity (Mae Whitman) at the school's "Grom" (the Demon Realm's prom).

The presence of queer characters (witch or not) in film and television has long been marred by the choices made by mainstream Hollywood, particularly its white, cishet, male population. Directors, writers, actors, producers and others have long made decisions regarding their presentation of LGBTQ+ characters, centering the narrative on stereotypical tropes. As Harry M. Benshoff and Sean Griffin describe, "They have been noble AIDS patients, witty next-door neighbors, sexy 'bisexual' lesbians, and colorful drag queens – but rarely have they been complex characters dealing with the realities of sexuality in America."[36] The intersection of queer and witch identities, as well as racial, economic and other identity markers, in films and television go a long way to complicate the narrative of what it means to be queer in the United States. The significance of this intersection will be further explored in the next chapter.

Conclusion

The film and television witches covered in this chapter are only a fraction of the characters who grace these mediums with their magical and witchy ways. Samantha and Agatha of the classic sitcom *Bewitched*, Diana Bishop and her aunts, Sarah and Emily, in *A Discovery of Witches*, *The Mayfair Witches*, *The Witches of Eastwick* and countless others not included in this chapter have grappled with the contrast between what it means to be good or normal, evil or wicked, the portrayal of their power as a threat and decidedly unfeminine, as well as forms of bigotry, hatred and even being put on trial. Several also explore themes of sexual and gender identity, rejecting norms of marriage and motherhood, and following spiritual and cultural paths that lead them to be seen as outsiders.

The question of "normal" for these witch characters relies upon which normal is being referred to: does the character strive to be a "normal" woman or does the character live up to society's perception of a typical witch? Often, the concepts are at odds with one another. As Blécourt points out, historical perceptions of the witch saw her as decidedly unfeminine; therefore, to be a witch (unfeminine) and a "normal" woman (feminine) is seemingly incompatible. Yet, the witches in these films and television shows, while grappling with societal norms of gender and sexuality, eventually define for themselves what it means to be a witch and what that means regarding their own identities. As will be discussed in the next chapter, the reclamation of the word "witch" allows for new narratives, forms of storytelling and openness across diverse identities and mediums.

Notes

1 Griffin Dunne, "Practical Magic" (Warner Bros, 1998), film.
2 Griffin Dunne, "Practical Magic" (Warner Bros, 1998), film.
3 Zuleyka Zevallos. "What is Otherness?" *The Other Sociologist* (2011), https://othersociologist.com/otherness-resources/.

TV/Movie Witches of the Twentieth and Twenty-First Centuries   97

4 Susan Faludi, *Backlash: The Undeclared War Against American Women* (New York: Three Rivers Press, 2000), 1.
5 Anonymous, "Too Late for Prince Charming," *Newsweek*, June 2, 1986, 55.
6 Andi Zeisler, *Feminism and Pop Culture* (Berkley, CA: Seal Press, 2008), 90.
7 Laura Mulvey, "Visual Pleasure and Narrative Cinema," *Screen* 16, no. 3 (Autumn 1975), 8.
8 Laura Mulvey, "Visual Pleasure and Narrative Cinema," *Screen* 16, no. 3 (Autumn 1975), 5.
9 Molly Haskell, "The Woman's Film," in *Feminist Film Theory*, ed. Sue Thornham (Edinburgh: Edinburgh University Press, 1999), 20.
10 Ann Kaplan, *Motherhood and Representation: The Mother in Popular Culture and Melodrama* (London: Routledge, 1992), 81–82.
11 Stuart Hall, "The Work of Representation," in *The Media Studies Reader*, ed. Laurie Ouellette (New York: Routledge, 2013),195.
12 Barbara Creed, "Horror and the Monstrous Feminine: An Imaginary Abjection," in *Feminist Film Theory*, ed. Sue Thornham (Edinburgh: Edinburgh University Press, 1999), 36.
13 Barbara Creed, "Horror and the Monstrous Feminine: An Imaginary Abjection," in *Feminist Film Theory*, ed. Sue Thornham (Edinburgh: Edinburgh University Press, 1999), 43.
14 Barbara Creed, "Horror and the Monstrous Feminine: An Imaginary Abjection," in *Feminist Film Theory*, ed. Sue Thornham (Edinburgh: Edinburgh University Press, 1999), 56.
15 bell hooks, "The Oppositional Gaze: Black Feminist Spectators," in *Feminist Film Theory*, ed. Sue Thornham (Edinburgh: Edinburgh University Press, 1999), 309.
16 bell hooks, "The Oppositional Gaze: Black Feminist Spectators," in *Feminist Film Theory*, ed. Sue Thornham (Edinburgh: Edinburgh University Press, 1999), 313.
17 *Agatha All Along*, Season 1, episode 2, "Circle Sewn with Fate/Unlock Thy Hidden Gate," directed by Jac Schaeffer. Aired September 18, 2024, on Disney Plus.
18 *Charmed*, Season 1, episode 2, "I've Got You Under My Skin," directed by John T. Kretchmer. Aired October 14, 1998, on WB.
19 *WandaVision*, Season 1, episode 5, "On a Very Special Episode," directed by Matt Shakman. Aired February 5, 2021, on Disney Plus.
20 Screen Slam, "*Practical Magic*: Sandra Bullock Interview," 2013, https://www.youtube.com/watch?v=vPpCtQYWoXk.
21 Janet Maslin, "'Practical Magic': Designer Witches in Lightweight Farce," Film Review, *The New York Times*, October 16, 1998.
22 Kayleigh Dray, "Why Practical Magic is the Ultimate Feminist Film," *Stylist*, 2018.
23 Andrew Fleming, "The Craft" (Columbia Pictures, 1996), film.
24 Willem de Blécourt, "Witches on Screen," in *The Oxford History of Witchcraft and Magic*, ed. Owen Davies (Oxford: Oxford University Press, 2023), 260.
25 *Mister Rogers' Neighborhood*, Season 8, episode 63, "Margaret Hamilton," directed by Bill Moates. Aired May 14, 1975, on PBS.
26 Willem de Blécourt, "Witches on Screen," in *The Oxford History of Witchcraft and Magic*, ed. Owen Davies (Oxford: Oxford University Press, 2023), 284.
27 Aisling Walsh, "JK Rowling's Awful Gender Politics Should Be No Surprise to Harry Potter Fans," *The Mary Sue* (2020), https://www.themarysue.com/jk-rowlings-awful-gender-politics-should-be-no-surprise-to-harry-potter-fans/.
28 *Harry Potter and the Deathly Hallows Part 2*, directed by David Yates (2011; Warner Bros: 2024; Max). Streaming.
29 *WandaVision*, Season 1, episode 7, "Breaking the Fourth Wall," directed by Matt Shakman. Aired February 19, 2021, on Disney Plus.
30 Caroline Framke and Adam B. Vary, "'WandaVision': A Marvel Expert and Casual Fan Unpack 'the Series Finale' and the Double-Edged Sword of Fan Theories,"

Variety (March 6, 2021), https://variety.com/2021/tv/opinion/wandavision-finale-review-marvel-wanda-vision-1234923117/.
31 *Agatha All Along*, Season 1, episode 2, "Circle Sewn with Fate/Unlock Thy Hidden Gate," directed by Jac Schaeffer. Aired September 18, 2024, on Disney Plus.
32 *Agatha All Along*, Season 1, episode 7, "Death's Hand in Mine," directed by Jac Schaeffer. Aired October 23, 2024 on Disney Plus.
33 *WandaVision*, Season 1, episode 9, "The Series Finale," directed by Matt Shakman. Aired March 5, 2021 on Disney Plus.
34 Mey Rude, "*Agatha All Along*'s Latest Episode Confirmed a Major Character is Gay," *Out* (October 24, 2024), https://www.out.com/gay-tv-shows/agatha-all-along-confirmed-gay.
35 Sanskriti Lodhi, "Kathryn Harkness Opens Up About Agatha Harkness' Sexuality in *Agatha All Along*," *Yardbarker* (October 8, 2024), https://www.yardbarker.com/entertainment/articles/kathryn_hahn_opens_up_about_agatha_harkness_sexuality_in_agatha_all_along/s1_17442_41019254.
36 Harry M. Benshoff and Sean Griffin, *Queer Images: A History of Gay and Lesbian Film in America* (Lanham: Rowman and Littlefield Publishers, 2006), 262–263.

6 "The Power to Write Your Own Story"

The Witch as Reclamation in the Twenty-First Century

Introduction

Witches seem to be everywhere in the twenty-first century. Not only in popular television shows, cozy romance novels and the Spirit Halloween store, but deeply engaged in social media, business, politics and culture, many seeking to reclaim their identity and power as a means of resistance to a capitalist-driven patriarchal society. Twenty-first-century witches see their identities as "witch" intersect with systems of oppression and marginalization, where not only is their practice a target of discrimination and ridicule, but other aspects of their identities (race, gender, sexuality, economic status, ethnicity, etc.) have historically been subjected to violence and denial of power and basic human rights. This chapter will explore the connections between empowerment and social justice among modern witches, using four categories for examination: resistance against a capitalist-driven society of productivity; a space for social justice; a place of belonging and inclusivity; and as a connection to ancestry, culture and heritage. These themes are examined through popular books on witchcraft, witch-focused podcasts and social media such as Instagram and TikTok, the latter of which has a popular subsection #WitchTok that has millions of posts containing the hashtag.

A Note on Language

Though the word "witch" has been used extensively throughout this book, those who might fall under the social category of "witch" do not necessarily use that term for themselves. Some may use "Wiccan" or "Pagan" to describe their practice or connect to culturally specific words such as "bruja," or identify themselves through specific specialties such as "tarot" or focal points such as "manifestation." This chapter will often use the word "witch," but does so with the knowledge that it serves as an umbrella term and is not necessarily the most accurate definition for individuals who might prescribe to various ideologies and practices associated with witchcraft but do not see themselves as "witch." When referencing individual stories or specific individuals, this chapter will use the language offered by the individual referenced.

In the histories recounted in this book, particularly prior to the rise of Gardnerian Wicca, the term "witch" almost always refers to a cisgender woman. This chapter will illustrate that witchcraft and related spiritual paths are practiced by any gender, sexuality, race and class, and sometimes are done in combination with other faith practices. The use of pronouns, cultural/ethnic identities and other language will align with the individual referenced.

A Note on Social Media

The social media platforms showcased within this chapter are limited to TikTok, Instagram and YouTube. Though there are many examples of social media outside these three, such as Facebook, Reddit, X (formerly Twitter) and Threads, as well as ones with specializations, such as the app Fable, which caters to book lovers, this chapter is limited to TikTok, Instagram, and YouTube as many of the content creators examined are across at least two, if not all three, of these platforms. Research began with TikTok to follow the phenomenon of "WitchTok" and then followed creators to other platforms they utilized, which included Instagram and YouTube more than other social media platforms. The creators chosen in this chapter are only a few of the witches on social media platforms and are not indicative of all opinions, ideas or perspectives on witchcraft. Instead, they provide examples of the various ways the online witch community uses the digital space to communicate their spiritual, cultural, educational and political values. This chapter does not include reference to or comments by "trolls," or other forms of hate these creators receive, though that does not mean those creators are not on the receiving end of vitriol or bigotry.

Witchcraft as Resistance Against a Capitalist-Driven Society of Productivity

Google the term "self-care" and thousands of definitions and practices will be at a person's fingertips, reminding them to eat well, be mindful, exercise, get proper sleep, avoid stress, engage in pleasurable activities, and other suggestions for health, wellness and improved satisfaction with daily life. As many people have noted, however, the concept of self-care has been commodified by capitalist practices, where caring for oneself includes expensive beauty products and routines, overpriced aromatherapy candles and trips to spas for massages, facials and other services that no doubt can aid in relaxation and bring moments of joy and pleasure but also drain bank accounts in the process. Even access to healthy foods, gym memberships or equipment, or hobbies require financial security and/or additional time that is not available to every individual seeking to devote more time to self-care. The onus of self-care falls, as one might imagine, on the individual, the self, yet access is hardly equitable. In a society that has historically oppressed the financially disadvantaged, for those who are food insecure, BIPOC individuals, those within the queer community and others, the act of self-care is even more difficult to access. How does one find time for self-care if they have to work longer hours, are unable to advance in their careers, have to rely on public transportation or are not welcome and/or cannot feel safe in spaces such as fitness centers? Yet those who are socially marginalized and/or disadvantaged are, perhaps, more in need of self-care as they struggle to exist in a society that oppresses them.

Karl Marx touted that the idea of productivity, or producing through work and labor, is the key to accumulation of wealth in a capitalist society. As Dung Bui-Xuan and Kien Thi-Pham point out,

> In the production process, productive forces in the relationship with workers and means of production will change the production of the society; the workers have a crucial role in making contributions to the production process through their productiveness. According to K. Marx, productiveness is the production capacity of specific productive labor. It reflects the results of men's purposeful production in a certain unit of time.[1]

Productivity, in general terms, is how much one can labor and produce within a specific timeframe. Silvia Federici addresses the expectations of women's productivity, particularly domestic work, in her research, connecting the rise of capitalism and the need for productivity to early European witch trials. Illustrating that control over women's bodies, particularly during the witch trials, facilitated a rapid growth of capitalism in an increasingly patriarchal society,[2] she argues

> that the body has been for women in capitalist society what the factory has been for male waged workers: the primary ground of their exploitation and resistance, as the female body has been appropriated by the state and men and forced to function as a means for the reproduction and accumulation of labor.

One major tenet of modern-day witchcraft is the practice of slowing down, mindfulness and connecting with the earth, moving away from capitalist-driven practices such as excessive productivity, denying rest and overconsumption. Rituals are one way in which witches can resist these capitalist urges. Rituals for moon phases, particularly the new and full moons, or rituals connected to the Wheel of the Year are common themes in witch-centered books, blogs and social media, as are daily rituals. These might include morning meditation or intentionality when cooking a meal, focusing on the moment in time rather than hurrying through a task to get to the next.

> [Witches] know that rituals don't mean anything on their own . . . it's the intention that makes a series of arbitrary actions powerful . . . The

act of deliberately choosing to apply significance to our actions and to cultivate a deeper meaning to them is powerful. We can use ritual to gain . . . a specific type of control that requires no one else's approval or permission.[3]

In this way, the ritual can act as resistance against a societal force that seeks to control an individual's sense of worth based on productivity and output. As one witch noted,

> At the heart of these practices is the fact that witchcraft enables me to see the world through a more balanced lens. I've felt the reassuring presence of the otherworldly in the midst of difficult circumstances, and I know that magic happens when I summon the strength to draw boundaries or stir away the guilt that bubbles up if I choose self-care over self-sacrifice.[4]

Catherine Hernandez notes that her otherness as a brown queer femme heightened her relationship with witchcraft, magic and divine practices. After existing in spaces marred by white colonization, including Catholicism and theater school, Hernandez realized that "decolonisation of my practice became essential to my being" and, through this journey, created a manifesto she calls "Femme Wisdom."[5] One of the tenets of this manifesto is "UNAPOLOGETIC REST AND SELF-CARE: *To know that caring for your body is a radical act in a world that seeks to shut it down.*" Within this section, Hernandez describes various mantras she repeats in order to aid her "sick body . . . in its healing process" from multiple mental and physical challenges.[6]

In this way, many witches see spiritual practice and self-care as intertwined but also caution against diving in too quickly or attempting to do too much too soon. As Arin Murphy-Hiscock says in *The Witch's Book of Self-Care: Magical Ways to Pamper, Soothe, and Care for Your Body and Spirit*, "Self-care is a complicated interwoven combination of hundreds of small acts and an attitude shift. Using just one of the rituals, spells, or practices in this book is not going to solve your problems," but doing a little bit at a time has the potential for creating a feeling of self-worth and dedication to "the time and attention you need."[7] TikTok creator @beyournottygirl posted in September 2023 that

> Spirituality is the study & wellness of the self. It is going within and bringing awareness to who you truly are so you can live in it. When you dive immediately trying to cast spells, connect with spirits, expecting a gain without facing your shadow, you set yourself up to run.

She encourages those just starting a spiritual journey to "start with the self . . . how you've been expressing it and navigating the world."[8]

Many authors and content creators emphasize that rituals do not require special equipment or materials to engage in the practice but can include being in nature or space with natural elements, reciting mantras or intention within a mundane task, such as focusing on the act of love and nourishment while cooking a meal. Yet, many of the complicated critiques of witchy authors, bloggers, podcasters and content creators are that both they and their followers are participating in the capitalist forces that major tenets of witchcraft profess to resist. They promote their books, provide paid services such as tarot readings, are sponsored by companies to sell products, or market their own products, courses or coaching services. In a study on the phenomenon of witches on TikTok, Chris Miller explores the tensions that exist between authenticity and consumerism in many of these online spaces. While consumerism is encouraged and content is monetized through views, shares and subscriptions, Miller notes that the users have agency in that they "decide in whom they invest authority" and use comments to claim agency or impart their sense of knowledge even if it deviates from or challenges the authority of the creator.[9] Hernandez's "Femme Wisdom" manifesto includes "SKILLS SHARING, LABOUR SHARINGS: *To understand that in order to survive as femmes, we need to join forces*," using examples such as languages and mental health strategies as part of this process of dismantling "labour stratification" and "celebrating such labour, asking for fair wages, and encouraging the sharing of work."[10] Through this lens, the work of witches who earn income from their practice could constitute a fight for fair wages and the creation of space where being a witch can include a means of financial survival. Many witches, particularly those who create content in digital spaces such as Instagram, TikTok and YouTube, provide a plethora of content that does not require purchase by the user, allowing for a flowing and sharing of work that can, but does not always, result in monetary gain.

A Space for Social Justice and Social Movements

In her work *Social Movements*, Suzanne Staggenborg describes social movements as "important means of bringing about political and cultural changes through collective action."[11] This idea of "bringing about political and cultural changes" doesn't mean that change is inevitable, only that the goals of a social movement are to create changes to the system at a political, social or cultural level. Staggenborg's emphasis on "collective action" demonstrates that a significant number of participants are needed to bring attention and awareness to the change that is called for. However, it is also important to recognize that, just because something might not meet the definition of social movement, it doesn't mean that there aren't people, groups and organizations striving for change. Staggenborg argues that the group ties, in this case the identity of "witch," encourage individuals that are a part of or connect to that group to engage in such collective action.

> If an individual is closely tied to a group of people engaging in collective action, he or she has a big stake in the group's fate and may find it

hard not to participate when everyone else is involved. When collective action is urgent, the person is likely to contribute his or her share even if the impact of that share is not noticeable.[12]

Starhawk, author of the 1979 classic *The Spiral Dance*, is an active participant in the intersection of magic and social justice. Her Instagram account, @starhawk_spiral, includes examples of magical activism, links to social movements and information on permaculture and environmental justice, the latter of which includes directing @earth_activist_training, defined as "permaculture design with a grounding in spirit and a focus on organizing and activism."[13] She regularly hosts meditation sessions, which she equates to collective movement in that magical activism can reveal inner power, allowing for "reviewing our power from within and joining it with others to strengthen our power together."[14] Starhawk's magical activism is an example of how many witches use digital spaces as cross-media, cross-platform, education, awareness, collective action and sharing knowledge, experience and information.

For some witches, this might include practices of social justice that run counter to generally accepted tenets of witchcraft. In her book *Brujas: The Magic and Power of Witches of Color*, Lorraine Monteagut writes,

> As their online communities grow, witches of color are gaining confidence in the unique perspectives they have to offer . . . they reject the whitewashed "love and light" that pervades social media. Instead they nurture conversations about shadow work, which involves honestly facing fear, traumas, and death.[15]

Similarly, Cassandra Snow, in *Queering Your Craft: Witchcraft from the Margins*, illustrates the problematic nature of the famous tenet "an ye harm none," as that type of "tone policing is a tool of white supremacy to silence dissenting viewpoints and serve the status quo instead of social justice."[16] On November 9, 2024, @thehoodwitch posted "Cussing them out is spiritual too," with a caption that encouraged users to "protect your well being, and overall happiness by any means! . . . I'm not sure who decided that being 'spiritual' also equated with being a doormat. We are no longer being shamed into this 'love and light' narrative," as the necessity to "protect your peace, speak your truth, and create strong psychic boundaries" is important in this time of uncertainty.[17] This perspective sees the disruption of the "love and light" narrative as permission to exist more authentically, calling for marginalized populations, repeatedly told by the capitalist white supremacy they were too angry, loud or defiant, to speak their truth and use their voice in a way that benefits themselves and their community.

A Place of Belonging and Inclusivity

In the foreword to *Queering Your Craft*, Mat Auryn, a gay witch who is the author of *Psychic Witch* and has an active online presence, writes that "Using the word *witch* for oneself is a potent act of reclamation and empowerment, very much in a similar manner to which we reclaim the word *queer*."[18] In an article on refinery29.com, a gender nonbinary witch named Krysta stated that witchcraft

> gave me a sense of my personal power . . . In this world, Black, indigenous, and queer people are told they have no power. So, to have something that gives me power and encourages me to use my voice and my will is invaluable.[19]

Not only has witchcraft of the last century or so been symbolic of resistance against an oppressive status quo, for those who are part of historically oppressed populations it is a space of inclusivity, empowerment and belonging. In "Queer Heresies," Kevin Talmer Whiteneir Jr, "a queer artist, an art historian of the African-diaspora, and a practicing occultist implementing the performative rituals and myths of witchcraft," sought to dig into the queer aspects of history and uncover how those histories shape the present and future. As he writes,

> Like witchcraft, sexual queerness is considered dangerous in that it disrupts familiar and accepted behaviors and boundaries of gender and sexuality. Because of this shared history, many have sought to reclaim the witch for its queer potential today. Much like witches, queerness exists in a liminal space, one which blurs accepted social boundaries and is considered by social gatekeepers as a threat to religious and civil order. Witchcraft and queerness both represent forbidden knowledge and power in practice. This knowledge and power can mobilize marginalized peoples to disestablish restrictive cultural systems and, in their place, manifest realities that extend the borders of prevailing hegemonic ideas.[20]

Finding a space of spiritual inclusivity is especially important for marginalized populations who have historically been denied access to or condemned by other faiths. The gay and queer liberation movements of the late twentieth century experienced intense backlash, particularly from Christian opponents who invoked biblical scripture in order to dehumanize and villainize members of the queer community. As Harry M. Benshoff and Sean Griffin argue in *Queer Images: A History of Gay and Lesbian Film in America*, "Scapegoating queers as symbols of moral decline and national turpitude, the so-called religious right (led by televangelists such as Jerry Falwell) became a formidable force within mainstream American politics."[21] The Religious Right was composed of politically powerful individuals who invoked elements of Christianity in order to further persuade the American public of Reagan's conservative ideals. They were instrumental in mobilizing influential Evangelical figures to help reshape party platforms and support for President Reagan. Their focus was on "family values," the teaching of "traditional American history" and questioning reform movements such as feminism. They were also a significant force in fueling the fear and stigma that accompanied the AIDS crisis. Many sufferers of AIDS, even gay men, were believers in God and held Christian beliefs, but, much like other oppressed groups, had to find their own path toward God as they were not welcome in many mainstream churches. The rise of Christian-based conversion therapy programs not only reinforced that queer people did not have an automatic place in Christianity, but that it could be dangerous and harmful to be "out" in that space.[22]

Though spiritual practices such as witchcraft have created more inclusivity for members of the queer community, the history of Wicca demonstrates that that hasn't always been the case. Gardnerian Wicca relied heavily on the gender binary, including the notion of male and female sexual partnerships, roles for men and women in the coven and stark differentiations between the masculine and feminine divine. Gardnerian Wicca was not designed as an inclusive space for queer practitioners. In *Dancing with Witches*, Lois Bourne, one of the "maidens" within Gardner's coven, wrote that "Gerald was homophobic. He had a deep hatred and detestation for homosexuality, which he regarded as a disgusting perversion and a flagrant transgression of natural law, negating the life force and fertility aspect represented by the God and Goddess."[23] She even once heard him shout that it was impossible to be a homosexual and be a witch, and no one argued with him.

Gardner might not have left any space for queer inclusivity in his vision for Wicca, but, as discussed in Chapter 4, his influence on witchcraft and spirituality in the twentieth century is undeniable. The tension between the problematic figure of Gardner and the desire to practice witchcraft, Wicca or paganism is not one that is easily resolved. Like many marginalized communities who occupy oppressive spaces, "queer people in this period did what queer people always do – they found a way to subvert and reclaim that witchcraft as their own."[24] Many queer witches have done just that, finding a place at the table while simultaneously grappling with the homophobic and transphobic history of Wicca. On the popular story-sharing site myumbrella.com, Parker writes about this tension in specific detail, noting that it isn't easy to rectify:

> If you see issues with Gardner, but you think the core of Wicca is good, and you want to build a tradition out of it which is LGBTQ+ inclusive, I respect that. If you're a Gardnerian and see how he was a problematic figure, but due to investing your whole life in Gardnerian Wicca you feel you need to change it from the inside rather than leaving it entirely, I respect that. If you are part of another Wiccan group, such as the Feri Tradition, that seeks to keep the "good" and discard the "bad," I respect that. There is no way that homophobia, a heavy focus on male–female polarity, and heteronormativity did not in some form bias in the rituals and affect the way they were performed and put together.

> If you insist on believing, despite the evidence, that all Wicca is flawless and perfect and that no one made mistakes in its creation, you're not a queer ally.[25]

Parker's respect goes toward those who are in a space of grappling with the tension, attempting to educate themselves and finding space for inclusivity. Burying one's head in the sand and refusing to acknowledge Wicca's – most notably Gardner's – problematic history only adds to the oppression and marginalization of the queer community.

In *Queering Your Craft*, Auryn argues that the story of Aradia in Leland's work demands justice for marginalized identities:

> In the myth, the lunar goddess Diana sends down her daughter Aradia to instruct the marginalized people in the art of witchery to overthrow their oppressors . . . the central theme . . . is that of magickal and spiritual powers being placed in the hands of the marginalized.[26]

Auryn is among the thousands of queer witches and spiritualists who use their platforms to illustrate that witchcraft can be a space of inclusivity and belonging. Another TikToker, @sapphicandspiritual, posted a video on April 23, 2024 stating that

> being queer is inherently spiritual . . . that leads us down a path of self-discovery, love, and wholeness . . . I created the Sapphic and Spiritual podcast as a way to start a discussion about queer spirituality. I noted that even within new-age, witchy spiritual spaces, sometimes I still felt a lack of inclusion.[27]

They note that spiritual discovery and finding oneself can be a result of necessity, particularly in a world that seeks to exclude. Kir Beaux, a trans, nonbinary psychic witch and tarot reader, describes their take on this intersection between queerness and witchcraft on their website www.itsqueermagic.com. Their website's homepage states that

> Queerness is wildness. It's a channel through which a more balanced and equitable world is possible. Its queer magic is creating space for queer witches and magic makers who are looking for support, education, and community that reflects their values.[28]

These creators demonstrate that all genders can find spiritual, ecological and social connection through witchcraft.

A Connection to Ancestry, Culture and Heritage

The history of witchcraft extends beyond the borders of Europe and the Americas, beyond those who were/are white and cisgender. Witchcraft has roots in African, Native American, Latinx and Asian cultures. Those who developed Wicca in its early days (like Gardner) borrowed from cultures without contextualizing, giving proper credit or including their voices in popular or academic works. Today, many witches across various racial and ethnic walks of life seek not only to decolonize their practice, but also to connect to their ancestral and cultural heritage to position their spirituality within the context of those whose stories, experiences and symbols have been co-opted for use and benefit by privileged communities.

On the "About" page of her blog "The Writing Witch," podcaster and witch influencer Afura Nefertiti Fareed writes, "I believe that magick is the power to write your own story." On an October 2022 episode of the "Alchemy of Affluence" podcast, Fareed, aka "The Writing Witch," described to listeners "How to Work with Our Ancestors at Samhain." Within the discussion, Fareed and her mother, Lisa, explored how examining her own family history allowed her space for shadow work, as it can help us "to better understand and appreciate some of our own experiences and tendencies" as well as open the door to bring to light "the lost history of African American families."[29] She also described her mother's penchant for family history and storytelling, demonstrating both "the link between ancestry, cultural heritage and manifestation" and "my mom's beliefs about ancestor spirit guides on the other side of the veil." The podcast, posted across platforms such as Spotify, Apple Podcasts, YouTube and thewritingwitch.com, garnered hundreds of comments from listeners who appreciated the perspective of ancestor work and connection to one's cultural heritage. One YouTube commenter, @Saturnarium, remarked,

> As a person who has mixed feelings about ancestor work (I am somehow afraid to unlock the shadow side of my ancestry), I really enjoyed this conversation to gain some clarity. I also have distant relatives from West Africa (as many Brazilians do, particularly from Benin) and African griot tradition fascinates me!

Another user, @Swanofdreamers, commented on the significance of understanding our ancestors to gain further clarity and insight into why a witch might be called toward a particular practice or element. They wrote,

> In my family, I felt like the odd duck being intuitive and doing readings though my mom encouraged it. I found out from my Aunt that my grandmother was psychic. I had no idea she was. Knowing that information gave me a new confidence. I was doing something that is part of bloodline.[30]

In addition to receiving these comments on her podcast, Fareed also responded to each of the YouTube user's comments, acknowledging their appreciation and extending gratitude for the sharing of information and stories.

Furthermore, Fareed sees witchcraft as a way to honor their ancestry and traditions while moving toward a path that allows them to find balance and a means of self-care.

Fareed also notes the feeling of not quite belonging to particular communities. Prior to taking DNA tests to examine her heritage, Fareed says that they would often

> consider ourselves black because that's our that's who that's what we look like and that's how we were raised but you know I would also I would often be around other black people who are like you're just weird and different and you don't fit in get out of here and then you know white people would also be like well you're you're cool or whatever but you're not one of us you know and so I've always kind of had to I think maybe that's for part of my spiritual um path comes from where I feel like souls are families as opposed to just you know specific groups of people who are necessarily related or seem to have the same ethnicity and that sort of thing but I mean come to find out maybe part of the reason for that is not only that I come from a line of people who transcend ethnicity with their you know their choice of friends but it also turns out that I'm not just black or just anything you know and that's just interesting to me.[31]

Fareed's description of her own experience of not neatly fitting into definitions of what it means to be a particular racial or ethnic identity illustrates an aspect of intersectionality. Coined by black feminist scholar Kimberlé Crenshaw, intersectionality

> is a lens through which you can see where power comes and collides, where it interlocks and intersects. It's not simply that there's a race problem here, a gender problem here, and a class or LBGTQ problem there. Many times that framework erases what happens to people who are subject to all of these things.[32]

The perspective of intersectionality is crucial to understanding issues of social justice, as it creates space for greater nuance for problem-solving and agency within the individual experience.

Articulating one's intersectional perspective is not as easy as making a list of various identity markers and seeing how they overlap. Often, so many find themselves experiencing an "in betweenness" of identity. Monteagut describes her own in-betweenness as a daughter of parents born in Colombia and Cuba who moved their family to Florida when she was just 9 years old.

> I had a sense that there were secrets my family wouldn't tell me, and for some reason, I was afraid to ask. Besides some old photos, they brought no heirlooms that I could use to access family memory. To

them, progress was a constant newness, the cold and hard aesthetic of Miami in the early 1990s.[33]

Witchcraft, particularly the witchcraft aesthetic of 1990s television shows such as *Charmed* and *Buffy the Vampire Slayer*, became a balm for her feeling of "in betweenness," of not belonging or understanding who she was. Though her wardrobe of "dog collars and baby tees" and "flowy skirts with combat boots" gave her a starting point of expression of her witch-coded spiritual self, Monteagut soon learned that it wouldn't be enough to reconcile the "in betweenness."[34] In her work *Brujas: The Magic and Power of Witches of Color*, Monteagut tells the story of her first encounter with a "bruja." After attending a Catholic mass with her mother and aunts, they took her to a house where

> they consulted someone dressed all in white. They appeared with something wrapped in burlap (and covered in blood?) and they told me not to tell anyone where we'd been. In my family, brujas were associated with dark magic and openly shunned, so they were sought in secret.

For years, she "held on to the word *bruja* because it was more right than the witch I associated with paganism" even if she didn't see her practice aligning with the dark magic that she'd been told was part of the bruja's craft.[35] Monteagut's story demonstrates that witches of color "are increasingly reclaiming their ancestries and speaking out against the internalized colonialism, cultural appropriation and spiritual consumerism that mars mainstream spirituality."[36] This includes challenging the history of Wicca as only "invented" by Gardner in the mid-twentieth century and rejecting narratives and tenets that silence the voices of the angry and oppressed.

Rituals and spells are another way in which today's witches can connect to their ancestors and cultural heritage. In *Sacred Woman: A Guide to Healing the Feminine Mind, Body, and Spirit*, Queen Afua defines an ancestor as

> a blood – or extended – family member who has died and made the transition into the spirit world. This person is now in a position to render service to those who call out his or her name for spiritual guidance in the material world.[37]

A search of #ancestorwork on TikTok shows several spiritualists and witches who provide encouragement, knowledge and guidance for how to work with ancestral spirits. One TikToker, @mazdamiles, argues that slave-holding oppressors had long-removed connection to ancestors from the oppressed, leaving generations of people of color without ancestral connection. She argues that the practitioner must "venerate and elevate" their ancestors prior to asking for guidance, being mindful of this violent and oppressive history.[38] TikToker @anastasiamoongirl describes that veneration can include sitting at a clean altar space with a white candle and clear fresh glass of water, then calling on ancestors who morally align with the practitioner, making sure to spend time getting to know them before asking for guidance.[39] Both TikTokers engage with the comments asking questions about offerings, language barriers, ways to hear the ancestor, further definitions of veneration, etc., allowing the space to be one of continued learning and engagement.

Though ancestral work can happen at any time, it is particularly associated with the festival of Samhain, often considered the time of year when the veil between the living and the dead is at its thinnest. In *Kitchen Witch: Food, Folklore, and Fairy Tale*, Sarah Robinson writes, "In many cultures, it was thought that one's ancestors and loved ones who had passed on could visit during this time, often people would prepare their favourite meal or leave out treats for spirits and souls."[40] Sometimes referred to as a "dumb supper" or "spirit supper," the ritual of honoring an ancestor through a meal includes seats and place settings for the number of expected ancestors visiting, food and drink that hold special connection or memory associated with the deceased and a photograph or an image with a representation of those being called upon. In an Instagram post from October 31, 2024, @brigantiasdaughter described her own "spirit supper" honoring her Ukrainian grandfather, Dido. The caption under the post highlights that working with and honoring ancestors isn't necessarily an easy process, especially if the practitioner knows of problematic elements of the deceased person's time on Earth.

> He had a hard life and was very hard on others. He fled occupied Ukraine during the world war after he had his warhorse shot from under him and he pretended to be dead in the snow . . . he self-medicated, lost his only son in a car accident, and refused to speak English for his new home in Canada. But he was gentle with me [gray heart emoji] we ate terrible food like Cheetos and Lucky Charms cereal . . . He taught me swear words and called me "Chu-pee" which to this day no one can translate for me . . . He's a controversial invite because he was such a hard man to be around in life. But not for me. I hope I was someone whom he could see all his trials come to a win . . . I am not in a war zone right now because of him, I'd be in Kyiv right now if he'd stayed, if he had not fled.[41]

This story told by @brigantiasdaughter illustrates the powerful yet complex connection of ancestral work, allowing space for today's witches to reconnect with past generations and honor their history while learning about who they are and where they come from.

Conclusion

The historical and traditional narrative of the witch has almost exclusively been synonymous with cisgender women, often white, presumably heterosexual. Today, partially through the rapidly evolving landscape of digital media, that narrative is changing. The term "witch" is not simply a label that defines a spiritual practice or outward aesthetic, but embodies the ideologies of resistance, intention and action. In "Lessons from the Other Realm: Being a Male Witch in 2019 is Complicated," Douglas Greenwood quotes a male witch, Michael, who argues that "the word 'witch' doesn't carry a gender – "it's a verb . . . something you do."[42] The "doings" of witches included in this chapter range from various ritualistic acts to education, raising awareness, posting content, performing spells, communicating with the divine, acting toward social change, resisting oppressive structures, and rewriting and reclaiming narratives in order to decolonize practices and increase inclusivity. As Monteagut writes,

> In the 2010s, as a new intersectional feminism emerged, so did the new witch. She stands at the borders of complicated racial, class, and gender identities. She's a reflection of the feminism of these times, always shifting in response to political, social, and environmental problems.[43]

Today's witch is more likely to be focused on inclusivity, reclamation, empowerment, environmental stewardship and social justice. Furthermore, today's witchy practitioners are more willing to grapple with the complexities of witchcraft, including Wiccan and Pagan histories and culture, recognizing that reconciliation can be a part of the spiritual path. Reflection on one's past, ancestry and identity as well as the awareness of injustices within one's community and beyond allow space for the witch to, as Fareed says, "use magic to tell their own story."

Notes

1 Dung Bui-Xuan and Kien Thi-Pham, "Karl Marx's View of the Productive Forces and Its Development Today," *Midwestern Marx Institute* (August 29, 2022), https://www.midwesternmarx.com/articles/karl-marxs-view-of-the-productive-forces-and-its-development-today-by-kien-thi-pham-dung-bui-xuan.
2 Silvia Federici, *Caliban and the Witch* (Brooklyn: Autonomedia, 2004), 17.
3 Kristen J. Sollee, "Foreword," in *Becoming Dangerous: Witchy Femmes, Queer Conjurers, and Magical Rebels*, ed. Katie West and Jasmine Elliott (Newburyport, MA: Weiser Books, 2019), xv.
4 Antonio Pagliarulo, "Why Paganism and Witchcraft Are Making a Comeback," *NBC News* (October 30, 2022), https://www.nbcnews.com/think/opinion/paganism-witchcraft-are-making-comeback-rcna54444.
5 Catherine Hernandez, "Femme as in Fuck You: Fucking with the Patriarchy One Lipstick Application at a Time," in *Becoming Dangerous: Witchy Femmes, Queer Conjurers, and Magical Rebels*, ed. Katie West and Jasmine Elliott (Brooklyn: Weiser Books, 2019), 50.
6 Catherine Hernandez, "Femme as in Fuck You: Fucking with the Patriarchy One Lipstick Application at a Time," in *Becoming Dangerous: Witchy Femmes, Queer Conjurers, and Magical Rebels*, ed. Katie West and Jasmine Elliott (Brooklyn: Weiser Books, 2019), 53–54.

7. Arin Murphy-Hiscock, *The Witch's Book of Self-Care: Magical Ways to Pamper, Soothe, and Care for Your Body and Spirit* (New York: Simon and Schuster, 2018), 12.
8. @beyournottygirl, "Casting Intricate Spells, Connecting with Ancestors, Doing Divination," TikTok, September 2023.
9. Chris Miller, "How Modern Witches Enchant TikTok: Intersections of Digital, Consumer, and Material Culture(s) on #Witchtok," *Religions* 13, no. 2 (2022), 118.
10. Catherine Hernandez, "Femme as in Fuck You: Fucking with the Patriarchy One Lipstick Application at a Time," in *Becoming Dangerous: Witchy Femmes, Queer Conjurers, and Magical Rebels*, ed. Katie West and Jasmine Elliott (Brooklyn: Weiser Books, 2019), 52.
11. Suzanne Staggenborg, *Social Movements 2nd Edition* (Oxford: Oxford University Press, 2016), vii.
12. Suzanne Staggenborg, *Social Movements 2nd Edition* (Oxford: Oxford University Press, 2016), 36.
13. Anonymous, "Earth Activist Training," https://earthactivisttraining.org/.
14. @starhawk_spiral, "Magical Activism: Inner Power," Instagram, November 15, 2024.
15. Lorraine Monteagut, *Brujas: The Magic and Power of Witches of Color* (Chicago: Chicago Review Press, 2022), 16.
16. Cassandra Snow, *Queering Your Craft: Witchcraft from the Margins* (Newburyport, MA: Weiser Books, 2020), xxii.
17. @thehoodwitch, "Cussing Them out Is Spiritual Too," Instagram, November 9, 2024.
18. Cassandra Snow, *Queering Your Craft: Witchcraft from the Margins* (Newburyport, MA: Weiser Books, 2020), xi.
19. Amanda Kohr, "Why Queer People Love Witchcraft" (June 17, 2020), https://www.refinery29.com/en-us/2020/06/9861310/queer-lgbt-witch-trend.
20. Kevin Talmer Whiteneir Jr, "Queer Heresies: Witchcraft and Magic as Sites of Queer Radicality," *The Activist History Review* (May 24, 2019), https://activisthistory.com/2019/05/24/queer-heresies-witchcraft-and-magic-as-sites-of-queer-radicality/.
21. Harry M. Benshoff and Sean Griffin, *Queer Images: A History of Gay and Lesbian Film in America* (Lanham: Rowman and Littlefield Publishers, 2006), 158.
22. Katherine Ott, "The History of Getting the Gay Out" (November 15, 2018), https://americanhistory.si.edu/explore/stories/history-getting-gay-out.
23. Lois Bourne, *Dancing with Witches* (London: Robert Hale, 1998), 38.
24. Cassandra Snow, *Queering Your Craft: Witchcraft from the Margins* (Newburyport, MA: Weiser Books, 2020), xxi.
25. Parker, "Queering Paganism: A Gay Practitioner's Perspective of Wicca Craft" (April 30, 2021), https://myumbrella.co/queering-paganism-a-gay-practitioners-perspective-of-wicca-craft/#:~:text=Some%20popular%20pagan%20traditions%20have,and%20cisnormativity%20in%20certain%20traditions.
26. Cassandra Snow, *Queering Your Craft: Witchcraft from the Margins* (Newburyport, MA: Weiser Books, 2020), xiii.
27. @sapphicandspiritual, "Queer is Inherently Spiritual," TikTok, April 30, 2024.
28. Kir Beaux, "It's Queer Magic," www.itsqueermagic.com, accessed December 12, 2024.
29. Afura Nefertiti Fareed, *Alchemy of Affluence*, Podcast audio: "How to Work with Ancestors at Samhain" (51m 03s), October 19, 2022, https://writingwitch.com/2022/10/19/how-to-work-with-our-ancestors/.
30. Afura Nefertiti Fareed, The Writing Witch, "How to Work with Our Ancestors + AncestryDNA – What Am I? (Witchy Chit Chat with My Mom)," YouTube, October 31, 2023, https://www.youtube.com/watch?v=DlSQPlgsdQM&t=1689s.
31. Afura Nefertiti Fareed, The Writing Witch, "How to Work with Our Ancestors + AncestryDNA – What Am I? (Witchy Chit Chat with My Mom)," YouTube, October 31, 2023, https://www.youtube.com/watch?v=DlSQPlgsdQM&t=1689s.

114 *Witchcraft: Gendered Perspectives*

32 Kimberlé Crenshaw, "Kimberlé Crenshaw on Intersectionality, More Than Two Decades Later," (June 8, 2017), https://www.law.columbia.edu/news/archive/kimberle-crenshaw-intersectionality-more-two-decades-later.
33 Lorraine Monteagut, *Brujas: The Magic and Power of Witches of Color* (Chicago: Chicago Review Press, 2022), 10.
34 Lorraine Monteagut, *Brujas: The Magic and Power of Witches of Color* (Chicago: Chicago Review Press, 2022), 11.
35 Lorraine Monteagut, *Brujas: The Magic and Power of Witches of Color* (Chicago: Chicago Review Press, 2022), 16.
36 Lorraine Monteagut, *Brujas: The Magic and Power of Witches of Color* (Chicago: Chicago Review Press, 2022), 12.
37 Queen Afua, *Sacred Woman: A Guide to Healing the Feminine Mind, Body, and Spirit* (New York: Ballantine Publishing, 2000), 126.
38 @mazdamiles, "veneration or elevation," TikTok, September 27, 2022.
39 @anastasiamoongirl, "Ancestor Veneration Pt1," TikTok, April 10, 2023.
40 Sarah Robinson, *Kitchen Witch: Food, Folklore, and Fairy Tale* (Cork, Ireland: Womancraft Publishing, 2022), 169.
41 @brigantiasdaughter, "Setting the Table for Our Spirit Supper," Instagram, October 31, 2024.
42 Douglas Greenwood, "Lessons from the Other Realm: Being a Male Witch in 2019 is Complicated" (October 30, 2019), https://www.dazeddigital.com/beauty/article/46549/1/male-witch-magic-magick-witchcraft-warlock-wizard.
43 Lorraine Monteagut, *Brujas: The Magic and Power of Witches of Color* (Chicago: Chicago Review Press, 2022), 14.

Conclusion

Final Thoughts

The study of witchcraft and research into its history has gained increasing traction in the latter half of the twentieth century and appears to have no sign of slowing down. As this book demonstrates, there are varying, and often intersecting, directions one can take into researching witchcraft. These include literary analysis, diving into historical records, examining it as a religious or spiritual practice, through pop culture and media representation, as a social media phenomenon and through the lens of international affairs, to name a few.

This book has examined the gendered components through which witchcraft can be viewed, both in its history and its culture. The field of gender studies goes far beyond the dynamics of gender identity and is a field that grapples with issues of power, marginalization and systemic injustice across many populations and identities. Those who have been marginalized, both historically and today, have been repeatedly labelled by hierarchical structures as somehow "less than" more privileged members of society but also as "dangerous threats" to the system as a whole.

Crenshaw's theory of intersectionality is also a crucial part of this discipline, as the fluidity of identity and worldviews allows for greater considerations of power structures, the inclusion of multiple voices and the validity of personal experiences. This enables a more nuanced understanding of both systems of privilege and of oppression, including how privilege exists within marginalized communities. This also allows us to understand that the experiences of those persecuted for alleged witchcraft are not monolithic and that many of the recorded testimonies that exist are of those who were white and spoke English. For example, older and elderly women were common targets of accusation, and though we have the testimonies of Sarah Goode and Sarah Osborne, those of women of color such as Tituba are few and far between. Assumptions about a woman of color's foreignness or communication skills led to poorer recordings of their testimony or no record at all.[1]

The original aim of this book was to examine how the culture and language around the "witch" moved from an accusation that could lead to death and most definitely to exile to its current iteration, at least in Western cultures, where being a witch is not only proudly claimed by some, but has become a symbol of empowerment, patriarchal resistance and social justice. What became clear through my research and writing was that the power of the word "witch" remained within the purview of those who wielded it.

Many of the people featured within this book were not actually witches but had had the label foisted onto them by institutional systems that sought to remove any perceived threat to their power. Those threats included anyone who might disrupt the societal order, where subjugated people would stay in their place and continue to contribute to the status quo. Those "witches" were primarily women on the margins of society in some fashion, leaving them with little agency or power, making them easy targets, even scapegoats, for the ills of society at large. Men like Institoris and Sprenger used their privilege and power as educated men to shape the discourse around the word "witch" (or "sorceress," depending on translation). By making connections between witchcraft or sorcery and the devil, disseminating that information through print to be distributed in a highly patriarchal Christian society and then accusing women who they perceived as blights or burdens to society of that same witchcraft, they infused the words with a power to dangerously harm those who did not fit in with the righteous perception of a Christian woman. As Hutton has pointed out, the idea of the witch as someone who performs "magical harm" has become so pervasive that early scholars of the subject had accepted this definition.[2] Fear has dominated the definition of witch for far too long.

This is not just a European and North American phenomenon. Prior to 1879, Okinawa was not a part of Japan but was known as the Ryukyu Islands with its own cultural and religious practices. Women called "noro" were respected High Priestesses, while "yuta" were spiritual mediums who did not necessarily need any training or affiliation to practice. Court records from the seventeenth century show that some yuta were persecuted, accused of destroying livestock and summoning evil spirits to commit murder.[3] Research shows that this persecution reemerged as recently as the 1940s, when Japanese Special Forces engaged in "shaman hunts."[4] In the twenty-first century, Japanese witchcraft is largely influenced by Western constructs of Wicca, which has relegated spiritual practices of Shinto to "custom" or "tradition" rather than a religious endeavor.[5]

Furthermore, witchcraft persecution and trials continue to persist in areas of the world today. In Ghana, elderly women survive in refuges called "witch camps," a space where they might be free from the persecutions in their communities but are also often exploited for labor and treated as slaves. Like other "witches" before them, the women in Ghana are accused of causing maladies and tragedy in their society, namely the deaths of people in their community. Ghanian beliefs in witchcraft connect it to all too familiar concepts, such as the notion that witches fly at night, eat the flesh and blood of humans and can transform livestock into humans and vice versa.[6] A 2022 *Newsweek* report states,

> the government has previously tried to shut down the settlements in an effort to dismantle the stigma placed on these women and reintroduce them to their communities. But [Human Global Charities activist Leo] Igwe said this was a problematic solution, and leaves the women without a refuge.[7]

On July 27, 2023, Parliament passed an act to not only outlaw, but criminalize accusations of witchcraft and acts of violence against those purported to be witches.[8]

The use of the word "witch" in these instances as well as in publications such as the *Malleus Maleficarum*, against women such as Agnes Sampson, Alizon Device and Tituba, and featured in folklore, fables and plays such as *Macbeth*, illustrates that the connotation of the word as describing one who performs "magical harm" was largely constructed by those with far more power and agency than those alleged to have been witches. The "witch" as evil, in league with the devil, vengeful, ugly, a destroyer complete with bodily scars, with the ability to cast dark magic and otherworldly power such as flight or to control the weather, is almost exclusively the invention of those who wrote the pamphlets, persecuted the women and inked the records and documents of the trials.

Though still connected to the idea of evil and destruction, and while some are unjustly persecuted for societal ills far beyond their control, the word "witch" has undergone a transformation. Pam Grossman, author of *Waking the Witch: Reflections on Women, Magic and Power*, argues that this reclamation

> kicked off in the 19th century when scholars started looking back at the witch hunts, and realizing that these women were actually sympathetic figures. They started romanticizing who these people were . . . saying: "Oh, they were the most brilliant minds of their age, or they had some kind of incredible power that was threatening to the church."[9]

While Grossman notes that this likely wasn't accurate, particularly due to the systems of power that existed at the time, the idea of looking at the victims through a lens of sympathy and humanity was tantamount to this reclamation. Coleridge and Dickinson also used their limited privilege as literate white women to write poetry that demonstrated both a reflection on past ills and recognition of present injustices, imbuing a new kind of power to the word "witch."

The power of the word "witch" has also come with an individual's connection to it as a spiritual practice. The intersection of gender studies and religion is also a significant part of the study of Wicca, paganism, mysticism, witchcraft, etc. Religion, as defined by the US government and as related to the First Amendment, "includes (A) all assertions of truth of and concerning the supernatural, (B) all assertions of truth flowing forth from supernatural beliefs, and (C) actions taken pursuant to such beliefs."[10] While this definition has undergone scrutiny and debate, it allows space for the inclusion of Wiccans, Pagans and witches. As Hutton argues,

> pagan witchcraft... has a common identity and a common institutional structure, of the coven supplemented by solitary practice of the same tradition... It is more than the veneration of a single deity or object, and has not separated off from a larger religious body or movement.[11]

With the *Dettmer v. Landon* Supreme Court case, Wicca earned protection under the US First Amendment in 1986.

Witchcraft, paganism and Wicca are hardly monolithic in their respective practices or use of language. Among the primary differences between them are language, origin and practice. For example, the term "Pagan" originated as a word to represent someone from a more rural area, eventually was used to describe someone as uncivilized and later became a word used as slander against those of another religion, becoming interchangeable with words such as "heathen."[12] Conversely, Wicca, as a term, became more widely used in the 1960s, with the work of Gardner, Valiente and others hitting the mainstream. Even within the practice of Wicca in the mid-twentieth century and beyond, the words take on new meanings as a result of shifting dynamics in language and belief systems. As noted in Chapter 6 with the story of Parker, one need not completely upend or ignore a practice because of outdated or problematic belief systems within the original cohort of organizers. For example, Gardner may have been homophobic, but Wiccans, Pagans and witches across cultures and generations have not only vehemently disagreed with Gardner's take but have actively welcomed LGBTQ+ members into their communities.

Many today have their own takes on what it means to be a Pagan, Wiccan or witch. For the HearthWitch on YouTube, there are three definitions of paganism. The first demonstrates that paganism is often associated with ancient polytheistic belief systems and rural people who lived in accordance with nature's seasons. The second definition comes from the development of the Abrahamic religions, as

> they were often trying to remove people from the traditions and the religions that came before and so paganism was considered to be a religion that follows false gods and so pagan was often considered a derogatory term to represent someone who didn't believe in the correct deities.

The third is a modern definition, but more closely aligns with the first.[13] Much like the use of the word "witch," these definitions illustrate that the meaning changes depending upon agency, if the word is used to describe one's identity or as a means of harm against another.

Well-known witches such as Starhawk have increasingly recognized that the use of language and considerations of inclusivity are significant tenets at the core of the practice. In the tenth anniversary edition of *The Spiral Dance*, published in 1989, Starhawk noted just how much the United States had changed both socially and politically through the 1980s. She'd always seen *The Spiral Dance* as a political book,

> but over the last decade, as the gap between the rich and poor widened, as our nuclear arsenals were rebuilt, as the homeless began to die in our streets and the jobless to crowd the bread lines, as the United States moved into covert and overt wars in Latin America, as the AIDS virus spread while legislators sat on funds for education and treatment, as the environment deteriorated, the national debt quadrupled, and the hole in the ozone layer grew ominously, a more active political engagement seemed called for.[14]

In the twentieth anniversary edition, Starhawk also notes her own growth regarding the gender binary from the original publication in 1979 to the eve of the twenty-first century.

> In the 1989 introduction, I wrote extensively about my shift away from the polarized view of the world as a dance of "female" and "male" qualities and energies, and toward a much more complex and inclusive view of gender and energy. That shift continues to deepen as I grow older and it is still the major change I would make in this book.[15]

This type of self-reflexivity is a crucial part of the field of gender studies, as it acknowledges the complexity of experience and the errors or unawareness of the past, reconciling it with the realities of the social and political fabric of the present.

Language and the written word have been a significant reason for the growth of Wicca and paganism and their proliferation in the political sphere in the last few decades of the twentieth century. Starhawk and other witch activists followed the lead of Valiente, who advocated for claiming agency and ownership over one's Wiccan identity rather than leaving it in the hands of hegemonic forces within the media. Wiccan and Neopagan organizations led to "newsletters, magazines, publishers, networking, and advocacy organizations" being given an "additional boost in the United States by the founding of Llewellyn, a publishing house based in Minnesota."[16] Dating back to 1901, today Llewellyn publishes books on astrology, tarot, spell work, nature-based spirituality and herbalism, as well as tarot decks, calendars, journals and more.[17]

Social media has only added to the consumption, combining oral and written content in order to increase the reach of Wicca, paganism and witchcraft.

Many consumers of witchcraft-related social media content receive information and inspiration from content creators, describing how they might incorporate it into their own beliefs, values and ideas. Commenters on social media, for example, will sometimes elaborate on how the content creator inspired them to perform a ritual, read about herbalism or become more aware of social injustices. Robinson, author of *The Witch and the Wildwood*, host of the podcast *This is Witch Country* and curator of @thisiswitchcountry and @yogaforwitches accounts on Instagram, often incorporates aspects of nature, folklore and food symbolism into her posts and other writings. In a post from February 19, 2024, Robinson posted, "Today's #wildmoment the crocuses are rising with a little support by the Green Man! What's your little pocket of wild today?" Inspired by the idea of a #wildmoment, several replies included seeing spring flowers emerging, feeling freedom in a yoga class and the sound of a woodpecker.[18]

It is clear that users and followers of witchcraft-related content are inspired and empowered by the emphasis on social justice and emotional wellness. On October 20, 2024, @thehoodwitch posted "Saying No is the Spell," encouraging her followers to recognize that they do not have to take on the physical, emotional or spiritual burdens of everyone they come across. Forty-one people commented their gratitude for her post.[19] Less than ten days later, @thehoodwitch posted "Ancestral Reverence is Resistance," calling for Samhain, traditionally a time to honor ancestors, to go beyond remembering their stories and "Honor the labor, the blood, the sweat, and the tears. Let's acknowledge the oppression, heartache and pain that our ancestors endured. Their struggles were not in vain!" Several commentors posted fire emojis out of their appreciation and one acknowledged the need to recognize the sacrifices of their grandparents.[20] This one account illustrates the emphasis on balance between self-care and social justice in the practices of witchcraft.

Yet one need not claim the identity of witch to find empowerment and inspiration within these types of posts. As a matter of fact, very few of the comments on the posts referenced in this book mention individual identities relating to witchcraft, Wicca, paganism, etc., making it unclear exactly how users of social media might identify. What is apparent is the emphasis on community and connection within the digital space of social media. With impending threats to social media usage, such as ongoing discussions about a ban of TikTok that began in 2020, witchy content creators emphasized one of the most significant aspects of their public practice, the facilitation of community. Several creators encouraged their followers to find community on other social media accounts, following links on their favorite creator's bios to "find other ways to stay connected." For example, commentors on @cocos.cauldron's January 13, 2025 post encouraged others to find spaces on YouTube, Instagram and RedNote in order to keep their community more or less intact.[21] These types of posts and comments demonstrate that the online community provides a space for greater authenticity and acceptance, regardless of whether or not they identify as a "witch."

Conclusion 121

As with other words used to harm and oppress, it is difficult to completely disentangle the prejudice and harm from empowerment and reclamation. As illustrated by examples in Tanzania and Ghana, the weight of the words "witch" and "witchcraft" still carries deadly consequences, particularly for marginalized communities such as elderly women, and the connotation of witches as being in league with the devil persists nearly six centuries after the publication of the *Malleus Maleficarum*. Furthermore, the "witch" is still largely considered to be a woman, leaving other words, such as "wizard" and "warlock," to be used for men who practice ritual magic and/or spell work in their craft. Even popular books such as the *Harry Potter* series draw this distinction, where boys are wizards and girls are witches. Not only is the binary construction of the language damaging regarding gender identity, but the history of the witch is also so fraught with violence and diabolism that it is nearly impossible to escape the implication that women who practice magic are inherently evil. Yet today, it is common to see and hear people, of all genders, cultures, ages, etc., regularly using the word "witch" as part of their identity. These people imbue the word "witch" with their own sense of power, as, even with the knowledge of a violent and oppressive history, they find connection, support, empowerment, spirituality and/or justice within the vast space of its reach.

Notes

1 Zachary McLeod Hutchins and Cassander L. Smith, "The Salem Witch Trials, the Testimony of Candy and Mary Black, 1692," in *The Earliest African American Literatures: A Critical Reader*, ed. Zachary McLeod Hutchins and Cassander L. Smith (Chapel Hill: University of North Carolina Press, 2021).
2 Ronald Hutton, *The Witch: A History of Fear from Ancient Times to the Present* (New Haven: Yale University Press, 2017), 12.
3 Adam Ledford, "The Yuta, the Noro, and the 'Okinawan Witch Trials': Japan's Lesser-Known Salem Witch Trials," *Tofugu* (April 16, 2014), https://www.tofugu.com/japan/yuta-noro-okinawa-witch-trials/.
4 Matthew Allen, "The Shaman Hunts and Postwar Revival and Reinvention of Okinawan Shamanism," *Japan Forum* 29, no. 2 (2017), 218–35.
5 Eriko Kawanishi, "The Western Witchcraft in Contemporary Japan," American Academy of Religion Annual Meeting, Denver, 2018.
6 Kwasi Atta Agyapong, *Witchcraft in Ghana: Belief, Practice, and Consequence* (Ghana: Noyam Publishers, 2021), 2–3.
7 Robyn White, "The Witch Camps Where Hundreds of Elderly Women Are Left to Die," *Newsweek* (October 30, 2022), https://www.newsweek.com/witch-camps-elderly-women-die-ghana-1754907.
8 Katherine Marshall, "Combatting Accusations of Witches in Ghana" (August 22, 2023), https://berkleycenter.georgetown.edu/posts/combatting-accusations-of-witches-in-ghana.
9 Pam Grossman, "Picturing Queer Witchcraft: A Conversation with Susan Aberth and Pam Grossman," by Ksenia M. Soboleva, *New York Historical Society* (June 22, 2023), https://www.nyhistory.org/blogs/picturing-queer-witchcraft-susan-aberth-pam-grossman.
10 Joseph Kerstiens, "A Historical, Philosophical, and Etymological Study of the Word 'Religion' as Used in the First Amendment: Coming to a Textually Based Definition," *George Mason Law Review* 31, no. 1 (2023), 75–118, 78.

11 Ronald Hutton, *The Triumph of the Moon: A History of Modern Pagan Witchcraft* (Oxford: Oxford University Press, 1999), 413.
12 David Waldron, "Paganism," in *Encyclopedia of Psychology and Religion*, ed. David A. Leeming (New York: Springer, 2020), 1683.
13 HearthWitch, "Witchcraft, Wicca, and Paganism: The Differences," YouTube, December 9, 2020, https://www.youtube.com/watch?v=RhfUqyxwJS0.
14 Starhawk, *The Spiral Dance: A Rebirth of the Ancient Religion of the Great Goddess 10th Anniversary Edition* (San Francisco: HarperSanFrancisco, 1989), 6–7.
15 Starhawk, *The Spiral Dance: A Rebirth of the Ancient Religion of the Great Goddess 20th Anniversary Edition* (San Francisco: HarperSanFrancisco, 1999), 27.
16 Linda J. Jencson, "Wicca," in *The Routledge History of Witchcraft*, ed. Johannes Dillinger (London: Routledge), 2021), 326–327.
17 Anonymous, "Publishing for Body, Mind, and Spirit," https://llewellyn.com/about/index.php.
18 @yogaforwitches, "Today's #Wildmoment," Instagram, February 19, 2024.
19 @thehoodwitch, "Saying No Is the Spell," Instagram, October 20, 2024.
20 @thehoodwitch, "Ancestral Reverence Is Resistance," Instagram, October 29, 2024.
21 @cocos.cauldron, "Let's All Remember to Stay Connected," TikTok, January 13, 2025.

Bibliography

Primary Manuscript Sources

Primary Sources

Allingham, William. "The Fairies." Scottish Poetry Library. https://www.scottishpoetrylibrary.org.uk/poem/fairies/, accessed August 22, 2024.

Andrews, Allen. "Calling All Covens." *Sunday Pictorial* (London, England), July 29, 1951.

Anonymous. "Confession of Agnes Sampson, One of the 'North Berwick' Witches." In *The National Archives*, January 29, 1590. https://www.nls.uk/learning-zone/literature-and-language/themes-in-focus/witches/source-1/#:~:text=The%20North%20Berwick%20witches&text=Agnes%20Sampson%20was%20one%20of,storm%20to%20shipwreck%20the%20king.

Anonymous. *Newes from Scotland, Declaring the Damnable Life of Doctor Fian a Notable Sorcerer, Who Was Burned at Edenbrough in Lanuarie Last*. London: University of Glasgow, 1591.

Anonymous. "Extraordinary Assault." *Birmingham Journal* (Birmingham, Warwickshire, England), April 14, 1827. www.britishnewspaperarchive.co.uk.

Anonymous. "Too Late for Prince Charming." *Newsweek*, June 2, 1986.

Apuleius. *The Golden Ass*. Transl. Robert Graves. New York: Farrar, Straus and Giroux, 1971.

Broads, Dudley. "Examination of Elizabeth Johnson Jr." Peabody Essex Museum: Essex Institute Collection, August 11, 1692. http://salem.lib.virginia.edu/n83.html.

Brontë, Charlotte. *Jane Eyre*. New York: Penguin Books, 2006.

Brontë, Emily. *Wuthering Heights*. Seattle: Amazon Classics, 2017.

Carroll, Lewis. *Alice in Wonderland: A Norton Critical Edition*. Edited by Norton Critical Editions, fourth edn. New York: W.W. Norton and Company, 2024.

Cotta, John. "The Infallible True and Assured Witch; or the Second Edition of the Tryall of Witch-Craft Shewing the Right and True Methode of the Discoverie with a Confutation of Erroneous Waies. Carefully Reviewed and More Fully Cleared and Augmented." In *Digital Witchcraft Collection*, edited by Cornell University. London: I.L. for Richard Higginbotham, 1624.

Council Fathers. "Fourth Lateran Council: 1215 Council Fathers." https://www.papalencyclicals.net/councils/ecum12-2.htm.

Crowley, Aleister. *The Book of the Law*. Newburyport, MA: Weiser Books, 2004 (reprint).

Culpeper, Nicholas. *Culpeper's Complete Herbal: Over 400 Herbs and Their Uses*. London: Arcturus Publishing Limited, 2012 (reprint).

Bibliography

Cunningham, Scott. *Wicca: A Guide for the Solitary Practitioner.* Woodbury, MN: Llewellyn Publications, 1989.
Dickens, Charles. *Great Expectations.* New York: Penguin Classics, 2010.
Dickinson, Emily. *The Complete Poems of Emily Dickinson.* Edited by Thomas H. Johnson. Boston: Little Brown and Company, 1960.
Farrar, Janet. *A Witches' Bible: The Complete Witches' Handbook.* London: Robert Hale, 1981.
Friedan, Betty. *The Feminine Mystique.* New York: W.W. Norton and Company, Inc., 1963.
Gardner, Gerald Brousseau. *Witchcraft Today.* New York: Magickal Childe Publishing Inc, 1982.
Gardner, Gerald Brousseau. *The Meaning of Witchcraft.* New York: Magickal Childe Publishing Inc, 1984.
Gardner, Gerald Brosseau. *High Magic's Aid.* Thame, England: Essex House, 1999.
Gardner, Gerald Brousseau. *The Gardnerian Book of Shadows.* London: Forgotten Books, 2008 (reprint).
Grimm, Jacob and Wilhelm Grimm. *The Complete Grimms' Fairy Tales.* New Delhi: Fingerprint! Publishing, 2020.
Hawkins, Peter. "No Witchcraft is Fun." *Sunday Pictorial,* June 12, 1955.
Kant, Immanuel. "An Answer to the Question: What is Enlightenment?" 1784. https://enlightenment.commons.gc.cuny.edu/files/2016/12/Kant-What-is-Enlightenment.pdf.
Keats, John. "La Belle Dame Sans Merci," 1819. https://www.poetryfoundation.org/poems/44475/la-belle-dame-sans-merci-a-ballad.
King James VI of Scotland. *Daemonologies, in Forme of a Dialogue, Divided into Three Bookes.* Edinburgh: Robert Walden-Grave, 1597.
Leland, Charles Godfrey. *Aradia, or the Gospel of Witches.* London: D. Nutt Publisher, 1899.
MacDonald, George. *The Princess and the Goblin.* London: Puffin Books, 1997.
Mackay, Charles. *Extraordinary Popular Delusions and the Madness of Crowds.* Boston: L.C. Page and Co., 1932 (reprint).
Maguire, Gregory. *Wicked: The Life and Times of the Wicked Witch of the West.* New York: William Morrow Publishing, 2004 (reprint).
Maslin, Janet. "'Practical Magic': Designer Witches in Lightweight Farce." Film Review, *The New York Times,* October 16, 1998.
Mather, Cotton. "Memorable Providences, Relating to Witchcrafts and Possessions, Clearly Manifesting, Not Only That There are Witches, but That Good Men (as Well as Others) May Possibly Have Their Lives Shortened," 1689. http://law2.umkc.edu/faculty/projects/ftrials/salem/ASA_MATH.HTM.
Murray, Margaret. *The Witch Cult in Western Europe: A Study of Anthropology.* Oxford: Clarendon Press, 1921.
Murray, Margaret. *The God of Witches.* London: Oxford University Press, 1970 (reprint).
Potts, Thomas. *The Wonderfull Discoverie of Witches.* Manchester: Charles Sims and Co., 1745.
Scot, Reginald. *The Discoverie of Witchcraft.* London: Elliot Stock, 1886.
Scott, Sir Walter. *The Lady of the Lake.* New York: American Book Company, 1893. https://www.gutenberg.org/files/45888/45888-h/45888-h.htm.
Shakespeare, William, ed. *Macbeth,* third edn. London: The Arden Shakespeare, 2015.
Shelley, Mary. *Frankenstein.* New York: Penguin Classics, 2006.
Shelley, Percy Bysshe. "The Witch of Atlas." https://knarf.english.upenn.edu/PShelley/witch.html.
Spottiswood, James. *The History of the Church of Scotland, Beginning the Year of Our Lord 203 and Continuing to the End of the Reign of King James VI Vol. 2.* Edinburgh: Spottiswood Society, 1874.
Summers, Rev. Montague. *Malleus Maleficarum.* London: John Rodker, 1928.

Valiente, Doreen. *Witchcraft for Tomorrow*. Custer, WA: Phoenix Publishing, 1978.
Valiente, Doreen. *The Rebirth of Witchcraft*. London: Robert Hale, 1989.
Weyer, Johann. *Pseudomonarchia Daemonum: Illustrated English Translation (On the Tricks of Demons)*. Fort Lee, NJ: Abracax House, 2014 (reprint).

Multimedia Primary Sources

Aguirre-Sacasa, Roberto. *Chilling Adventures of Sabrina*. Kiernan Shipka, 2018; Netflix. Television show.
Barone, Eric. *Stardew Valley*. 2016; Concerned Ape. Nintendo Switch.
Chu, Jon M., dir. *Wicked*. 2024; Universal Pictures: Amazon Prime Video, 2024. Streaming.
Dunne, Griffin, dir. *Practical Magic*. 1998; Warner Bros: Amazon Prime Video, 2024. Streaming.
Fleming, Andrew, dir. *The Craft*. 1996; Columbia Pictures: Peacock, 2024. Streaming.
Fleming, Victor, dir. *The Wizard of Oz*. 1939; Warner Bros: Max, 2024. Streaming.
Fletcher, Anne, dir. *Hocus Pocus 2*. 2022; Disney Plus. Streaming.
Friedkin, William, dir. *The Exorcist*. 1973; Peacock. Streaming.
Gillard, Stuart, dir. *Charmed*. 2018; The CW: Netflix, 2024. Streaming.
HearthWitch. "Witchcraft, Wicca, and Paganism: The Differences." YouTube, December 9, 2020. https://www.youtube.com/watch?v=RhfUqyxwJS0.
Kretchmer, John T., dir. *Charmed*, Season 1, episode 2, "I've Got You Under My Skin." Aired October 14, 1998, on WB.
Moates, Bill, dir. *Mister Rogers' Neighborhood*, Season 8, episode 63, "Margaret Hamilton." Aired May 14, 1975.
Nefertiti Fareed, Afura. "How to Work with Ancestors at Samhain." *Alchemy of Affluence*, October 19, 2022. Podcast, 51:33. https://writingwitch.com/2022/10/19/how-to-work-with-our-ancestors/.
Nefertiti Fareed, Afura. The Writing Witch. "How to Work with Our Ancestors + AncestryDNA – What Am I? (Witchy Chit Chat with My Mom)." YouTube, October 31, 2023. https://www.youtube.com/watch?v=DlSQPlgsdQM&t=1689s.
Robinson, Sarah. "This is Witch Country." Podcast. YouTube, 2024. https://music.youtube.com/channel/UCT440I1Eyyceva8xY8BGOAA.
Schaeffer, Jac, dir. *Agatha All Along*, Season 1, episode 2, "Circle Sewn with Fate/Unlock Thy Hidden Gate." Aired September 18, 2024, on Disney Plus.
Schaeffer, Jac, dir. *Agatha All Along*, Season 1, episode 7, "Death's Hand in Mine." Aired October 23, 2024, on Disney Plus.
Schmock, Jonathan and Nell Scovell. *Sabrina the Teenage Witch*. 1996; ABC: 2024; Peacock. Streaming.
Shakman, Matt, dir. *WandaVision*, Season 1, episode 5, "On a Very Special Episode." Aired February 5, 2021, on Disney Plus.
Shakman, Matt, dir. *WandaVision*, Season 1, episode 7, "Breaking the Fourth Wall." Aired February 19, 2021, on Disney Plus.
Shakman, Matt, dir. *WandaVision*, Season 1, episode 9, "The Series Finale." Aired March 5, 2021, on Disney Plus.
Walgrave, David. *Baldur's Gate 3*. 2023; Lorian Studios. PlayStation 5.
Whedon, Joss. *Buffy the Vampire Slayer*. 1997; The CW: 2024, Hulu. Streaming.
Wisinski, Wade. *The Owl House*. 2020; Disney: 2024, Disney Plus. Streaming.
Yates, David. *Harry Potter and the Deathly Hallows Part 2*. 2011; Warner Bros: 2024, Max. Streaming.

Social Media Primary Sources

@anastasiamoongirl. "Ancestor Veneration Pt1." TikTok, April 10, 2023.

@beyournottygirl. "Casting Intricate Spells, Connecting with Ancestors, Doing Divination." TikTok, September 2023.
@brigantiasdaughter. "Setting the Table for Our Spirit Supper." Instagram, October 31, 2024.
@cocos.cauldron. "Let's All Remember to Stay Connected." TikTok, January 13, 2025.
@mazdamiles. "veneration and elevation." TikTok, September 27, 2022.
@sapphicandspiritual. "Queer is Inherently Spiritual." TikTok, April 30, 2024.
@starhawk_spiral. "Magical Activism: Inner Power." Instagram, November 15, 2024.
@thehoodwitch. "Saying No is the Spell." Instagram, October 20, 2024.
@thehoodwitch. "Ancestral Reverence is Resistance." Instagram, October 29, 2024.
@thehoodwitch. "Cussing Them Out is Spiritual Too." Instagram, November 9, 2024.
@yogaforwitches. "Today's #Wildmoment." Instagram, February 19, 2024.

Secondary Sources

Books

Adler, Margot. *Drawing Down the Moon: Witches, Druids, Goddess Worshippers, and Other Pagans in America*. Boston: Beacon Press, 1979.
Agyapong, Kwasi Atta. *Witchcraft in Ghana: Belief, Practice, and Consequence*. Ghana: Noyam Publishers, 2021.
Avery, Simon. Selected Poems of Mary Coleridge. Exeter: Shearsman Books, 2010.
Behringer, Wolfgang. "Climate Change and Witch Hunting: The Impact of the Little Ice Age on Mentalities." In Climate Variability in Sixteenth-Century Europe and Its Social Dimension, edited by Rudolf Brazdil and Christian Pfister. Rudiger Glaser: Springer Science and Business Media Dordrecht, 1999.
Benshoff, Harry M. and Sean Griffin. *Queer Images: A History of Gay and Lesbian Film in America*. Lanham: Rowman and Littlefield Publishers, 2006.
Bergin, Joseph, Hans Broedel, Penny Roberts and William G. Naphy, eds. '*The Malleus Maleficarum*' *and the Construction of Witchcraft: Theology and Popular Belief*. Manchester: Manchester University Press, 2004.
Blécourt, Willem de. "Witches on Screen." In *The Oxford History of Witchcraft and Magic*, edited by Owen Davies. Oxford: Oxford University Press, 2023.
Bloom, Harold. "The Witch of Atlas." In *Modern Judgements*, edited by R.B. Woodings. London: Palgrave, 1968.
Bourne, Lois. *Dancing with Witches*. London: Robert Hale, 1998.
Breslaw, Elaine. *Tituba, Reluctant Witch of Salem: Devilish Indians and Puritan Fantasies*. New York: New York University Press, 1996.
Creed, Barbara. "Horror and the Monstrous Feminine: An Imaginary Abjection." In *Feminist Film Theory*, edited by Sue Thornham. Edinburgh: Edinburgh University Press, 1999.
Crook, Nora. "Shelley and Women." In *The Oxford Handbook of Percy Bysshe Shelley*, edited by Michael O'Neill. Oxford: Oxford University Press, 2012.
Crumbley, Paul. "Dickinson's Use of Spiritualism: 'Nature' of Democratic Belief." In *A Companion to Emily Dickinson*, edited by Martha Nell Smith and Mary Loeffelholz. Malden, MA: Blackwell Publishing, 2008.
Davies, Owen and Willem de Blécourt. *Beyond the Witch Trials: Witchcraft and Magic in Enlightenment Europe*. Manchester: Manchester University Press, 2004.
Davies, Owen. "Witchcraft Accusations." In *The Routledge History of Witchcraft*, edited by Johannes Dillinger. London: Routledge, 2021.
Dillinger, Johannes. "Germany – 'the Mother of Witches'." In *The Routledge History of Witchcraft*, edited by Johannes Dillinger. New York: Routledge, 2020.
Dworkin, Andrea. *Woman Hating: A Radical Look at Sexuality*. New York: Penguin Books, 1974.

Ehrenreich, Barbara and Deirdre English. *Witches, Midwives, and Nurses 2nd Edition: A History of Women Healers*. New York: Feminist Press, 2010.
Faludi, Susan. *Backlash: The Undeclared War against American Women*. New York: Three Rivers Press, 2000.
Farr, Judith. *The Passion of Emily Dickinson*. Cambridge: Harvard University Press, 1992.
Farrar, Janet and Stewart Farrar. *The Witches' Way: Principles, Rituals and Beliefs of Modern Witchcraft*. Blaine, WA: Phoenix Publishing, 1984.
Farrar, Janet and Stewart Farrar. *A Witches' Bible: The Complete Witches' Handbook*. London: Robert Hale, 1996.
Faxneld, Per. "Disciples of Hell: The History of Satanism." In *The Routledge History of Witchcraft*, edited by Johannes Dillinger. London: Taylor and Francis, 2021.
Federici, Silvia. *Caliban and the Witch*. Brooklyn: Autonomedia, 2004.
Francis, Richard. *Judge Sewall's Apology: The Salem Witch Trials and the Forming of an American Conscience*. New York: Harper Perennial, 2006.
Geschiere, Peter. "Shifting Figures of the Witch in Colonial and Postcolonial Africa." In *The Routledge History of Witchcraft*, edited by Johannes Dillinger. London: Routledge, 2020.
Gibson, Marion. "Thomas Pott's 'Dusty Memory': Reconstructing Justice in *The Wonderfull Discoverie of Witches*." In *The Lancashire Witches: Histories and Stories*, edited by Robert Poole. Manchester: Manchester University Press, 2002.
Gilbert, Sandra and Susan Gubar. *The Madwoman in the Attic: The Woman Writer and the Nineteenth-Century Literary Imagination*. London: Yale University Press, 1979.
Grossman, Pam. *Waking the Witch: Reflections on Women, Magic and Power*. New York: Gallery Books, 2019.
Hall, Stuart. "The Work of Representation." In *The Media Studies Reader*, edited by Laurie Ouellette. New York: Routledge, 2013.
Haskell, Molly. "The Woman's Film." In *Feminist Film Theory*, edited by Sue Thornham. Edinburgh: Edinburgh University Press, 1999.
Hernandez, Catherine. "Femme as in Fuck You: Fucking with the Patriarchy One Lipstick Application at a Time." In *Becoming Dangerous: Witchy Femmes, Queer Conjurers, and Magical Rebels*, edited by Katie West and Jasmine Elliott. Brooklyn: Weiser Books, 2019.
Herzig, Tamar. "The Bestselling Demonologist: Heinrich Institoris' *Malleus Maleficarum*." In *The Science of Demons: Early Modern Authors Facing Witchcraft and the Devil*, edited by Jan Michaelson. London: Taylor and Francis, 2020.
hooks, bell. "The Oppositional Gaze: Black Feminist Spectators." In *Feminist Film Theory*, edited by Sue Thornham. Edinburgh: Edinburgh University Press, 1999.
hooks, bell. *Feminism is for Everybody: Passionate Politics*. Cambridge, MA: South End Press, 2000.
Horowitz, Daniel. *Betty Friedan and the Making of the 'Feminine Mystique': The American Left, the Cold War and Modern Feminism*. Amherst: University of Massachusetts Press, 2000.
Howard, Michael. *Modern Wicca: A History from Gerald Gardner to the Present*. Woodbury, MN: Llewellyn Publications, 2010.
Hutchins, Zachary McLeod and Cassander L. Smith. "The Salem Witch Trials, the Testimony of Candy and Mary Black, 1692." In *The Earliest African American Literatures: A Critical Reader*, edited by Zachary McLeod and Cassander L. Smith. Chapel Hill: University of North Carolina Press, 2021.
Hutton, Ronald. *The Triumph of the Moon: A History of Modern Pagan Witchcraft*. Oxford: Oxford University Press, 1999.
Hutton, Ronald. *The Witch: A History of Fear from Ancient Times to the Present*. New Haven: Yale University Press, 2017.

Jencson, Linda J. "Wicca." In *The Routledge History of Witchcraft*, edited by Johannes Dillinger. London: Routledge, 2021.
Kaplan, Ann. *Motherhood and Representation: The Mother in Popular Culture and Melodrama*. London: Routledge, 1992.
Levack, Brian P. "General Reasons for Decline in Prosecutions." In *Witchcraft and Magic in Europe: The Eighteenth and Nineteenth Centuries*, edited by Bengt Ankarloo and Stuart Clark. Philadelphia: University of Pennsylvania Press, 1999.
Levack, Brian P. *The Witch-Hunt in Early Modern Europe*. London: Routledge, 2006.
Levack, Brian P. *The Witchcraft Sourcebook 2nd Edition*. London: Routledge, 2015.
Mackay, Christopher S. *The Hammer of Witches: A Complete Translation of the Malleus Maleficarum*. Cambridge: Cambridge University Press, 2009.
Maxwell-Stuart, P.G. "A Royal Witch Theorist: James VI's *Daemonologie*." In *The Science of Demons: Early Modern Authors Facing Witchcraft and the Devil*, edited by Jan Machielse. London: Routledge, 2020.
Mitchell, Domhnall. *Emily Dickinson: Monarch of Perception*. Amherst: University of Massachusetts Press, 2000.
Monteagut, Lorraine. *Brujas: The Magic and Power of Witches of Color*. Chicago: Chicago Review Press, 2022.
Mueller, Michelle. "The Chalice and the Rainbow: Conflicts between Women's Spirituality and Transgender Rights in US Wicca in the 2010s." In *Female Leaders in New Religious Movements*, edited by Christian Giudice: Palgrave Macmillan Cham.
Murphy-Hiscock, Arin. *The Witch's Book of Self-Care: Magical Ways to Pamper, Soothe, and Care for Your Body and Spirit*. New York: Simon and Schuster, 2018.
Novy, Marianne. *Shakespeare and Feminist Theory*. London: Bloomsbury Arden Shakespeare, 2017.
Pomfrey, Stephen. "Potts, Plots, and Politics: James I *Daemonologie* and *The Wonderfull Discoverie of Witches*." In *The Lancashire Witches: Histories and Stories*, edited by Robert Poole. Manchester: Manchester University Press, 2002.
Purkiss, Diane. *The Witch in History: Early Modern and Twentieth-Century Representation*. London: Routledge, 1996.
Queen Afua. *Sacred Woman: A Guide to Healing the Feminine Mind, Body, and Spirit*. New York: Ballantine Publishing, 2000.
Riddle, John M. *Eve's Herbs: A History of Contraception and Abortion in the West*. Cambridge: Harvard University Press, 1997.
Roach, Marilynne K. *The Salem Witch Trials: A Day-by-Day Chronicle of a Community Under Siege*. Lanham, MD: Taylor Trade Publishing, 2003.
Robinson, Sarah. *Kitchen Witch: Food, Folklore, and Fairy Tale*. Cork, Ireland: Womancraft Publishing, 2022.
Robinson, Sarah. *The Witch and the Wildwood*. Cork, Ireland: Womancraft Publishing, 2024.
Roper, Lyndal. *The Witch in the Western Imagination*. Charlottesville: University of Virginia Press, 2012.
Seymour, Miranda. *Mary Shelley*. New York: Grove Press, 2000.
Sharpe, James. "Introduction: The Lancashire Witches in Historical Context." In *The Lancashire Witches: Histories and Stories*, edited by Robert Poole. Manchester: Manchester University Press, 2002.
Snow, Cassandra. *Queering Your Craft: Witchcraft from the Margins*. Newburyport, MA: Weiser Books, 2020.
Sollee, Kristen J. "Foreword." In *Becoming Dangerous: Witchy Femmes, Queer Conjurers, and Magical Rebels*, edited by Katie West and Jasmine Elliott. Newburyport, MA: Weiser Books, 2019.
Spengeman, William C. *Nineteenth-Century American Poetry*. London: Penguin Books, 1996.

Staggenborg, Suzanne. *Social Movements 2nd Edition*. Oxford: Oxford University Press, 2016.
Starhawk. *The Spiral Dance: A Rebirth of the Ancient Religion of the Great Goddess 10th Anniversary Edition*. San Francisco: HarperSanFrancisco, 1989.
Starhawk. *The Spiral Dance: A Rebirth of the Ancient Religion of the Great Goddess 20th Anniversary Edition*. San Francisco: HarperSanFrancisco, 1999.
Thomas, Keith. *Religion and the Decline of Magic: Studies in Popular Beliefs in Sixteenth- and Seventeenth-Century England*. London: Weidenfeld and Nicolson, 1971.
Thurston, Robert W. "The Salem Witch Hunt." In *The Routledge History of Witchcraft*, edited by Johannes Dillinger. New York: Routledge, 2020.
Topolski, Anya. "What Do Women Have to Do with It? Race, Religion and the Witch Hunts." In *Purple Brains: Feminisms at the Limits of Philosophy*, edited by Annabelle Dufourcq, Annemie Halsema, Katrine Smiet and Karen Vintges. Nijmegen, Netherlands: Radboud University Press, 2024.
Van Engen, Abram C. *City On a Hill: A History of American Exceptionalism*. New Haven: Yale University Press, 2020.
Waldron, David. "Paganism." In *Encyclopedia of Psychology and Religion*, edited by David A. Leeming. New York: Springer, 2020, 1683–87.
Weigand, Kate. *Red Feminism: American Communism and the Making of Women's Liberation*. Baltimore: Johns Hopkins University Press, 2002.
Willis, Deborah. *Malevolent Nurture: Witch-Hunting and Maternal Power in Early Modern England*. Ithaca: Cornell University Press, 1995.
Willumsen, Liv Helene. *The Voices of Women in Witchcraft: Northern Europe. Routledge Studies in the History of Witchcraft, Demonology, and Magic*. London: Routledge, 2022.
Wilson, Richard. "The Pilot's Thumb: *Macbeth* and the Jesuits." In *The Lancashire Witches: Histories and Stories*, edited by Robert Poole. Manchester: Manchester University Press, 2002.
Zeisler, Andi. *Feminism and Pop Culture*. Berkley, CA: Seal Press, 2008.

Articles

Allen, Matthew. "The Shaman Hunts and Postwar Revival and Reinvention of Okinawan Shamanism." *Japan Forum* 29, no. 2 (2017): 218–235.
Baker, Emerson W. and James Kences. "Maine, Indian Land Speculation, and the Essex County Witchcraft Outbreak of 1692." *Maine History* 40, no. 3 (2001): 158–189.
Braun, Heather L. "'Set the Crystal Surface Free!': Mary E. Coleridge and the Self-Conscious Femme Fatale." *Women's Writing* 14, no. 3 (2007).
Bravo, Maria del Pilar. "Literary Creation and the Supernatural in English Romanticism." *GIST – Education and Learning Research Journal* 1 (2007).
Cowdell, Paul. "Margaret Murray: Who *Didn't* Believe Her and Why." *TFH: The Journal of Folklore and History* 39/40 (2023).
Crisman, William. "Psychological Realism and Narrative Manner in Shelley's 'Alastor' and 'The Witch of Atlas'." *Keats–Shelley Journal* 35 (1986).
Dennis, Matthew. "American Indians, Witchcraft, and Witchhunting." *OAH Magazine of History* 17, no. 4 (July 2003): 21–27.
Dray, Kayleigh. "Why Practical Magic is the Ultimate Feminist Film." *Stylist* (2018).
Kerstiens, Joseph. "A Historical, Philosophical, and Etymological Study of the Word 'Religion' as Used in the First Amendment: Coming to a Textually Based Definition." *George Mason Law Review* 31, no. 1 (2023): 75–118.
Leeson, Peter T. and Jacob W. Russ. "Witch Trials." *The Economic Journal* 128 (August 2018): 2066–2105.

Maxwell, Lynn. "Wax Magic and *The Duchess of Malfi*." *Journal for Early Modern Cultural Studies* 14, no. 3 (Summer 2014): 31–54.

Miller, Chris. "How Modern Witches Enchant TikTok: Intersections of Digital, Consumer, and Material Culture(s) on #Witchtok." *Religions* 13, no. 2 (2022).

Mulvey, Laura. "Visual Pleasure and Narrative Cinema." *Screen* 16, no. 3 (Autumn 1975).

Murrey, Amber. "Decolonising the Imagined Geographies of 'Witchcraft'." *Third World Thematics: A TWQ Journal* (2017).

Ring, Nicola A. "Healers and Midwives Accused of Witchcraft (1563–1736) – What Secondary Analysis of the Scottish Survey of Witchcraft Can Contribute to the Teaching of Nursing and Midwifery History." *Nurse Education Today* 133 (2024).

Smith, Moira. "The Flying Phallus and the Laughing Inquisitor: Penis Theft in the *Malleus Maleficarum*." *Journal of Folklore Research* 39, no. 1 (January–April 2002): 85–117.

Tucker, Veta Smith. "Purloined Identity: The Racial Metamorphosis of Tituba of Salem Village." *Journal of Black Studies* 30, no. 4 (March 2000): 624–634.

Web Sources

Anonymous. "Emily Dickinson and Gardening." https://www.emilydickinsonmuseum.org/emily-dickinson/biography/special-topics/emily-dickinson-and-gardening/.

Anonymous. "The Last Witch: A Documentary 330 Years in the Making" (2023). https://www.thelastwitchfilm.com/.

Anonymous. "Earth Activist Training." https://earthactivisttraining.org/.

Anonymous. "Reclaiming, a Tradition, a Community." www.reclaimingcollective.wordpress.com.

Anonymous. "Publishing for Body, Mind, and Spirit." https://llewellyn.com/about/index.php.

Beaux, Kir. "It's Queer Magic." www.itsqueermagic.com.

Bui-Xuan, Dung and Kien Thi-Pham. "Karl Marx's View of the Productive Forces and Its Development Today." Midwestern Marx Institute (August 29, 2022). https://www.midwesternmarx.com/articles/karl-marxs-view-of-the-productive-forces-and-its-development-today-by-kien-thi-pham-dung-bui-xuan.

Camping-Harris, Marnie. "The Pendle Witches: How a Nine-Year-Old Girl Sentenced Her Family to Death," *Retrospect Journal* (October 23, 2022). https://retrospectjournal.com/2022/10/23/the-pendle-witches-how-a-nine-year-old-girl-sentenced-her-family-to-death/.

Crenshaw, Kimberlé. "Kimberlé Crenshaw on Intersectionality, More Than Two Decades Later" (June 8, 2017). https://www.law.columbia.edu/news/archive/kimberle-crenshaw-intersectionality-more-two-decades-later.

Dobbins, Peggy. "W.I.T.C.H. Zora Burden's Introduction to Interview with Peggy for Zora's Collection of Verbatim Interviews with *Women of the Underground Resistance*," by Zora Burden (2020). http://peggydobbins.net/womensmovement/witchzorapeggy.html.

Fearnow, Benjamin. "Number of Witches Rises Dramatically across U.S. As Millennials Reject Christianity," *Newsweek* (March 25, 2020). https://www.newsweek.com/witchcraft-wiccans-mysticism-astrology-witches-millennials-pagans-religion-1221019.

Framke, Caroline and Adam B. Vary. "'WandaVision': A Marvel Expert and Casual Fan Unpack 'the Series Finale' and the Double-Edged Sword of Fan Theories," *Variety* (March 6, 2021). https://variety.com/2021/tv/opinion/wandavision-finale-review-marvel-wanda-vision-1234923117/.

Greenwood, Douglas. "Lessons from the Other Realm: Being a Male Witch in 2019 is Complicated" (October 30, 2019). https://www.dazeddigital.com/beauty/article/46549/1/male-witch-magic-magick-witchcraft-warlock-wizard.

Grossman, Pam. "Picturing Queer Witchcraft: A Conversation with Susan Aberth and Pam Grossman," by Ksenia M. Soboleva, *New York Historical Society* (June 22, 2023). https://www.nyhistory.org/blogs/picturing-queer-witchcraft-susan-aberth-pam-grossman.

Katz, Brigit. "Last Convicted Salem 'Witch' is Finally Cleared," *Smithsonian Magazine* (August 3, 2022). https://www.smithsonianmag.com/smart-news/last-convicted-salem-witch-is-finally-cleared-180980516/, accessed January 13, 2024.

Kenny, Emmaline. "The Last Salem Witch Has Been Exonerated," *Ms. Magazine* (October 30, 2023). https://msmagazine.com/2023/10/30/salem-witch-trial-exonerated-movie-documentary/, accessed January 21, 2024.

Kohr, Amanda. "Why Queer People Love Witchcraft" (June 17, 2020). https://www.refinery29.com/en-us/2020/06/9861310/queer-lgbt-witch-trend.

Ledford, Adam. "The Yuta, the Noro, and the 'Okinawan Witch Trials': Japan's Lesser-Known Salem Witch Trials," *Tofugu* (April 16, 2014). https://www.tofugu.com/japan/yuta-noro-okinawa-witch-trials/.

Lodhi, Sanskriti. "Kathryn Harkness Opens Up About Agatha Harkness' Sexuality in *Agatha All Along*," *Yardbarker* (October 8, 2024). https://www.yardbarker.com/entertainment/articles/kathryn_hahn_opens_up_about_agatha_harkness_sexuality_in_agatha_all_along/s1_17442_41019254.

Marshall, Katherine. "Combatting Accusations of Witches in Ghana" (August 22, 2023). https://berkleycenter.georgetown.edu/posts/combatting-accusations-of-witches-in-ghana.

Moreno, Manny. "UN Council Adopts Historic Resolution Condemning Harmful Practices Related to Accusations of Witchcraft and Ritual Attacks" (July 28, 2021). https://wildhunt.org/2021/07/un-council-adopts-historic-resolution-condemning-harmful-practices-related-to-accusations-of-witchcraft-and-ritual-attacks.html.

Onyulo, Tonny. "Witch Hunts Increase in Tanzania as Albino Deaths Jump," *USA Today* (February 26, 2015). https://www.usatoday.com/story/news/world/2015/02/26/tanzania-witchcraft/23929143/.

Ott, Katherine. "The History of Getting the Gay Out" (November 15, 2018). https://americanhistory.si.edu/explore/stories/history-getting-gay-out.

Pagliarulo, Antonio. "Why Paganism and Witchcraft Are Making a Comeback," *NBC News* (October 30, 2022). https://www.nbcnews.com/think/opinion/paganism-witchcraft-are-making-comeback-rcna54444.

Parker. "Queering Paganism: A Gay Practitioner's Perspective of Wicca Craft" (April 30, 2021). https://myumbrella.co/queering-paganism-a-gay-practitioners-perspective-of-wicca-craft/#:~:text=Some%20popular%20pagan%20traditions%20have,and%20cisnormativity%20in%20certain%20traditions.

Rude, Mey. "*Agatha All Along*'s Latest Episode Confirmed a Major Character is Gay," *Out* (October 24, 2024). https://www.out.com/gay-tv-shows/agatha-all-along-confirmed-gay.

Screen Slam. "*Practical Magic*: Sandra Bullock Interview," 2013. https://www.youtube.com/watch?v=vPpCtQYWoXk&embeds_referring_euri=https%3A%2F%2Fwww.bing.com%2F&embeds_referring_origin=https%3A%2F%2Fwww.bing.com&source_ve_path=Mjg2NjY.

Tousignant, Lauren. "Woman Cleared of Witchcraft 300 Years Later, Thanks to Eighth-Grade Class," *Jezebel* (May 26, 2022). www.jezebel.com/woman-cleared-of-witchcraft-300-years-later-thanks-to-1848983594.

United Nations. "Concept Note on the Elimination of Harmful Practices Related to Witchcraft Accusations and Ritual Killings" (March 19, 2020). https://www.ohchr.

org/en/documents/tools-and-resources/concept-note-elimination-harmful-practices-related-witchcraft.

Walsh, Aisling. "JK Rowling's Awful Gender Politics Should Be No Surprise to *Harry Potter* Fans," *The Mary Sue* (2020). https://www.themarysue.com/jk-rowlings-awful-gender-politics-should-be-no-surprise-to-harry-potter-fans/.

Walsh, Brendan. "'Witches' Are Still Killed All Over the World. Pardoning Past Victims Could End the Practice" (May 10, 2024). https://www.uq.edu.au/research/article/2024/05/%E2%80%98witches%E2%80%99-are-still-killed-all-over-world-pardoning-past-victims-could-end-practice.

White, Robyn. "The Witch Camps Where Hundreds of Elderly Women Are Left to Die," *Newsweek* (October 30, 2022). https://www.newsweek.com/witch-camps-elderly-women-die-ghana-1754907.

Whiteneir Jr, Kevin Talmer. "Queer Heresies: Witchcraft and Magic as Sites of Queer Radicality," *The Activist History Review* (May 24, 2019). https://activisthistory.com/2019/05/24/queer-heresies-witchcraft-and-magic-as-sites-of-queer-radicality/.

Zevallos, Zuleyka. "What is Otherness?" *The Other Sociologist* (2011). https://othersociologist.com/otherness-resources/.

Theses and Dissertations

McTier, Rosemary J. "'An Insect View of Its Plain': Nature and Insects in Thoreau, Dickinson, and Muir." PhD Dissertation, Duquesne University, 2009.

Conference Papers

Kawanishi, Eriko. "The Western Witchcraft in Contemporary Japan." American Academy of Religion Annual Meeting, Denver, 2018.

Index

activism 4, 6–7, 16–17, 75–7, 104, 117–19
Adams, Abigail 86
Adler, Margot: *Drawing Down the Moon* 77; relationship with Starhawk 77–8
Agatha All Along 6, 84, 88, 93–5, 97, 98
age of Enlightenment 48–9
age of Romanticism 49
Allingham, William 51

Baldur's Gate 92
Bewitched 96
Bronte, Charlotte 51
Bronte, Emily 51
Buffy the Vampire Slayer 84, 85, 91, 92–3, 96, 110

Carroll, Lewis 51
Charmed (1998) 83, 89, 93, 97, 110
Charmed (2018) 95
The Chilling Adventures of Sabrina 95
Christianity 2–3, 8, 12, 16, 19, 37–8, 41, 52, 59, 63, 69; Catholic Church 4, 13, 18–19, 25, 35–6, 78, 90, 102, 110; Eve 13; Religious Right 105–6; representations of the devil 11, 18–19, 26, 50–1; scripture 18, 19–20, 26, 34, 71, 105
class 49, 52, 83, 85–6, 88, 100, 109, 112; capitalism 6, 99–100, 103–4; and labor 75, 95, 101, 103,116, 120; and self–care 100–1
Cleaver, June 86
Coleridge, Mary 5, 52, 59, 62, 117; education 55; relationship to Samuel 55; "The Witch" 48, 55–7, 60, 64
The Craft 83, 88, 90–2, 98

Creed, Barbara 86–7, 97
Crenshaw, Kimberle 114–15
Crowley, Aleister 63, 66, 71–3
Culpeper, Nicholas 15
Cunningham, Scott. *see* Wicca

Darwin, Charles 55
devil: and witch association 3–4, 8, 11–13, 15–16, 18–19, 21–3, 25–6, 31–5, 39–40, 42, 50–1, 68–9, 73, 90–1, 116–17, 121
Dickens, Charles 51
Dickinson, Emily 5, 53; family 57; education 57–8; "The Murmur of the Bee" 48, 58–9; "Witchcraft has not a pedigree" 59; "Witchcraft was hung, in History" 59
A Discovery of Witches 96

Ehrenreich, Barbara 77
The Exorcist 87

fairy tales 13, 49–50; Grimm's fairy tales 51, 60; *Hansel and Gretel* 51; *Snow White and the Seven Dwarves* 2
feminism 37, 84, 90, 106, 112; activism in 1960s 75–8; backlash against 84; beauty standards 2–3, 6, 52, 54–5, 76, 82–3, 85, 88, 92–3, 100–1; Daly, Mary 77; Dworkin, Andrea 16–7, 27, 77; Friedan, Betty 75–6, 80–1; girl power 84–5; Inman, Mary 75; intersectionality 5, 7, 77, 109, 112, 115; marriage and motherhood 5–6, 20, 22–3, 75–6, 83–8, 95–6; Sexual violence 22–3, 35, 71, 76; W.I.T.C.H. 76–7, 81
Fiske, Thomas 1

Index

Gardner, Gerald 5, 8, 63, 65–7, 78–9, 100, 106–7, 108, 110; childhood 67; education 67; media 68–9, 73–4 relationship with "Old Dorothy" 67–8; relationship with Crowley 63, 66, 72–3; relationship with Valiente 67, 70–75; written works 68–76;
Germany 4, 11–12, 30
Ghana 9, 116–17, 121
Gold Star Mothers 86
Grossman, Pam 117

Hall, Stuart 86
Harry Potter 93, 98
Haskell, Molly 86
Hawkins, Peter 68–9, 73

Ibsen, Henrik 55
Institoris, Heinrich 18–9, 21, 116; background 11–3; on women 13, 16–18, 19–20, 22–6; writing and printing of *Malleus Maleficarum* 13, 15–16

James, William 55
Japan 116

Kaplan, Ann 86, 93
Keats, John 60
King James VI 4, 36, 50–1, 59; *Daemonologie* 26, 30, 33, 38, 39, 43; participation in Sampson interrogation 32–3; reign 31, 36, 48
Kristeva, Julia 86–7

The Last Witch 1
Leland, Charles Godfrey 63–4, 67; *Aradia* 64–6, 71, 72, 107; relationship with Maddalena 64–5
Little Ice Age 12

MacBeth 30, 36–7, 39, 43, 52, 54, 60, 93, 117
MacDonald, George 51
Mackay, Charles 50–1, 52, 59, 61
Maguire, Gregory 92
Maleficent 91
The Malleus Maleficarum 4, 6, 11–12, 33–4, 40, 52, 54, 60, 77–8, 117, 121; language 14–15; part one 18–20; part two 20–3; part three 23–6; Summers, Rev. Montague 14, 16–17; translations 13–14

Mary Shelley's *Frankenstein* 51
Mather, Cotton. *see* Puritans.
The Mayfair Witches 96
Mulvey, Laura 85, 87–8
Murray, Margaret 63–6

Newsweek 84
Nicholas, Mary 64
The New York Times 90

The Owl House 95

pagan 2–3, 5–7, 55, 63, 65, 74–5, 78–9, 106; various definitions 99, 110, 112, 117–120
Pendle Witch Trials 4–5, 37–41; Device, Alizon 37–8, 40, 117; Device, Jennet 37–8; Southerns, Elizabeth (Old Demdike) 38–40
Pope Innocent VIII 12–13
Potts, Thomas 30, 38–40, 43
The Powerpuff Girls 85
Practical Magic 6, 82–4, 89–90, 96, 97
Puritans 41

Queen Elizabeth I 34
Queer Identity 7–8, 101, 102, 104–05; AIDS 105–06; and the witch in film/TV 94–6; as spiritual 8, 105–06, 107; exclusion from early Wicca 8, 106–07

race/racism: and ancestry 6, 99, 107–08; bell hooks 77, 87; "bruja" 99, 14, 110; decolonization of practices 102, 108, 112; and identity as witch 104, 105, 107–11; and the witch in film 87–8, 90–1

Sabrina the Teenage Witch 89
Salem Trials: Goode, Sarah 42, 115; Johnson Jr., Elizabeth 1–2; and Native Americans 7–8; Osborne, Sarah 42, 115; Parris, Samuel 41–2; Phips, William 1; Putnam, Joseph 43; Putnam, Thomas 42; Sewall, Samuel 1; Tituba 5, 7–8, 41–3, 115, 117
Scot, Reginald 16, 33
Scotland: Duncan, Geillis 31–3, 36, 50–1; *Newes from Scotland* 31–2; North Berwick 4, 31–4; Sampson, Agnes 4, 31–5, 50–1, 59, 117; Seton, David 31

Scott, Sir Walter 5, 51
Shakespeare, William *see MacBeth*.
Shelley, Percy Bysshe 5, 48; health 52–3; marriage to Mary 52–3, 55; "The Witch of Atlas" 52–5, 59–60
social justice *see* activism
social media: Fable 100; Facebook 100; Instagram 99, 100, 103, 104, 111, 120; Reddit 100; Threads 100; TikTok 2, 99–100, 102–03, 107, 110–11, 120; X (formerly Twitter) 100; YouTube 100, 103, 108, 118, 120
Spirited Away 2–3
Sprenger, Jakob 11–12, 15–16, 21, 116
Stardew Valley 92
Starhawk 63, 77–8, 104, 119
Switzerland 48
The Sword in the Stone 2–3

Tanzania 7, 9
Thomas, Keith 16
Tolstoy, Leo 55

Valiente, Doreen 5, 63, 67–8, 78, 118–19; background 70–1; marriage 70; role as high priestess 70, 74–5; split from Gardner 73–4; writing of "The Charge" 71–2
Variety 94

WandaVision 83, 89, 93–5, 97, 98
Weyer Johann 33

Wicca 2, 5–6, 8, 63, 70, 72–5, 77–9, 99–100, 106–110, 116–120; Cunningham, Scott 8; Goddess 3, 8, 63, 65–9, 72, 74–5, 78, 106–07; Horned God 65, 68–9, 71; Moon rituals 63, 69–70, 72, 74, 101–02; "Old Religion" 4, 63, 65, 67–9, 71, 74, 77; Wheel of the Year 5, 63, 70, 74; Wiccan Rede 63, 66, 91
Wicked see Maguire, Gregory
Winthrop, John *see* Puritans.
The Witches of Eastwick 96
Witchcraft Act of 1735 48, 73
witchcraft symbols and rituals: black cat 2; black hat 2, 77; broomstick 2, 16; cauldron 2, 16, 70; dance 70, 72; dumb supper 111; fire 70; tarot 2–4, 71
witches, accusations against: as healers and midwives 21, 30–2, 35–6, 77; due to alleged promiscuity 4, 11, 15–17, 20–3, 34–5, 40; male accused 21; weather/nature magic 12–13, 21, 36, 117
witch trials: executions 1, 4, 7, 11–12, 25–6, 30–3, 43, 48–9, 78, 83; inquisition and interrogation 4, 21, 23, 32–4, 42, 78; torture 23, 25, 31, 33, 43, 48, 59
The Wizard of Oz 2–3, 88, 91–3
The Wonderful Discoverie of Witches see Potts, Thomas.

Yeats, W.B. 55